SNOWFLAKE

TRAPPED BETWEEN WORLDS

THE SNOWFLAKE SERIES

In reading order:

Snowflake: Trapped Between Worlds

Take Care While You Still Can…Snowflake

Have a Little Faith…Snowflake

It's Different This Time…Snowflake

MARTHESE BONAQUI

SNOWFLAKE

TRAPPED BETWEEN WORLDS

For my soulmate, Mark,
our blessings, Kelly, Celine, and the one on the way,
and our guardian angel, Jamie.

Every choice comes with a consequence.
Once you make a choice,
you must accept responsibility.
You cannot escape the consequences of your choices,
whether you like them or not.
—Roy T. Bennett

CHAPTER ONE

James's eyes darted away from the array of omniscient street lenses. Jaw clenched, black cap lowered. He kept his head bowed away from the menacing stare of the cameras.

The afternoon streets were empty. The warmth of the spring sun induced a hushed laze. He turned round another corner, keeping a brisk pace, until he came to the gray garage door.

He made a furtive glance up and down the road, reached for the key in his pocket, and let himself in.

The smell of what had become his home for the past eight weeks—musty sawdust—filled his nostrils. He quickly scanned the room. Everything was as he'd left it. The tools positioned at particular angles, seemingly random to the untrained eye, were still in place; no one had entered the garage.

He closed and locked the door. The faint light coming through the garage door vents, was just enough to see his steps as he went to the back of the garage. His hunger pangs called out to the smell of the freshly baked bread he'd bought.

There was a black swirl of fur on the cot, “Hey, cat,” he whispered as he switched on the small lamp on the nearby table. A purred meow replied, its head stretched out to sniff at the paper bag in his hand.

“Making a habit of this, aren't you?” he continued. The cot creaked beneath his weight as he sat.

The cat climbed onto his lap, its nose diving into the bag, racing with his hand to the small tin.

Impatient meows pierced the silence and only ceased once the tin clinked on the ground. The cat remained alert of its surroundings as she ate, ready to flee if need be. Just like James.

He took out the plain baguette. It was still warm and its crust gently crisp. Inside; light and airy. He devoured it. Satisfying his cravings for sustenance. For now.

He reached for the small bottle of water on the table and gulped it down. His rations; an open packet of peanuts, four apples, an orange, three rice crackers—and for his furry companion, two cans of cat food. He hoped it'd last the next two days. He was saving up for a pair of new shoes. His current pair were beyond mending; the soles were cracked and a chunk about to fall off.

If his hunger got to be too much, he could dive into the ocean, breathe its icy cold waters, and eat seaweed—like he'd done previously when he lived in the sea—for his safety. A perfect hideout where all but one person and a few of his men, wouldn't suspect a human of living.

But his boss, Connor, was always on time with an envelope of cash to pay James. He'd take the wood and leave another tower of pallets. He was due in another three days. James would have to stretch his rations but he'd make it on what he had left.

The cat jumped onto the cot again and pressed her head against James, purrs vibrating the pair. James stroked her back as she twirled, angling for more pets.

A familiar roar of an engine broke the silence on the street. It got louder as it approached, then cut off right outside the garage, followed by a door slam. Keys jingled at the garage lock; Connor was early.

James sprang up, ready to dash—activating his escape plan—

"Andrew, you here?" Connor called to James, and flicked the light switch. The humming fluorescence flooded the room with dim light.

A slim, teenage boy followed Connor. He'd mentioned he'd find someone to help out with the pallets; this was probably him.

"Yeah," James replied as he stepped forward—aborting his panicked escape.

"This is Matthew," Connor said. "He'll be helping out with the work load."

"Hi," Matthew said.

James gave Matthew a brief nod and studied him the way he'd been trained; inconspicuous—appearing as though he was giving him barely a thought. His heightened senses could measure vitals only machines and he himself could process. Matthew's pulse was steady, a smile in his eyes, normal pupil dilation, breath even, demeanor at ease; Matthew posed no threat. James determined he was not one of Ricin's men.

"Matthew starts on Monday," Connor continued. "Two hours in the afternoon, three times a week. I'll be bringing more pallets as of this Friday—make sure you finish them all," Connor added sternly. His gaze ascended the untouched stack of pallets and he fidgeted impatiently with his overgrown moustache.

"I always have," James reminded Connor.

"Right, kid. So—uh—Andrew and Matthew," Connor said, "listen; I haven't had any trouble so far and that's how I want to keep it. Understood?"

Connor squinted sharply at Matthew. Matthew nodded eagerly in agreement.

"Great. I got to get going. I'll see you on Friday." Connor walked out of the garage and into the sun.

Matthew eyed the neatly stacked planks of wood, "You been working long here?" he asked.

"A few weeks," James said.

"Cool."

Matthew scanned the room with a curious gaze and wandered to the back of the garage.

James continued to work on the piece of wood he had started earlier. He had to finish at least seven more pallets before midnight.

"You wash your clothes here?" Matthew asked, thumb jabbed toward clothes hanging on a line on the tiny patch of grass serving as a backyard.

"I live here," James said, and pulled out the last nail in the plank.

Awkward pause.

"Connor said you're my age; fifteen." There was a lilt of confusion in Matthew's voice.

"Yep."

"So—no family?"

James glanced over at Matthew, recognizing sympathy in his voice.

"Mother died. Never knew my father," he invented.

“Oh.” Another awkward pause. “So sorry to hear,” Matthew said, and quickly cleared his throat. “How many pallets do you work on each day?”

“Not enough—apparently,” James said. Then asked, “What about you? From around here?”

“Yeah; two blocks up the road.”

A rap song ringtone went off in Matthew's pocket. He pulled it out and tapped the screen, “Hey mom,” he answered. “…Yeah I'll grab some on the way home—five?—Okay bye.”

Conversation fell silent and the loud bangs of the hammer echoed off the walls until all the planks of the pallet were separated. Matthew followed James's lead in earnest.

“Do we cut them too?” Matthew asked.

“Only half of the planks.”

“Hm. All right,” Matthew said. James remained focused on the task. “What does Connor sell them for anyway?” Matthew grabbed the claw hammer to have a closer look at it.

“Long planks for fences. Cut ones for firewood.”

Matthew's phone rang again, the rap song ringtone muffled in his pocket. “What?” Matthew sounded irritated. “Will get some of those too—okay? Bye.” Matthew heaved a heavy sigh and pocketed his cell phone again. “She'll probably call two more times,” Matthew scoffed. “I don't know why she can't just text me a list.”

“Cool ringtone though.”

“It is, right?” Matthew glanced around the room again. “Is there a laptop—radio? Something?”

“No. There was a stereo here but Connor took it.”

"Do you mind if I bring one next time?"

James hesitated, his eyes on Matthew. He was wary of anything that might attract attention to the garage.

"Don't you like music?" Matthew asked.

"I just don't want to get into any trouble with Connor—the noise—"

"We'll keep it low," Matthew assured. "It'll help the time pass, this is boring."

James gave a hesitant, "Okay."

"I should get going. I'll see you on Monday after school then."

"Yeah. See you."

Matthew left and James watched him pull the door shut behind him. Once alone, his nerves mounted with alarm—he had to be careful. He needed to remain in the shadows; protect his identity. One picture of his face on social media, one short recording of his voice, any slip could easily raise a red flag and alert Ricin to his whereabouts. It was not only for James's sake, but for everyone else's, too.

CHAPTER TWO

Standing in a large courtyard, the high sun squeezing sweat from pores, a man, a young boy, and a battered man kneeling.

"You can't?" Ricin said, the rise in his calm voice belied his frustration.

"I—," James squeaked. The weight of his finger was on the trigger in his outstretched arms. The barrel aimed at the man locked in supplication.

"You were engineered for this, son. Pull that trigger," Ricin urged. "He's already dead. Finish the job, make it quick for him." Ricin's tone was that of a father encouraging his water wary child to jump into the pool.

James took a shuddering breath. He locked eyes with the supplicated man and steadied his aim through grit teeth.

"Please," the man cried. He raised his bound hands to his face in a feeble attempt at stopping a bullet. "I've got two young kids; I'm all they've got!" Tears and blood streamed down his face, each diluting the other.

James tensed his finger on the trigger and attempted to block out the pleas. He prepared himself for the kick of the gun when the trigger was pulled. He was ready for the smell of gun powder to sting his nose. He was ready—but he froze. “I can't do this.” His voice a weak whisper; his head hung in shame as his tense stance melted.

Ricin grabbed his shoulder with a gentle gesture, “It's all right,” Ricin said with a forced smile. “Next time,” he assured with a firm pat on James's back.

Ricin pulled the gun from his belt and turned to the man, “One day,” he said to James, “you'll become all that I am and more.” Ricin raised his aim to the man's head. Desperate pleas from the hoarse throat were cut short by the pop of gunfire. The bullet pierced the man's skull, his body fell with a thud on the hard dirt, and warm droplets of blood spattered the side of James's face.

James awoke with a sharp gasp for air, soaked in sweat, and clattered to the floor off his cot. He leaped blindly to his feet, terror iced through his veins, as the memories of Ricin tormented his dreams.

The same nightmare haunted him all week. He plopped on the edge of the bed and slumped with his chest tight. He forced his eyes shut in an effort to cast out Ricin's image. To no avail.

He went to the washbasin and splashed cold water onto his face. He steadied his breaths, easing his angst. He couldn't keep living like this; capsized by Ricin every time he tried to rest.

A merry chirp caught his attention and he traced the sound to the backyard and lifted his eyes toward a sparrow flying into vast purple skies—freedom that every living being deserved. James inhaled the crisp air of dawn and repeated his only comforting thought; They won't find me.

A dark shadow descended the tangerine tree. It was the black cat.

“Morning,” James said with a smile as she sauntered toward him. She rubbed against his ankles, her tail stretched upward. He picked up the black ball of fur and headed inside, her loud purrs vibrated her body. He lay her down on the cot to grab a can of food.

“Give me a sec,” he said. James pulled the tab from the tin can and set it on the ground with a gentle clink. He watched the cat eat peacefully, her tail huddled close to her feet.

The day ticked by and James kept himself occupied with the woodwork. Five in the afternoon, a loud thump on the door startled him. He peeked through the eyehole and opened the door for Matthew.

“Hey,” Matthew said, and stepped inside. Whatever verve pepped his step drained from him as he took in the piles and piles of pallets that now owned half the space of the garage. He frowned, “Oh—these have to be ready by—?”

“Next Friday,” James replied. “We’ll get them done.”

“Right,” Matthew said, sounding doubtful, and put his bag down. “I got a laptop—and an awesome playlist,” he continued, taking it out from his bag.

“Can I see something real quick?” James asked, his hand reaching out to take it.

“Sure,” Matthew replied, trying to hide the squint of his russet brown eyes. “Login is Parlor; my last name.”

James took the laptop and opened it, his thumb carefully placed to keep the camera covered. He began rapidly clacking at the keys with one hand while Matthew kept a close eye on what he was doing.

"Are you—looking for something?" Matthew asked as James clicked on another desktop icon.

After a brief pause James said, "Yes but it's all good." He was confident Matthew's laptop wasn't bugged.

"Looks like you've worked on computers before," Matthew noted.

"Yeah—it's a virus thing. Some record your mic and camera and send it to—I don't know really but I'm not interested in anybody else knowing a fifteen-year-old kid is living by himself in a garage. Just a little paranoid, I guess," James said, and was pretty happy he could tell the truth even if Matthew didn't know what it meant.

"Uh, weird but I guess I get it. So, you ready to listen to some rap and R&B?" Matthew asked.

"Sure."

They worked at a steady pace and exchanged conversation between the pounding of their hammers. James laughed at Matthew's jokes. Initially, James was nervous about Matthew's presence but it felt great to be around someone his age; normal almost.

"So do you have a girlfriend—or boyfriend?—I don't judge," Matthew asked, and placed cleaned planks to one side.

"Yeah of course I have a girlfriend; I invite her over and we build sawdust castles together," James replied. Matthew burst out laughing.

"Me neither," Matthew then said. "Apparently I'm good at saying all the wrong things at the wrong time." Matthew's gaze turned into a thousand yard stare—clearly talking from experience. "Welp—live and learn, right?" Matthew shrugged. "I was thinking maybe building muscle would help since talking sure isn't helping. I wanna be part of the muscle gang—how do I do that?"

"Pull-ups, push-ups, sit-ups…anything that helps with anger."

"Someone did you wrong?" Matthew asked.

"Life," James said. Matthew's presence reminded him that he was still just a teenager and teenagers weren't supposed to take on the evils of the world.

"I'm hungry," Matthew said, and put his hammer down. "My mom made me dinner, lawl. She gave me enough for the both of us. We should eat. You hungry?"

"Am I hungry? I'm starving. What do you have?" James asked, surprised by the kind gesture.

"Grilled veggie wraps and homemade ginger cookies. My mom's cookies are better than from the store."

James felt like a normal teenager for just a moment in time. Ricin's image was but a hazy billow of memory smoke. He savoured the meal; it felt like a gift. A shot of hope surged through James—maybe he could have a simple life, a teenage life, but no—he knew it was only naïve to underestimate Ricin's determination.

CHAPTER THREE

Months passed. Matthew routinely showed up to help with pallets on his days off and always brought enough food from home for the both of them. James wondered if this was what having a brother was like.

It was the end of the work day for the pair, an off day for Matthew, yet another he showed up to assist James. Their bellies were full from dinner and they huddled over a live soccer game on Matthew's laptop.

Matthew yelled at the players on screen. He begged one to pass the ball but the recalcitrant player refused to heed Matthew's direction. Matthew lamented in a not very quiet voice how he'd cost them the ball. But as another play was being executed the pair shouted '*Come on! Come on!*' over and over, and louder and louder, their bums raising up with each shout as the ball teased toward the goal. The cat shot her head up at the commotion, her stupefied gaze bouncing between them. Finally, the player obeyed Matthew's distance coaching and the ball was lobbed through the goalie's hands and into the back of the net. Matthew and James sprang to their feet as they called out long and loud *GOAL*, each pumping their fists in victory.

“Good game,” Matthew remarked, completely rapt, and they sat back down again.

“Nice,” James said, following the ball. His hand groped for some salted popcorn from the bowl on the chair between them.

They watched on attentively until the final whistle was blown.

“They never disappoint, eh?” Matthew said elated, stretching back in his chair. “Want to play a match before I head home?”

“Sure, ready to lose again?”

“Bruh. Nah. I gotchu now. I’m winning this time,” Matthew said resolutely, and handed James a controller.

They played against each other. Matthew laughed when his team took the ball and scored the game winning point in a clutch victory.

“You should come over to my house sometime. Losing on a big screen feels much nicer, I promise,” Matthew laughed when his team took the ball again.

“I mean, yeah, you would know,” James countered.

James was running out of excuses to dodge Matthew's out-of-garage invites. He could never be too cautious, but having concluded that Matthew's parents couldn't be involved in Ricin's organisation—as if they were; a fifteen-year-old with no family, living in the garage where he worked, would have definitely aroused their suspicion by now—he decided to accept.

“So you’ll be coming over?” Matthew asked again, his players getting closer to the goal post once more.

“Yeah, sure. Why not?”

Matthew's players were trying to score and he leaned forward in his chair, closer to the laptop.

"Move! Move!" Matthew ordered his players. "Goal!" he called out but did his best to restrain its volume and length. "I win, bro. Four-one—just saying!"

"I'm just tired—"

"Yeah, yeah right!" Matthew cut in, mocking his response.

James chuckled and got to his feet. He grabbed their empty glasses from the chair and put them in the washbasin while Matthew put away the laptop and devices.

"I'll join the morning tutorial class tomorrow," Matthew said, looking at the remaining pallets. "I'll finish school earlier and come by sooner. We got to get at least half of those done otherwise we won't finish them."

"Yeah. I'll try to do as much as I can in the morning."

"Maybe you should ask Connor for a raise—he's bringing too much."

"He is," James sighed. "But I cannot risk him kicking me out—I'll get them done," he added confidently, and yawned, his eyes tearing up with exhaustion.

"I'll see you tomorrow. And we'll decide when you could come over and have the pleasure of watching yourself lose on a bigger screen," Matthew bantered.

"Right," James snickered. "Goodnight, bro."

"Goodnight to you," Matthew said, his hand raising to his forehead in salute, and he stepped outside.

The bright moon was dimming the lamp posts along the road. Cumulus clouds chasing each other. Matthew disappeared up the road and James locked the pedestrian door.

***

They agreed to go to Matthew's house the following Wednesday. James tried not to overthink it but his nerves were screaming at him—exposing himself closely to people was definitely not a good idea.

Still, that Wednesday evening, James was there as Matthew turned the key and pushed the front door of his house open.

“You’re sure your parents won't mind?” James asked.

“Of course. As long as you don't break any of my mom's useless porcelain figurines in the hallway that only exist to collect dust,” Matthew answered with a smirk, and stepped inside.

These are good people, James told himself, and followed Matthew into their home.

He had barely set a foot inside, when the delightful smell of baked goods embraced his appetite.

“Mom?” Matthew called, hanging his keys behind the door.

“In here, Matt,” a female voice replied from the other end of the hallway.

“I brought Andrew over—he was just about to trip on your favorite swan statue,” Matthew said.

James nudged Matthew's arm, feeling somewhat diffident.

“Very funny, Matt!” the voice remarked with an air of sarcasm. “Come on in and have a cup of tea. I just baked a chocolate cake.”

A woman popped her head out of a room, smiling at them in the most amicable manner as they made their way through the corridor.

"Hi," James uttered as they came next to her, consciously ignoring his apprehension.

"Hi, Andrew! Pleased to finally meet you. I'm Katy," she replied with a broad grin. "Have a seat. Tea, coffee? Or hot chocolate?" she continued, inviting him into the kitchen.

"Tea, please. Thanks."

"Matt, you?" she asked.

"Same, please," Matthew replied, and they sat down at the table while Katy started brewing some tea.

Matthew had Katy's shade of brown hair and both their skin tones were naturally tanned. Her hair was in a tidy up-do. Her mint, spotted apron fitting loosely around her waist.

She took out three mugs from a top cupboard and grabbed a teaspoon from the drawer. The kitchen was of medium size, the oval table they were sitting at, centered in the room. The cupboards and kitchen tops were made of wood, coated with deep blue and white post forms. On the window sill, above the kitchen sink, were small planters with basil, mint and thyme. Stuck to the fridge, a long shopping list and a heart-shaped note reading 'I love you.'

"One? Two? Sugar," Katy asked, raising the teaspoon in her hand.

"No sugar. Thanks," James replied.

"Matt, one?" she asked.

"You know it's two but you still always put one, or less," Matthew said, his eyebrows raised.

"You still drink it," Katy replied. "Too much sugar is not good for anyone."

“That definitely cannot be your motto if you open up the bakery,” Matthew said.

“Right,” Katy laughed, putting down the mugs of tea on the table. “Well, moderation is key to everything. And I do use healthier substitutes in my baking, thank you very much,” she added merrily, and placed a plate of sliced chocolate cake and another of ginger biscuits in front of them. “Help yourselves.”

“Thanks,” James replied. “And I wanted to thank you for the meals you send with Matt.”

“Oh, don't mention it, hon!” Katy said. “My pleasure, really!”

A dry cough from the corridor caught their attention and a lean, dark-skinned man appeared through the doorway, his face a map of wrinkles.

“Hey, Grandpa. This is Andrew,” Matthew said.

“Pleased to meet you,” the man greeted with the warmest of smiles. “I'm John Edwin Meli.”

“Pleased to meet you too.”

“Tea, Dad?” Katy asked.

“Yes, please, with a teaspoon of honey,” John replied, pulling out the chair next to James, and sat down.

“So, how is work going boys?” John asked.

“It's work,” Matthew replied shortly with a sigh of irritation. “Pallet after pallet after pallet after pallet.”

“Tiring isn't it?” John said, empathy echoing through his voice. “Well, we all have to start from somewhere, right?” John added, turning to James, waiting for his response.

“It's not—that bad,” James replied. “Pay could be better but—it's okay.”

John nodded in thought.

"I used to work on a farm back in the day," John said. "It was my grandfather's farm. Manual work is tough but it is greatly rewarding in its own way."

Katy put down a mug in front of John and joined them at the table.

"Thanks, dear," John told her, and reached for the plate of cookies and pulled it toward James. "Have you tried Katy's ginger cookies?"

"Yes," James replied. "Matt always brings some over at the garage; best ones I ever tasted."

"See?" John remarked, turning to Katy, "You should open that bakery. I'll definitely help—with the tasting mostly."

"Oh, Dad," Katy replied, almost shy, and picked up her mug cautiously. "You know Paul was against taking the risk for such an investment. And maybe he's right; people are becoming more health conscious these days which means that unless—"

"Which means that you don't believe in yourself enough," John interrupted. "Paul has his own managing career going; good for him, but it's about time that you follow your passion too."

"I'm in for it," Matthew said. "Would be nice working in a family business."

"Right. That is exactly what Paul would want to hear," Katy laughed nervously. "That instead of getting a degree you'd end up behind a counter selling cakes."

"I could always work part-time and continue studying."

"Okay, let's just drop it, shall we?" Katy concluded.

John took a slow, deep breath and reached for a ginger cookie.

“As my beloved Martha used to say,” John said, looking at the orange tinged biscuit in his hand, “‘Baking sweets is your pleasure, eating them is mine.’”

They all smiled and James watched John dip the cookie in his tea before biting into it.

It had never really occurred to James before that family wasn't just about parents and siblings, but also about grandparents and other relatives. Ricin had told him he hadn't any biological parents, let alone other relatives.

From what James was told, his first body cells were created in a petri dish during yet another trial experiment which to Ricin and all his scientists’ delight, fused perfectly right that time. And for some bizarre, unknown reason, the elaborate procedure could never again be successfully reproduced, leaving him as the only human weapon to serve Ricin. Or so that was the goal. To Ricin's great disappointment, James turned out to be a dud. Despite Ricin's most stringent efforts, James's sense of compassion and empathy was a plague upon him.

The thought of Ricin sent crippling chills down James's spine and he forced himself to shift his focus. That was all behind him now, he thought as he sipped his tea and heard Katy's comment about the weather. Life had been good to him lately; a brother was more than he could have ever wished or hoped for. And Ricin seemed to be fading perfectly into the past, right where he belonged.

CHAPTER FOUR

Apart from the weekday dinners at Matthew's house, Sundays weren't the same again. Katy insisted that James came over for Sunday family lunches and always made sure he felt right at home with them.

"Does anyone want a second helping?" Paul asked, looking from one to another around the table.

"No, thanks, Dad," Matthew replied.

"Thanks," James voiced, signalling to Paul he had had enough. "Food was very good. As always," he added to Katy.

"Thanks, hon," Katy replied. "I learned from the best. Right, Dad?"

"Well, if you insist on giving me the credit," John said, raising his glass of water in cheers, "why should I object? You're all welcome," he laughed.

"So, Andrew, any thoughts about returning to school?" Paul asked, wiping his mouth with a napkin. "You could always get a good student loan," Paul added, and took a sip of his red wine.

"Maybe next year," James replied with a polite nod.

“You should. A good education is required if you are to move forward in life,” Paul said. “Working on pallets; well, I don't think you see yourself doing that all your life. I mean, where can that get you?”

“Maybe next year,” James repeated in a respectful manner. He had long come to his own conclusion that Paul, although always meaning well, was the kind of person to impose his opinions on others.

“Education is important but there is no age limit,” Katy said. “Everyone gets there at their own pace,” she continued, giving Paul a firm nod.

“Right—but it's harder to get an education the older you get, Andrew,” Paul insisted.

“I want dessert,” Matthew blurted out, looking expectantly at his mom.

But Paul's persistence did not evoke any intimidation for James.

“I always liked sciences,” James began, putting a smile on Paul's long face. “But life has taught me so much already—probably more than I could have ever learned in school. Isn't learning more important than education?”

Matthew burst out laughing, almost spitting out his drink.

“Well, that diplomacy is definitely not taught at school,” Matthew said.

Paul bobbed his head in thought, his eyes resting on his empty wine glass.

“Still, education opens many doors,” Paul said. “But I get what you mean—I see where you're coming from.”

There was a degrading undertone in Paul's voice everyone picked up on—Katy's eyes locked with Paul's in a rebuking manner, Matthew began tapping his index finger on his glass—but Paul's remark simply rolled off James's shoulders.

"Not everyone walks on a paved road, Paul," John said, his tone solemn. "And experience will teach you the ones that don't, often end up making more out of their life. There are doors in life which only pain and humbleness can open."

"You always lose me there, John," Paul said blithely. "Philosophy was never my thing, but I'm sure it makes total sense to those that do get it."

Unlike Paul, James had understood John completely. He only hoped Ricin would not be able to slam shut more doors in his life.

"Dessert?" Katy announced, getting to her feet.

"Yes, please," Matthew replied, stretching back in his chair.

Katy went to the fridge and took out a light pink cheesecake. It was topped with chopped strawberries encircled by whirls of whipped cream.

"Hope you like," Katy said as she put it down on the table.

"Isn't that simply gorgeous?" John said, his eyes feasting on the cake.

"As gorgeous as my lovely wife," Paul said, quickly standing up, and took the cake knife from her hand. "Do sit down, sweetheart. I'll take it from here."

"Oh, thank you," Katy said with a broad smile, and sat down again.

"Ah, Dad," Matthew sighed. "So romantic. We all know you always offer to cut the dessert yourself to take the largest slice."

Loud laughter followed and Paul simply shrug his shoulders.

"What can I say—your mom's desserts are the key to my heart."

"Washing the dishes for a change would certainly be the key to mine," Katy said.

"Okay, okay, fine. I'll do the dishes today," Paul replied.

"Woohoo! Pass the bottle of wine will you?" Katy said. "I can hop right into bed for a siesta after dessert."

They enjoyed the cheesecake, sprinkled with a light conversation. Then played a few card games, Paul taking all the wins.

Katy went to bed and James helped Paul with the dishes while Matthew showed John how to use some new apps on his phone.

"And what's the point of being alerted that it is raining outside?" John asked with a chuckle. "Are people that lazy to look out of a window nowadays?"

"It's about time efficiency," Matthew replied.

"I prefer to call it laziness," John said. "Back in the day, we didn't have all these technological advances yet we still got more work done every day."

"I like it," Matthew shrugged. "It's almost like a superpower—you're not looking outside, yet you know exactly what the weather is like."

"Right," John said, getting off the sofa. "The older I get, the more I question human evolution. What do you think, Andrew?" John asked James, who was standing by the sofa listening to their conversation.

"It has its good and bad—but everything's subjective," James replied. Subjective—like the fact that for him, his own body advancements were nothing other than his curse.

***

The sun set earlier again and James was back at the garage before the moon watched over the skies. The air in the garage was cold even though the door to the backyard was also closed. A frigid winter was said to be coming, its bleak breath announced its awaited presence.

James got up early the next morning and began cleaning planks; removing nails from pieces of separated wood he had left aside for when it was too early or too late to bang a hammer.

Dark clouds drizzled fitfully in the afternoon, just enough to cause peril on the roads. Matthew came straight from school, popping in at his house to grab their dinners.

"Physics class was fun. Mirabelle and Tiffany always know how to entertain with their obvious rivalry—diva war problems," Matthew laughed as he put a plank of wood to the side.

"Bet Miss Zammit was thrilled," James remarked, amused by the stories of school life.

"Oh, that teacher's patience deserves a Nobel Peace Prize. Though maybe she gets her revenge on us through the homework she gives," Matthew said, squinting in suspicion. "Got another paper for Thursday and am not looking forward to it; read the first question and my brain was like no; not happening today."

"What's the topic?"

"The mega boring electromagnetic spectrum."

"Light waves," James replied. "Cool."

"Cool? Is there any topic you actually dislike? You would be the perfect student; full attention, full focus," Matthew laughed.

"I don't know about school but science magazines made everything sound awesome."

"Right. By the way, I signed up for Mister Larry's afternoon gym class. It's once a week, on Tuesdays. I need to start building muscle, man. Heck, even the men working on the street look like the marines. Did you see them? Each one of them is totally ripped and all."

"Workmen? On the street?" he asked, unaware roadwork was going to take place again so soon.

"Yeah, they were setting up orange cones to block the road when I got here."

The thrum of a helicopter began approaching, another one right behind it. That was odd—James could only recall one other time a helicopter flew close by and now there were two.

"I think I might start taking those protein shakes. Mom is against—"

"How many men did you see on the street?" James cut in. The helicopters seemed to remain hovering close by. His mind racing.

"Um, don't know, seven—maybe eight—why?"

James hurried to the pedestrian door and looked through the eyehole. All appeared normal outside, just two neighbors talking to each other across the street.

"What is it?" Matthew asked.

But James kept listening carefully to the sound of the blades—the helicopters were circling the area.

"Matt, you need to leave!" James said, panicked. "Walk out of here calmly and go home before they come."

"What—who's coming?"

"I don't have time to explain, Matt; they can't find you here," he replied, chasing his words.

"Who? What are you talking about?"

"Matt, please listen," he cried, convinced those helicopters were Ricin's and those workmen were actually trained like the marines if not better. "You need to get home and stay out of this."

"Andrew, wh—"

"Matt, just leave!" James ordered. "If they find you here they'll kill you."

Matthew's face turned ashen and he put down the hammer.

"Should I call the police?" Matthew asked, reaching for his phone in his pocket.

"You'll be dead before they get here."

Every cell in James's body was yelling at him to take off before it was too late—with Ricin behind a plan, every second counted. But he couldn't just leave and let them find Matthew there.

"Listen to me, Matt; leave now while they're still setting up. Please, just go; now."

Matthew's eyes bulged in bewilderment. He grabbed his backpack and rushed through the pedestrian door.

James watched Matthew through the eyehole and listened carefully, making sure that Matthew walked away safely.

The two neighbors were still enjoying their pleasant chat beneath the apple tree—if the workmen had made a move on Matthew, the commotion would have surely drawn their attention.

James could not stay a second longer. The helicopters were still monitoring the area; any moment now men could swarm into the garage. He dashed to the door of the yard and scanned the top of the stone fence—there was no suspicious movement, the usual hush bouncing off the limestone.

He went to the fence and effortlessly jumped over it into the cobbled alley. He looked both ways, no one was in sight, and he hurried down the narrow passageway.

Stepping out of the alley, the horrid nightmare came to life—the exact tormenting night terror he had been having ever since he had escaped from Ricin. Numerous men were closing in on him from everywhere, each approaching with precision. Black vehicles roared in his direction and the helicopters ranged in on him.

He took off; parkoured up walls, roofs, and fences in a frantic effort to get away. His unnatural ability enabled him to leap heights unlike anyone—and soon, the men were far behind. The persistent rotor blades of the helicopters sliced through the air. And on he ran in a desperate flee.

The helicopters chased him—right into Ricin's trap. Dark vans screeched into a circle around him, men poured out of the vehicles, each of their aims pinned on him. The helicopters descended to within shooting range, and his chance of escape was the only thing getting away.

He hesitated his next move—a wrong step could further entrap him—but with his adapted reflexes engaged, he dodged an ambush of tranq bullets and leaped over the closest van.

He hit the ground and a shimmer caught his eye just as he was about to launch into a run. A young girl rode her bicycle heading to the one way street, oblivious to the black van revving in her direction. James calculated their trajectories on a collision course.

Ignoring his reflexes, he dashed toward her and snatched her off the bike just in time. The van smashed it; its lilac seat hurled into the air.

“Run!” he told her as he put her down, and her little feet took off in haste.

The men close behind, James mapped his exit, but a heaviness began spreading through his limbs. He looked down at his leg and his heart stopped; a tranquillizer dart. He yanked it out, but it was too late. He couldn't even take a step. A heavy lethargy drowned his body, his vision blurred. A hand grabbed his arm, he tried to pull away, his balance off—dark uniforms—Ricin's men—and everything faded to black.

CHAPTER FIVE

James's body ached. His head throbbed. His leaden eyelids couldn't lift, around him dead silence. Beneath him was a familiar cold, hard surface; he was back at Ricin's headquarters. The chase. The dart. His failure. His stomach churned. He rolled over and threw up.

The too-familiar sound of the metal gate sliding, broke the silence. He looked up—his vision hazy yet the outline of the hefty man recognizable as he walked into the cell; it was Ricin himself.

"You're here, James," Ricin said. The particular timber of his deep voice impaled James's heart. "It was only a matter of time you know." Ricin kicked him forcefully in the stomach.

The effect of the drug had not worn off completely and James just lay there drowsing. Ricin walked out of the cell, the metal bars slamming shut behind him.

Hours seemed to have gone by and James's sight was now back to normal. He sat up and slid to one side of the cell, resting his back against the metal wall. The cell was just as he had left it; bare, suffocating in the absence of natural light. Its three metallic walls reflecting nothing other than Ricin's ruthlessness. The small toilet and washbasin were still standing in the same corner, the deep dent on the bottom of the washbasin still visible.

Outside the cell was an empty, medium-sized room where guards stood by while cameras monitored everyone's every move.

After outgrowing the nursery, this cell was practically his room. Ricin had set up a bedroom for him and James remembered that heavenly feeling of sinking into the soft pillows after long hours of physical training with Wang Gu or target practice with Garth. But Ricin's idea of discipline didn't allow for him to be the child he was back then and punishments meant endless cell time with no food, only allowed out for more lessons and practice, and a shower. As he grew older, the more his thinking began clashing with what Ricin expected out of him, and his defiance soon turned him into Ricin's prisoner.

His mind had suppressed many memories in an effort to cope with living, but he still clearly recalled what Ricin had warned him he would do, if he dared ever escape from him.

James swallowed hard, his pulse beginning to pelt at the recollection. The electric door of the room outside his cell, swooshed open. Ricin strode in, approached James's cell, and glared down at him.

"Almost two whole years, James," Ricin began. "Two —that is how much of my precious time you have wasted. I thought you had understood me clearly when I told you I own you and you'll work for me regardless of what your opinion on that matter was. I created all that you are; mutant and all. I invested so much in you; you don't have any say."

Ricin's piercing blue eyes pinned James, his words debilitated James's soul.

"You're just going to wish I'd kill you instead," Ricin continued. "I'm going to make sure you think twice, if running away ever crosses your mind again." Ricin paused, wrath highlighting his face. "Let him have it."

James knew he would not be able to avoid what came next. Embedded in the cell walls were weapons which ensured that James was certainly hit. This was proven several times—one particular occasion had left James with eight stitches on the back of his right forearm.

His warning reflexes tripped and he sprung up. A small opening in one of the walls appeared and a thick, metal muzzle came forward.

It began activating, its sound increasing in pitch as the red glow in the barrel got brighter. Extreme panic flushed through James's veins, his reflexes overwhelming his conscious. He swiftly turned his back to it, crouching down and burying his head between his shoulders, beneath his arms.

Sharp laser beams fired a fusillade of red throughout the whole cell. It was as though hot spears pierced through James's back, burning his flesh as they penetrated through his skin. He stiffened in response to the pain—excruciating. He fell to his knees—helpless—as each breath expanded his torso and pulled at his wounds.

His back was bare and bloody. It would heal much faster than would normally be expected; that was the way his body was designed to restore to health. But right then, it was a raw wound, engaging nerve fibers in screams of burning agony.

He remained there, kneeling on the ground, petrified of the pronounced pain he would feel if he moved a muscle. His body began shaking as he slowly inhaled shallow breaths, fighting back tears that would only satisfy Ricin's barbarity.

"Not that I ever needed to prove anything," Ricin said, "but I am a man of my word; you knew this would inevitably happen if you ran away." His voice lacked any pity. "Oh, and I almost forgot, son, we wouldn't want those wounds to get infected now, would we?"

A liquid sprayed onto James's back, setting the cuts on fire; submerging him into a deep wave of torment that drowned his conscious into merciful suspension as he collapsed to the cement floor and all went blank.

***

It was the ping of a glass vial against the floor of the cell that awoke him. His eyes opened but he dared not budge, the pain unbearable.

"James?"

It was Edgar, his medical consultant ever since he could remember, the only one at Ricin's headquarters that had sometimes stood up for him. Yet still, Edgar was also Ricin's right-hand man.

"James?" Edgar called again, gently tapping on his shoulder.

James opened his eyes again, continuing to focus on his breathing; slow, steady breaths moved his torso the least.

"Here, you need to drink, and move for better circulation to help with your healing; you've been in the same position for too long. Come on," Edgar said, attempting to pull at his arm to get him to move.

But James lacked any strength or will and remained there on the floor.

"James, please, come on," Edgar said, pulling harder at his arm. "Ramon, give me a hand, will you?" Edgar called to one of the guards outside the cell.

Ramon hurried toward them. They each took James by an arm and lifted him up slowly to a kneeling position. James gasped; his flesh snapped under the tension and seeped fresh blood. But then, the numbing exhaustion came over him again, his energy wasted on stifling the agony. Edgar held a bottle to his lips while they kept his body upright.

"Drink—it's added with vitamins and salts," Edgar said.

James managed to swallow a few sips of the sweet drink.

"Can you stand?" Edgar asked.

James's legs were melted rubber. He shook his head ever so slightly.

"Here, have some more," Edgar said, holding the bottle to his mouth again.

They helped him lie down, then left his cell and the bars closed behind them.

The next two days dragged by, the blink of his eyelids the only rapid movement he was able to do. The wounds were healing; quick as expected.

Apart from the guards that stood outside his cell, Edgar was the only person who came to him. Edgar kept monitoring his recovery, making sure he kept hydrated. He wasn't given food; one of Ricin's standard punishments.

Edgar's words were bare minimum, like they had always been throughout the years. Nothing about Edgar had changed, except for a deep scar just above his right eyebrow. And there was this odd, vague look Edgar kept giving James, as though he could not look him in the eye.

Movement for James was still painful, his posture stiff. He was standing over the washbasin, cold water droplets trickling down his face, pulling him into reminiscence of the ocean. The electric door opened and Ricin stepped in. James turned to face him, trying hard not to wince in pain.

"Having a rather speedy recovery, aren't you?" Ricin said. "Well, thanks to the way I designed you, right?"

James kept looking straight at Ricin. He might be his prisoner once again but he was not going to submit to him. He was no longer afraid of physical pain or hunger; there was only so much Ricin could do to him without killing him.

"When are you going to show some respect, James?" Ricin asked.

But James's eyes remained steady, his gaze defiant.

"Open up," Ricin said into a security camera in the room.

The guards present exchanged nervous looks. The gate swiftly opened and Ricin tread right up to James.

"You better start showing some deference," Ricin snarled into his face.

A tense aura jounced between them as James's eyes locked fiercely with Ricin's. Ricin pursed his lips in chagrin and grabbed him savagely by the throat.

"If you won't, I'll make you," Ricin threatened through clenched teeth.

But James kept looking Ricin in the eye. And spat forcefully in his face.

Ricin rammed harder on his throat, shoving him against the wall with one hand, and began punching him in the chest with the other.

James was still too weak to fight back. Ricin's strong blows drained all that was left of him.

"Ricin stop!" Edgar shouted as he ran into the room out of breath. "You're going to kill him. Stop!"

Edgar grabbed Ricin's fist.

"You're going to kill him!" Edgar repeated in anger. Ricin finally let go of James's neck and he tumbled to the ground, coughing up blood.

"You *will* show respect," Ricin said, and left the room.

"James, don't be foolish." Edgar sounded nervous. "He'll only make you pay harder for your actions. There is no point in having an attitude."

But James's mind was set. He'd rather have Ricin kill him than live under his supremacy. He was glad that for the first time in his life, he stood up to Ricin and let him know he was no longer his moldable accomplice or criminal servant—merely his prisoner.

The next afternoon, thunderous claps disrupted the hush that had fallen. James tried to keep his mind off the physical, replaying and reliving great memories involving frothy waves rolling onto sandy shores and meals full of laughter with Matthew's family.

Thunder kept rumbling closer to the building, the walls quivered in the chill air. Ricin came to the room. The guard accompanying Ricin stood in the doorway, drawing more attention to the muffled, odd sounds that were coming from the corridor.

"I thought long and hard yesterday," Ricin began, looking at him through the closed bars. "You must know by now that I always get what I want—one way or another. You clearly are not on the same page when it comes to your predestined role, but I am not going to let that stand in my way. Remember I had once told you I will obtain great power and control over practically the whole world? Well, that time is here. All I need is two more pieces of the puzzle for the ball to get rolling. Once I have the remaining information and a specific biological agent, I can begin the much awaited biological warfare."

Biological warfare; those two words hauled James back to the exact moment he had decided he was done with being Ricin's puppet. He was about nine years old and had finished target practice earlier that day. He was about to enter the kitchen when he overheard Ricin and Edgar's conversation from behind the door. They kept mentioning that phrase, *biological warfare*, Edgar sounding unusually tense. The next day, he had asked Wang Gu what biological warfare actually meant and he had never seen Wang Gu's face turn so solemn. *Listen carefully*, Wang Gu had told him, looking him straight in the eye, hammering the words into him, *that war will have a beginning but no real end. Countless innocent people will continue to die and those that remain standing, will not deserve to breathe; may you never allow yourself to be Ricin's means to bring hell upon Earth.*

"Infiltrating the air with a deadly pathogen," Ricin continued, "and being the only one who has and controls the antidote needed—which only reverses effects temporarily making people dependent on it—would create an uproar of chaos. Every other person in power will have no choice but to bow down to me. Wouldn't that kind of control be spectacular? Thing is, I need your mutant abilities to obtain the last two pieces left. I tried to get them several other ways since you were such a cretin and escaped, but unfortunately, none were successful. Now, having reaffirmed the dunce that you are and your disinclination to fulfil your role, I decided to give you a very, very clear perspective on the matter."

Ricin signalled to the guard by the door and the latter moved aside. A slim boy, most likely in his teens, was pushed into the room. Head covered with a black cloth bag, hands bound behind his back. An older man was forced to follow, him too, covered and bound.

"From what I got to know," Ricin said, "I'm more than sure these two are going to make you forget you ever had an opinion about your job."

James's eyes remained fixed on the covered faces. His chest tight, his heart pounding vigorously in anticipation. The guard uncovered the man's face; a dark-skinned, wrinkled countenance, and then that of the teenager; John and Matthew.

All the air seemed to be sucked out of the room. James's hands began to shake in trepidation—in Ricin's captivity, no life was guaranteed.

John and Matthew's mouths were gagged, dry blood smeared beneath a cut on Matthew's forehead.

"It's simple now, James," Ricin said. "You follow orders; they live."

James's eyes shifted to Ricin and he let his head fall in submission; a subconscious movement. Ricin, at last, appeared pleased.

“Rest, my boy,” Ricin said. “Rest well—you are going to need it.”

CHAPTER SIX

Ricin paraded out of the room, his smirk playing the tune of triumph. Once the door closed shut behind him, the four guards that remained cut the zip ties that bound Matthew and John's hands.

Matthew quickly pulled out his gag. "Andrew? What's going on?" he asked, his voice quavering with fear.

"I'm so sorry," James whispered weakly. "I'm so sorry."

Shock was still setting in James, blood draining from his head, sinking with the unbearable reality that was elucidating by the second—Ricin had him right in the palm of his hand and Matthew and John's lives were on the line.

"What is this place? Where are we? Why are you in a cell?" he heard Matthew ask. But James's head was spinning, his body paralyzed.

"Andrew?" Matthew called.

Matthew was standing right outside the metal bars. John right behind him. Both their gazes begging for answers.

James stood up slowly, ignoring his own pain.

“I’m so sorry,” he repeated, guilt weighing on him. “I’m not—who I said I was. I had to lie; I didn't want Ricin to find me.”

“Wh-What do you mean? Why? He told you to follow orders and we live; what orders, Andrew?” Matthew asked.

“My name is not Andrew—it's James,” he began. And for the next hour, he told them all they wanted to know about his past, about Ricin, and why they were there—consciously detached from any emotion that little mutant boy had gone through.

“So it's James, right?” Matthew asked, sitting on the floor outside the cell, eyes wide open, still digesting everything.

“Yeah—it actually stands for Junior Accomplice Mutant Evolutionary Species.”

“How was Ricin never arrested? How was he never caught?” Matthew asked, shaking his head in disbelief.

“Like I said; Ricin's undercover agents are everywhere. He's always steps ahead of everyone and manipulation gets him exactly where he wants to be.”

“You can breathe under water and sense danger? Apart from healing quicker and having abnormal strength?” Matthew voiced to himself in incredulity as much as in awe.

James's countenance fell to the floor; those were the exact symptoms of his plague.

A lingering silence dimmed the room, Matthew and John both ill at ease.

“I’m really sorry I dragged you into this; I never thought I'd—”

"It's not your fault that we're here," John interrupted. "This is not on you."

But James's thoughts were still yelling at him; rebuking his actions for allowing himself to get close to people.

"This war Ricin intends to start," John said, "how sure are you that he will be successful?"

"If I get what he needs—" James paused. "Ricin never fails," he said, and a wave of emotions slammed him violently against the edged rocks of his mind.

John nodded to himself in thought and they went quiet again.

Their heads soon turned to the loud swoosh of the door. Edgar came in, carrying a large plastic box.

Edgar was James's only hope for Matthew and John; their only chance if they were to make it out of there alive.

"Edgar," James called, getting to his feet, waiting for Edgar to look at him. But Edgar purposefully ignored him and put down the box right next to John.

"You've all got food and a change of clothes. And there is a shower and toilet right behind that curtain," Edgar said, pointing to the restroom the guards used.

"Edgar, they don't deserve to be here," James cried, but Edgar's face remained turned away. "Edgar please; Ricin knows about them now, they will still serve their purpose, they don't need to be kept in here."

"That's not for me to decide," Edgar replied.

"Please, Edgar," he repeated, almost begging.

Edgar paused to look him in the eye for the first time since he was caught. James searched deeply for the shred of pity Edgar once had, but to no avail. Instead, Edgar's face grew more solemn, bitterness lining his dark eyes.

"Their fate—is in your hands," Edgar said. "Wrap your head around that, James."

Edgar left the room. Matthew began shaking his head, then stood up abruptly, his feet keeping a swift gait as they paced from wall to wall, ignoring the four guards present.

"I'll figure something out, Matt. I promise," James said, trying to sound confident, but mostly, attempting to convince himself that that was even a possibility.

When he had managed to escape from Ricin, it was solely because of a mistake Edgar had made which James had fortunately noticed before anyone else did. Escaping with Matthew and John could never happen.

"We're going to die; we're going to be tortured and killed," Matthew said, still pacing anxiously. "I'm never going to see mom again."

"Hey, Matt, come here," John called firmly, but Matthew paid no attention.

"Mom's going to break down," Matthew continued to himself, chasing his breath. "The life she built—all's going to come crashing down on her—her only son, her father; it's going to destroy her."

"Matt, come here," John said, getting to his feet.

"Grandpa, this is bad; this is really—"

"Matthew, stop it!" John said, grabbing Matthew's shoulders, holding him steady. "Enough! It's not good, but it *will* be! Don't let Ricin get to you; don't give him that power; don't give him what he wants."

Matthew's eyes kept resting heavily on John's, the love of family building each other up, holding each other from falling apart. John pulled Matthew toward him and hugged him tightly, tapping strongly on his back.

"It's not good, but it will be," John repeated.

Matthew took a deep breath, nodding his head in hope.

"Let's eat," John said, looking at the both of them, forcing a smile.

They sat down on the floor, the metal gate between them a reminder of their captivity. Edgar had got some rice with vegetables and they began eating in silence. James had not eaten in days; food always tasted better thereafter.

"Food is good," John said, looking over at Matthew who had barely touched his portion. "Do eat, Matt, there is only so much one can do on an empty stomach."

Matthew hesitated, then heaped his fork and ate, soon finishing his rice. Edgar had brought some bottles of water too, sweetened with added vitamins and salts.

Matthew kept avoiding James's eyes, unusually keeping to himself. But could James blame him? There was no real light at the end of the tunnel for neither Matthew nor John, nor himself for that matter. The more he thought about it, the more fear constricted the air out of his lungs, choking him and making him light-headed. He sipped some water and forced himself to shift his focus on the relatively calm present.

John turned to the box and began taking out the clothes, then paused.

"See it's not that bad," John said with a rather cheerful tone. "We even got candy."

Candy? That was odd. James peered over into the box and there were three sweets at the bottom. Three half yellow, half red, hard candy; James's favorite candy; the same candy Edgar used to secretly give him every time he took him up to the roof to watch the night sky together. And Edgar would always utter the same phrase as he dropped one into his hand; *In the end, everything's okay. So if it's not okay, it's not the end. Just have a little faith.*

CHAPTER SEVEN

"Breakfast," Ramon said the next morning as he put down a colorful bowl of fresh fruit on the floor.

"Thanks," John replied with a smile.

Matthew was still dozing in a corner, arms crossed over his knees, his head resting against the wall. John had been up since the night guards had changed and kept pacing calmly across the room, absorbed in deep thought.

James himself had barely managed to get any sleep, hopelessness consuming his peace of mind.

"Fruit?" John asked him, holding the bowl close to the metal bars where James sat.

James shook his head, his appetite masked by nausea. John picked up one of the red apples and dropped it into his lap.

"Eat," John said. "Those wounds on your back—you need to eat to recover."

James had become accustomed to the dull ache. He had been allowed out of his cell to take a shower, cold water had soothed the burn.

The door to the room opened and Garth walked in. His stride was as arrogant as James remembered it to be, his hair still shabbily shadowing most of his face.

"Look who's home," Garth said with a smirk. "Pity I missed the chase."

James glared a thousand deadly daggers at Garth. Garth chuckled at his silence, then looked down on John and Matthew before stepping out of the room again.

"Who was that?" John asked James.

"Garth Mendes."

Matthew was now awake, his face less ashen than it had been yesterday. He took a tangerine from the fruit bowl and came over to the bars and sat down.

"Y'know, I thought *I* had been through a lot before this…" Matthew said, "with school and all."

"I'm going to get you both out of this, Matt," James promised, more of a hope than a plan.

"I know you will," Matthew said, and began peeling the tangerine. "Maybe the almighty Ricin can spare a big screen in the meantime," he added, raising his voice at one of the cameras in the room.

John came next to them and sat down, his old body cracking as it sat on the cold floor.

"Bet you know how many tiles there are," Matthew said, his eyes following the rows of tiles that covered the walls of the room.

"No idea," James replied.

"Seriously?" Matthew said. "All those long hours just sitting here; I'm tempted to start counting already," Matthew laughed.

They chatted away time, conversations drifting in and out of seriousness, and four days ticked by.

"I was about your age when I did that," John told them, a mischief smile on his face. "I managed to keep it hidden in the shed for nearly a month."

"How did they get to know about it?" Matthew asked.

John scratched his eyebrow, "I nearly gave my poor mama a heart attack," he chuckled.

"*She* found it?!" Matthew laughed.

"Not exactly," John replied, "I must have forgotten to close the lid properly and—"

The swoosh of the door cut John's words short and Ricin walked in.

"You look nicely settled," Ricin said to John and Matthew.

Matthew scowled at Ricin. John glanced up at him, then looked away and smiled to himself.

"Something amusing you, old man?" Ricin asked.

"No," John replied. His tone disconcertingly serene.

Ricin paused, the sharp squint of his eyes on John. Ricin then turned to face the cell, his hands calmly behind his back.

"James," Ricin began. "I believe, Matthew and John do mean something to you. However, following the mishap which led to your escape, I decided that a permanent solution demands to be implemented."

Ricin's calm demeanour trebled James's pulse—it only implied guaranteed success for his next move.

"I cannot lose track of you ever again, James," Ricin said. "The way to ensure that, is to insert a tracer into your body. This will enable us to know your exact location at all times, even in the deepest of seas. So if you are idiotic enough to attempt to run away again, well, how shall I put it? You will be more like a pathetic rabbit in my maze, bouncing around until you have nowhere else to hop but into my hands again. Do you understand?"

James remained staring helplessly at Ricin, desperately hoping to wake up from the nightmare.

"Enough time has now passed James and your body has practically healed," Ricin continued, "Edgar will be here very shortly and the procedure will take place today."

"Today?" James repeated. "Whe—Where will the tracer be?"

Ricin's phone beeped in his pocket and he calmly reached for it and tapped the screen, before putting it away again.

"You won't be able to get rid of it without killing yourself," Ricin said. "It's going to be attached to your heart muscle."

James heard the electric door close behind Ricin, then the thump of his heart getting louder and faster. The walls of the cell caved in and he gasped for air.

"Just because they will know where you are, still doesn't mean they own you, James," John said. "Heads up, son, one day, all this will be behind you."

He looked up at John, the rest of his body numb; a tracer in his heart meant Ricin would forever have him.

Not a minute was wasted, Edgar appeared through the doorway. He was followed by a man and woman who were pushing a gurney. The door closed shut behind them before the cell started to open.

"Ricin told you what we are about to do," Edgar said to James. "We'll sedate you here, then transport you to the operating room."

James stood up, extreme panic clouding his thinking. He did not want to be Ricin's prisoner, even more so, forever.

"Lie down," Edgar instructed, pointing to the gurney.

James shook his head and his feet took him a step backward.

"James, this is going to be done, whether you want it or not," Edgar said.

Edgar kept a steady gaze on James—awaiting, expecting. James broke out in a cold sweat, his angst loud in every pound of his heart. Edgar then looked away impatiently and cleared his throat.

"Fine," Edgar said, and turned to nod at Wayne, the closest guard to Matthew.

Wayne immediately cocked his gun and aimed straight at Matthew's head.

"Stop! Okay," James shouted, veiling Matthew's gasp, and walked heavily over to the gurney and sat down.

Wayne lowered his firearm. Matthew still held his breath.

Edgar began filling a syringe. James's lungs were as though failing; the air too dense to inhale. His nerves drove his head in circles, his stomach into twists.

"James," Edgar called, waiting for him to look up. "Breathe—and calm down," Edgar said, patient, maintaining eye contact with him.

James inhaled deeply and forced his eyes shut—Matthew and John's life depended on his cooperation with Ricin; he had to let them do it.

Edgar injected a warm fluid into his arm.

"Lie down," Edgar said, and James did as he was told. "It will just take a few seconds," he heard Edgar's voice say and everything around him began to fade away. That was the last thing he remembered.

A burning soreness in his chest shook him into consciousness. He had no perception of time and it took him a while to come around. He was on a bed, tubes snaking from his arms, a medical dressing covering his torso; it was done; Ricin's tracer was in him.

He was hit by a hurricane of emotions. His gaze a thousand yard stare. Then he noticed something peculiar about his cell—no one was beside him, yet the metal gate was open. He had always associated those metal bars with hope; hope that one day he would be free and out of that gate. Now those bars were wide open; he could just walk out. Because now, the bars were in his heart.

Despondency came upon him, the last thread of hope escaped. He lifted his hand over his face and for the first time in years, he wept quietly.

"Hey," John's voice called gently, up close to him. "You're still free. So what if they know where you are. They still cannot read your mind or heart, and most importantly, they can never have control on what you believe in and that is what makes us free."

James sniffed, gritting his teeth in an attempt to suppress his tears. He removed his hand from his face and turned to John.

"It's still okay. It's still okay," John repeated, looking steadily into his eyes as he sat down on the edge of the bed.

"Thanks," James whispered.

Matthew stood next to them; he, too, looked disheartened.

"How are you feeling; are you in a lot of pain?" Matthew asked.

"Not really—everywhere is just numb."

"Edgar just added something in the drip bag; pain medication I suppose." John said.

They all went quiet, occasional beeps from the medical monitor shifting John and Matthew's eyes.

"My grandfather," John said, grabbing their attention, "was a man of a few words. My grandmother used to tease him, saying you have to pay him to talk. But whenever he did say something, it was always food for thought. I remember this one time, I had just come home from school. I was so upset—angry, sad. I was being picked on at school because of the color of my skin. Something I couldn't change or at least hide. And when I told him what had happened and that I was being called names—his mouth became a hard line—I can still see him, holding his head high, and telling me, '*You are your own worst enemy and your own best friend. You can decide to let something destroy you, or you can learn how to live with it and use it to your advantage.*'"

"Wasn't he wise," Ricin mocked, coming up from behind them.

John stood up slowly. His grim expression on Ricin.

"Step aside, old man," Ricin said, his tone threatening.

John and Ricin exchanged fierce looks. Then John calmly walked away, Ricin's eyes stabbing him in the back.

"Such a success," Ricin said, turning to James with a smirk.

"Nothing's changed," James replied, avoiding any eye contact.

Ricin gave a hearty laugh. “Nothing's changed? Is that why you were crying a few minutes ago? Because nothing's changed?” Ricin chuckled in derision.

James kept his eyes down, too exhausted to feel Ricin's sting.

“Trying to be brave won't alter the facts James. I created you; you’ll do as I please; and there is no escape now. As soon as you recover from the surgery, you will be carrying out your first task. You will be collecting some very important documents—let's just say—collecting valuable leverage prior to your other missions.”

CHAPTER EIGHT

Almost three weeks went by and James's body healed perfectly; the only thing left scarred—his mind.

He spent hours listening to John talk about life. Matthew—mostly lost in his own world—had heard John's stories many times before.

James listened in awe at the way John handled what life had put him through. All he could think of as he listened, was how unfair life could be. But John would surprise him every time by how he had managed to turn those wounds into wisdom and use that to help others. John was the kind of man to aspire to become like; a man of value.

None of them were allowed out of the room, the walls seemed to inch closer every day. They were given ample food; fresh fruit for breakfast and two hot meals during the day.

Clean clothes for all three of them were always neatly stacked on the shelf near the washed towels. And Edgar had brought a shaving razor and gel for John.

Edgar came by every morning and evening and always asked the same two questions—if they had managed to get any sleep and if they were given enough food—but he looked at each of them carefully, as though making sure they were all doing okay.

Ricin had not set foot inside the room since the day of the surgery—the further away Ricin kept, all the better.

"I remember, the first time I had gone fishing with Edward," John said. "It was a beautiful day—cloudless sky with a gentle breeze. We were fishing down by the lake near Stella's fish market. Edward was four years old. Katy wasn't even born yet. He was so happy to catch his first fish. It was a bluegill. He was so excited, showing off with this fish in his hands. But when he went to put it in the bucket, it slipped right out of his fingers, back into the water. He cried so hard—he wanted to show his mother what he had caught. But I told him, '*Son, you don't need to prove anything to anyone, not to me, not to your mother: you only have to prove things to yourself.*' If you know the truth, no matter how many people deny it, proving it to them will only be a waste of time; people will only believe what they want to believe."

"Did he catch another one that day?" James asked.

"No. Even though he tried so hard to. But he did learn something that day—as soon as he saw his mother he told her; '*Mom, I'm not going to waste time proving to you that I caught a bluegill, but I did. Now let's go home,*'" John chuckled as he mimicked the tone of a four-year-old, and they laughed with him.

The door swooshed open and Ricin entered the room, killing the laughter. Both Matthew and John inhaled deeply, Matthew's breath highlighted by a quiver.

James disciplined his nerves; he couldn't let his emotions derail clear thinking.

“On your feet, James,” Ricin said firmly. “Time to get back to work.”

James stood up, avoiding John and Matthew's gaze, and walked out of the doorway after Ricin. Two guards that were waiting in the corridor began following him. Ricin led the way.

James was taken to a large room on the third floor. The steel gray of the curtains a continuation of the clouds that overlooked the river outside the wide windows.

“Have a seat,” Ricin told him, pointing to a chair around the oval, teak table at which Edgar, Garth, and another man and woman were already sitting. Ricin took his place at the head of the table. The woman sat up in her chair and took a sip from the bottle of water in front of her.

“As I had already told you, James,” Ricin said, resting his elbows on the table, locking his fingers together, “your first mission is to collect some very important documents. Documents which many people, other than myself, wish to possess. Too bad for them, but I have you and I know you are capable of obtaining these documents without getting a bullet in the back.”

James kept staring down at the table, anticipation fueling his angst.

“You will be going to the president's residence,” Ricin continued, “to get a file named Z.T.”

The president's residence? The other crimes he was forced to do when he was younger had never involved such extents.

“This file is exclusively found on the president's laptop and only he has access to it; so only he can give it to you,” Ricin said. “He will transfer it to us via an external device you will give him to attach to his laptop. At that same time, we will be able to check if it's the real thing. You will be wearing an earpiece and a camera at all times through which we shall be watching and communicating with you. And you will obviously be given a gun."

James remained silent, his gaze low.

"Are you even following?" Ricin asked him, impatient.

James slid up in his chair and nodded. Edgar stared at him intently from across the table.

"They will be taking you as close as they can to the residence," Ricin said. "The president is there today and will be having a meeting in the boardroom. This is the blueprint of the place." Ricin pulled out the large plan of the building from the stack of papers on the table.

James leaned forward, pretending to take interest in the layout. He had to let Ricin think he was on board with the mission, both for Matthew and John's sake, as well as to remain in Ricin's loop—he had to make sure Ricin kept relying on him to get the last two pieces he needed to start that war.

"This is where he'll be," Ricin said, tapping on a room on the floor plan. "It's on the second floor, left side of the building as you can see. You can enter through this terrace right here. When you get the file, get out of there and go to the food festival that is being held five blocks away at the Fun Park. Lose anyone following you and meet them at the fountain," Ricin said, pointing to the man and woman.

The man's long beard moved as though he was saying something, but no words were heard. The woman kept staring at Ricin, her light eyes hidden behind her red curls.

"They will give you a different hoodie, and hat. You will wear them and pretend you three are a family. Walk out of the park with them and Garth will drive you all back here. Any queries?"

James's thoughts were racing, but he shook his head. He just had to do it, hopefully having to hurt no one in the process.

"Great—you leave now," Ricin said, rolling up the blueprint.

Garth came over to James and attached a mini camera to his t-shirt.

"Put this in your ear," Garth said, handing him an aural device. "Now, this is the external device the president has to attach to his laptop," Garth continued, then took out a gun from his belt pocket. "This, you'll be given at your drop point. I'm sure you still remember how to use it—hope your lack of practice didn't ruin your perfect aim."

James arranged his earpiece that kept falling out of place and inserted the external device into the zipped pocket of his trousers.

"Okay, James—go and make me proud," Ricin said. "And James—I know you are more than capable of doing what is being requested of you; don't play the fool or Matthew or John will end up begging me to just shoot them."

James kept looking straight at Ricin, struggling to ease the tenseness in his fist.

"Come on, James " Garth called as he headed toward the door.

Edgar's eyes were still studying James's every move; ready to give orders.

James let out his rage in a restrained sigh and followed Garth.

The man and woman joined him and they all went to the elevator. Garth began humming a song as they waited for the door to open.

"That song gives me the chills," the man said to Garth, his voice harsh.

They entered the elevator and Garth pressed the button.

"I gotta go watch them play it live someday," Garth said.

"Count me in," the man replied. "The guitar solo is a masterpiece; never heard anything like it."

"True that," Garth said. "Cannot wait for their next album to come out."

"Next month right?" the woman asked.

"On the eighteenth," the man replied, and they stepped out of the elevator to the underground carpark.

James was the last to step out and Garth waited for him.

"Just like the good old days, right?" Garth told him as they walked past some parked cars. "Kinda missed working with you," he added with a light chuckle. "You always know how to surprise with your mutant skills."

James paid Garth no attention.

"You surely must have missed me just a tad, right?" Garth sneered. "Or at least missed having a real purpose? Pallet work, huh? What were you trying to accomplish? Build the Taj Mahal with planks? Oh wait, you became part of a family, right?" Garth added, placing his right hand on his heart, his expression mocking compassion. "Did that make you feel less mutanty?"

James ignored Garth and continued walking.

"Bet your brother, Matty, surely regrets it now," Garth said. "You should have heard him squeal when we snatched him and his grandpa as they came out of the grocery store," he snickered. "Katy was supposed to be with them but she got held up talking to the cashier—bet she regrets it too—not knowing where the hell her son and—"

"You haven't changed one bit," James said, keeping a lid on his boiling anger. "True that; empty vessels make the most noise."

"And the antisocial freak speaks," Garth said, stopping next to an SUV with tinted windows. "You know what I certainly didn't miss, James? Your lack of social skills, all reserved as though what's on your mind is beyond anyone else's comprehension. Maybe the social part is suppressed when one is a freak." Garth sniggered to himself and clicked his tongue. "Get in the front," Garth told James as he unlocked the car, and he got behind the wheel while the man and woman got into the back seat.

"Nice perfume you got on, Tasha," Garth remarked as they were all inside, citrus scenting the air.

"Thanks," she replied. "It was a buy one get one free kinda deal—but I got the free one only, if you know what I mean."

"A sister gotta do what she gotta do to live, right?" Garth said.

"Amen to that," she replied. "Amen to that."

The sun was bright, its warmth on James's pale skin rekindling a sense of hope for freedom. But the next heartbeat felt heavy—the tracer; Ricin's tight leash on him—freedom was now but a memory.

The streets were busy, the noise of vehicles drowning any other sound of life.

James kept looking out of the passenger side window, catching glimpses of people going about their normal life; wishing he could miraculously trade places. The gravity of the task he was about to do became more and more lucid, and his pulse throbbed in his throat, his anxiety poisoning his sense of sanity.

He kept hoping the car would just break down or better still, crash, but none of that happened and they were soon in the street heading to the president's residence. Garth slowly pulled over to one side of the road and turned to face him.

"This is where we drop you off. We will be watching through the camera and communicating with you through your earpiece. Do you copy, Ricin?" Garth asked.

"Crystal clear," Ricin was heard replying in his ear and through Garth's hand piece.

"These are yours," Garth said, holding out the gun and extra clip to him.

James paused, his eyes fixated on the deadly weapon. He couldn't go through with this; he shouldn't. But Matthew and John's lives hung in the balance; he just had to. He inhaled deeply and took the gun and clip from Garth's hands.

The cold steel in his hand awoke many vivid memories; memories he had tried so hard to forget, blood staining each one of them. He had never killed anyone though, he could never bring himself to do that. But things were very different now.

There is a line, the memory of Wang Gu's voice resounded in his head, *once crossed, there is no turning back. Killing a man makes you a murderer for life. After that, one of two things will happen—your conscience is forever silenced or your soul will forever scream.*

But wasn't that still much better than living with the weight of Matthew or John's coffin on his conscience? He hoped he wasn't about to find out.

CHAPTER NINE

James made sure the gun's safety was off—he had to act quick if anyone got in his way. He shoved the gun into his waistband and pulled his sweater over it. He forced himself out of the car, the cold wind slapped him in the face.

He steeled his nerves as he walked up to the residence. There was no room for failure to obtain that file. Matthew and John's safety depended on it.

The large building was fenced by a high iron gate, cameras capturing every move within them. Security guards posted at the main door.

He paused in front of the gate, chest tight; his next move would trigger the alarm; chaos would ensue.

"Get on with it, James," Ricin said through his earpiece.

James exhaled forcefully; he had no choice. He leaped up the fence and swung over it. A sharp siren pierced the air before his feet even hit the ground. He dashed toward the residence, alert security guards in quick pursuit.

"STOP!" a deep voice boomed.

James raced even faster and ran up the wall to the terrace on the second floor. He barged through the door. Nobody was there.

"He's not in here," he told Ricin.

"They probably moved the meeting to another room last minute," Ricin replied.

Three security guards darted into the room, guns drawn, aimed at James.

"On your knees! Hands in the air!" one yelled.

"Make do, James," Ricin said.

"I need to speak to the president," James told the guards.

"I will not repeat. Hands up and on your knees!" the same man ordered as more guards flooded the room.

"I need to speak to the president," James repeated, determined.

"Last warning! Don't make us shoot you!"

He dashed out again, the man's shouts muffled by the wind. He climbed up another storey and entered through the only open window.

A plump woman sitting in front of a computer gasped, "Are you crazy?!"

"I need to speak to the president; where is he?"

"Kid, if you know what's good..."

His gun, now aimed close to her face, silenced her words.

"I … I … I don't know," she stammered as she raised her trembling hands in the air.

"Find out who does," he instructed, extending the gun closer to her head.

She grabbed the phone on the desk, and quickly dialled a number.

"They're not picking up," she said, putting the receiver down and raising her hands in front of her face. "Please, I have a five-year-old daughter, please," she cried, her eyes glazed with tears.

The clonk-clunk of boots clattered through the hallway; guards were coming.

"Please," she whispered, the heavy boots getting closer.

He put the gun back into his waistband and fled out of the window.

"How am I supposed to find the president?" he asked Ricin as he leaped to ledges on his way to the rooftop.

"Oh, you're smart enough. Figure something out," Ricin replied.

James clenched his teeth hard in anger and continued up to the roof.

Dark clouds had gathered and a distinctive thrum was taking over the skies; two helicopters were racing toward the residence.

He sprinted across the rooftop, to the edge, and jumped onto a small balcony. He glanced through the door, there was no one there, and he stepped inside.

His eyes swiftly swept the room, searching for any inspiration. He then paused, looking at the sofa, and without further dither, he sat down.

"What on Earth are you doing, James?" Ricin shouted.

"I got this," he replied, rubbing his sweaty palms against his trousers.

Guards swarmed the room, weapons aimed, ready to shoot.

He stood up slowly and raised both his hands.

"James," Ricin said, "if you're giving yourself up—"

“I need to speak to the president,” James said, Ricin still yelling in his ear.

“That's not going to happen! On your knees and keep your hands where I can see them!” a guard ordered.

James lowered his hands and stood straight.

“It's in the president's interest that I speak to him. I’m only a messenger. If I don't speak to the president now, his family will get hurt.”

“Very nice,” Ricin remarked.

“Boy, listen to me: you are already in serious trouble. Hand yourself in and if you cooperate, you might not spend the rest of your life in prison,” the same man declared.

“It's your choice, I tried. The president's family is in danger. I have to go,” James said.

“Wait!” the president called as he strode into the room. “Well it's true. How old are you, son?”

“I need a file on your laptop,” James said, not taking time for banal conversation.

“Son, I don't know who sent you or what's his deal,” the president began, “but he's quite irresponsible to send a boy to break into my residence. Though I must admit, I am quite impressed you managed. You are one smart kid—what's your name?” the president asked, stepping closer toward him. All the guards maintained their steady aim.

“I need you to give me a file that is on your laptop,” James repeated.

The president feigned a smile, then glanced over at the guard that had walked in with him.

“You are under arrest,” the guard said, stepping in front of the president with handcuffs in his hand.

James shoved the guard and grabbed the president's arm, twisting it behind his back. Gun in the other hand, muzzle pressed against the president's temple, he forced him to move back, out of the pool of security. Everyone in the room stood stupefied.

"You don't want to do this," the president cried out, pain in his voice.

"Tell the guards to get out and get your laptop. NOW!"

"You're making a huge mistake," a brawny guard said. Their eyes met and James could see deadly focus.

James fired his weapon in the air then took aim at the guard.

"Everyone out. Out!" the president ordered, and the guard exchanged one last fierce scowl with James before leaving the room after the others.

"Get his laptop; you have five minutes," he warned the guard as he was stepping out, then forced the president to move toward the door, and locked it.

"Sit," he instructed, letting go of the president's arm.

"You are making me so proud," Ricin said.

James ignored Ricin's comment; he had to remain focused and get this over with. He locked the balcony window and door, and drew the curtains. Then went to the armchair facing the president, and sat down. The president's gaze fixated on the gun in his hand.

The bang of a gunshot blasted through the earpiece, seizing both their attention. James sprung to his feet, pulling the device out of his ringing ear.

Ricin roared in the distance. James put the earpiece back in and whatever Ricin was saying, wasn't to him.

"What just happened?" James called to Ricin.

There was yelling and the sound of a kerfuffle but James dared not ask who was shot or who had fired the gun.

James pointed his gun back at the president.

“Tell them to bring your laptop here, NOW!” James ordered.

The president picked up the phone from the coffee table and dialled.

“It's me. Tell Dave to bring my laptop, please. Thanks…Yes I’m okay,” the president said, and hung up the phone. “Whenever you are ready, son…we can help you,” he added, looking past the firearm, straight at James.

“When they bring your laptop, I’ll give you a device to attach to it and transfer File Z.T. They are able to check it out as it is being transferred, so make sure it is the real file.”

“File Z.T.? Is that what all this is about?” the president asked irritated, and pursed his lips.

A strong knock at the door broke the silence and James went to it.

“When the door opens, place the laptop on the floor in the room and walk away,” James called out, and unlocked the door and moved it ajar—standing firmly behind it.

A hand put the laptop on the floor together with two small bottles of water and moved back. James shut the door and locked it again, then grabbed the laptop and gave it to the president.

“File Z.T.,” James said, and took out the external device from his pocket and put it on the table.

“Sure…ummm…would you like some water? I’m quite thirsty myself.”

“I’m sure they’re drugged,” James replied. The president's smile disappeared.

The president opened his laptop and began going through his files.

“Hmmmm, that's strange,” the president began, “it's not here...I must have left it on my other—”

The resonating blast of James's gunshot cut the words short; the president yelled in pain as blood spattered the carpet and couch upholstery. The bullet went through the fleshy part of the president's thigh and his pants began to soak up blood.

“I’m not playing,” James said.

“Mr. President, are you okay? Mr. President?!” men shouted as heavy thumps vibrated on the door.

“I’m fine!” the president called back, maintaining eye contact with James. “Just a misunderstanding,” his voice croaked as he attempted to disguise his pain. He clenched his hand to the wound, blood oozed between his fingers.

The president picked up the device from the table and paused, “This file, if in the wrong hands, can do serious damage—”

“I don't have a choice. Transfer it.”

James's gun was still aimed at the president. The president gave a grim nod and attached the device to his laptop.

“Are you getting it?” James asked Ricin, when the transfer initiated.

There was a lengthy pause, then Ricin replied, “We got it. Now get out.”

James pulled the device from the laptop.

“I’m sorry,” he mouthed.

The president stared, shock setting in. James dashed to the balcony door and hurried out. Security and soldiers were everywhere he went. The two helicopters hovered.

A fusillade of bullets darted at him and he dodged every one as he rushed down the building. He ran toward the barricade of armed men, blindly going through them, avoiding every grasp.

"Five blocks to your left, James; to The Fun Park," Ricin said as James jumped over the iron fence.

James was surrounded by police cars and more bullets shot at him. His warning reflexes spiked high, and he had to veer and run faster than he had ever done before in his life. He ran left and leaped over a police car.

His feet kept up the pace and he soon caught sight of the colorful flags of the Fun Park. He was almost there, the last sprint toward the entrance, but a strong, sharp pain flooded his heart and he tumbled to the ground.

"James," Ricin yelled.

He struggled to get back up, the agony in his chest unbearable. He gasped for air, forcing himself to move and continue to the park, but the stabbing pain struck another time and his knees gave way.

"Ricin," he uttered feebly, unable to draw in enough air. "The tracer—"

"Just get to the park!" Ricin roared, his voice competing with the sirens.

But James couldn't catch his breath and remained on his knees, succumbing to his defeated body—while the sirens wailed closer and the helicopters ranged in for a clear shot.

CHAPTER TEN

"Ricin," James called, his voice hushed with pain, "I can't; I swear."

Ricin made no response and James attempted to get up again.

A black SUV revved in his direction, its tires screeching as they came to a halt right beside him.

Garth pounced out and grabbed him by the arm, shoving him onto the back seat. Garth took the wheel again and spun the car around, the air fumed with the smell of burnout tires.

Beads of sweat rolled down James's face, his chest in one tight ache.

"Ricin," Garth called as he drove steadily ahead, "tell Edgar to be ready; something's not right with James."

Garth deftly manoeuvred through traffic; speeding and braking as obstacles presented—hard turns of the steering wheel to overtake puttering cars and accelerating at long stretches of road before a hard brake and a sudden swerve around another slow moving vehicle.

The thrum of rotors persisted in close pursuit and Garth sped into an underground carpark. He parked haphazardly and hopped out.

"Come on," Garth said as he rushed to help James out of the car.

Lethargy drugged James's body and Garth helped him into the back seat of a white car—an emergency swop vehicle; one of Ricin's several that were stationed all over the country. Garth then got in the driver's seat and drove to the exit, following the other vehicles, losing all eyes from the sky.

"Hey," James heard Garth call to him, "how are you holding up?"

The pain in James's chest had subsided, but the profound weakness was still upon him. He kept his eyes shut, his head against the headrest.

"James? Say something, damn it," Garth said.

"Just…focus…on driving," James rasped.

Back at Ricin's headquarters, Edgar and Wayne were waiting for them in the carpark. Edgar lacking his normal composure.

Edgar opened the car door for James. "Can you walk?" he asked. "Do you want to lie down?" he added as he pulled the stretcher closer.

"No, I'm good to walk," James replied.

James got out of the car, his steps dragging.

They all got into the elevator and James was taken to the infirmary.

"Sit down," Edgar said, pointing to the hospital bed at one end of the room.

James sat down, the strong smell of sanitizer nauseating. Steel medical cabinets ran along all the four walls, pill bottles stacked in the ones with glass doors. At the other end of the large room, a gurney and dead medical machines.

Edgar gave James a bottle of water, then began talking to the infirmary staff, giving instructions on which tests they were to perform first to resolve the tracer's issue.

James lay down and closed his eyes, too tired to follow their conversation. His thoughts merged with a parallel world—the touch of a hand, the latex pegging his index finger, low voices, occasionally pulling him back to reality.

All was quiet around him now, the smell of coffee strong. He opened his eyes. He was still on the hospital bed, outside the window—pitch black.

"Hey," Edgar said, stepping closer with a mug in hand.

"What time is it?" James asked.

"Eight-thirty," Edgar replied. "We ran some tests—still working on some results as we speak, but what we concl—"

"Are Matthew and John okay?" James asked, sitting up.

"They're um—doing fine," Edgar replied. "As I was saying, we ran tests and it seems that your heart went through a severe state of fibrillation—this irregular heartbeat had to be due to the tracer and so we are going to have to replace it. The new tracer will be smaller, lighter—and although it will still use the same frequency to detect your location, it will radiate less electrical pulses; so it should not interfere with your heart activity."

"Right," James replied, glad he wouldn't be able to carry out missions for the next few weeks.

“We are performing the last few tests on the new tracer and we’ll be operating in a day or two,” Edgar continued. “In the meantime, you need to keep your heartbeat low.”

“Sorry to interrupt, Edgar,” a woman said as she came into the room, “the test results are ready—and you should come take a look.”

“Is the blood work all done too?” Edgar asked.

Blood—that word flashed the vivid memory of the president's leg bleeding. And it hit James with a ton of guilt—he had shot the president.

“James?” he heard Edgar call.

James lifted his face to Edgar, a black hole crushing his conscience.

“You okay?” Edgar asked.

“Yeah,” James lied. Nothing could be done about it now anyway.

“Feel free to freshen up in the shower room right here,” Edgar told him, pointing to the door at the back of the room. “I put some clean clothes on the rack for you. Wait for me here when you’re done.”

Edgar left the room with the woman. Ramon and Wayne stood by the door of the infirmary, their watch eliminating any possibility of privacy.

James went to take a shower. He kept the water running cold, his way of detaching and numbing everything.

Edgar was already waiting for him when he came out of the shower room. A fresh mug of coffee in hand.

“You hungry?” Edgar asked him.

“Yeah,” he replied, arranging the collar of his hoodie.

“Good, let's go to the kitchen, grab a bite.”

James followed Edgar to the kitchen. Ramon and Wayne took their posts by the kitchen door. It was the same enormous, classic kitchen made from solid wood with a whitish coating. The quartz countertops, a shade of pale blue. The ceramic knobs, white with a blue buttercup painted on them. The kitchen cabinets formed a u-shaped array that occupied half the room. Two standing freezers next to a wide fridge on one side of the rectangular table, filled the other half.

"The chef cooked a delicious leek and mushroom pie today," Edgar said. "Heat you up a slice?"

"Thanks," James replied with a nod, and opened the cupboard where small bottles of water used to be stored. The water was still kept there and he took one.

James went to the table and sat down. There were some fresh, orange flowers in a glass vase on the tabletop. He never remembered there being any flowers in the kitchen before.

The smell of baked pastry enhanced his appetite and Edgar soon put down two portions of pie on the table. Edgar sat down on the chair facing him and they both began eating.

"Good, isn't it?" Edgar said.

"Yeah," James replied, enjoying the flaky crust. "Dolan still the chef?"

"Mmm, no, Dolan had to stop working—he had some problems with his back—couldn't spend too many hours on his feet anymore," Edgar replied. "But the new chef, Gina, is great, right? Never tasted food better than hers."

"It is really good," he agreed. As a young boy, Dolan used to terrify him—he was a big man with a black beard and had a deep scar that ran across half of his face. He was always sharpening knives and his voice was gruff. Every time Dolan used to speak to him, he used to say whoever didn't obey, Ricin might order a stew made out of them. It was Dolan's way of joking, yet as a kid, the thought haunted him.

"Pastry dishes still your favorite?" Edgar asked.

James nodded.

"I will let Gina know," Edgar said. "She'll be happy to bake them—pastries are her favorite too."

Edgar finished his plate and sipped his coffee.

"Did you sell the watch?" Edgar asked.

That watch was one of the few gifts James had ever been given, and the only one that had meant something to him. It was a beautiful sports watch, black with blue features. On the back, the engraving; *Not everything is as it seems*. Edgar had given it to him for his tenth birthday. He had worn it every single day since then but had decided to remove it when he escaped, fearing it was trackable.

"I got rid of it—wasn't sure if it was bugged."

"Right," Edgar replied, escaping James's gaze.

James had long concluded that it wasn't though. He had purposefully hid it several times in different locations, only to go back for it and find the hideout untouched.

"Whoever has it is lucky," Edgar added, staring blankly.

It was just a watch, maybe worth some money, but lucky? He was still the one who had it, unless someone had now dug it up and found it.

Edgar went quiet, occasionally tapping his index finger nervously against the mug. James finished his pie and gulped down the rest of his water.

"James," Edgar began, shifting forward in his chair, his tone awkward, "there is something I need to tell you."

He stared at Edgar, dread highlighting his expectation.

"While you were carrying out the mission," Edgar said, and cleared his throat, "um—everyone is okay now but—John was shot. He's stable; he'll make it."

"What?" James voiced in shock, his heartbeat tripling.

"When you left, Matthew, he um—Matthew just wants to get out of here real bad. He kept pushing it and Ricin shot at him. John jumped right in front of him and took the bullet."

James's hands began shaking.

"None of this would have happened if they weren't being held here; they don't deserve any of this," James said, his breathing heavy.

"James, I need you to keep calm; your heart cannot go through another—"

"You need me to keep calm?" James snapped. "The only people that ever meant something to me just got hurt because of that psychopath and you just expect me to keep calm?"

James stood up. His jaw clenched tight.

"Where are they?" he asked.

"I will take you to them," Edgar said, getting to his feet. "And I promise you, John's going to make it."

"You were never in a position to promise anything, so save it," James replied, eyes locked with Edgar's.

Edgar remained silent, then began walking out of the room. James followed him to the elevator and they began ascending.

"Where did the bullet hit him?" James asked.

"He was quite lucky actually; it only hit his collar bone—nothing serious."

They walked past the infirmary and Edgar stopped in front of a door.

"They're in here," Edgar said. "I need to get going, I'll come by later," he added, and continued walking down the corridor while Ramon and Wayne took their posts by the wall.

James opened the door slowly, not wanting to wake them up if they had already fallen asleep. The room was dim, the heating on. Logan, the guard with the ponytail, right by the window.

John was propped up on some pillows on a bed, his left arm in a sling over his chest. Matthew slumped in an armchair right beside him, looking beyond worn out.

"Hey," John greeted James with a smile.

Matthew turned to James, his face blank.

"I'm so sorry," James said as he closed the door behind him.

"It's not your fault," John said. "And it's not your fault either," he added, turning to Matthew.

Matthew's eyes dropped to the floor, his leg jiggled.

"I'm going to get you both out of here," James said.

"The only way we are going to get out of here, is in body bags," Matthew replied, getting to his feet. "I'll be right back—I need some air," Matthew told John, and walked past James, out of the room.

"James, come sit down," John said, when Matthew closed the door behind him.

James sat down on the armchair Matthew had been on, guilt gnawing at him.

"I'm so sorry, John. I'm doing all I can to keep you both safe; I even had to…" he said, unable to finish his sentence.

"Don't you worry about me," John replied. "But if there is any way that you can get Matthew out; do it."

John's eyes rested heavily on him, the responsibility of Matthew's freedom weighing down harder on his shoulders. James nodded, his countenance quickly falling to the floor, helplessness suffocating his soul.

"Are you in pain?" James then asked.

"No, Edgar has me on medication. I'm okay, really," John replied. "It's Matthew I'm worried about."

The door opened again and Matthew hurried in, his face ashen, his brow furrowed.

"Ricin's coming," Matthew said, looking at James.

James leaped off the armchair and stepped out of the room, shutting the door behind him.

"There you are, James," Ricin said. "Great job."

"You shot John," James replied, anger coating his words.

"Well, Matthew was throwing quite the tantrum. Order is something everyone in this building ought to respect," Ricin replied.

"You shot at Matthew and John took a bullet," James repeated. "I'm doing exactly what you want me to do; I got that file. They don't need to be here—Matthew and his family are still your assets whether in here or out there so—please, just let them go."

"You do one job and you feel entitled to ask for their freedom?" Ricin said, his eyebrows raised in disbelief.

"You've got a tracer in me and I'm a highly wanted criminal now; I have nowhere to go. I know you can still get to them so why keep them locked up? Please, I'm begging you. They don't deserve this—I'll do anything—just let them go."

"Anything?" Ricin sneered. "Tell you what—there is this CIA agent that keeps poking her nose into my business far more than I approve of and she's costing me resources to throw her off each time. I need her to go away—kill her—I let them go."

"You want me to kill someone and Matthew and John are *still* going to be targets?"

"See?" Ricin replied. "Someone that would actually want to work for me knowing the way I do business, would have jumped at the opportunity. You are not even willing to sacrifice the life of someone you don't know for them, so why should I believe you will do anything for me?" Ricin said, impatient.

James remained silent, defeated.

"Look on the bright side, James," Ricin said, "with or without John and Matthew, the world is still going on."

James's anger shot up, his muscles tense.

"I'm not sure Katy's world is still going on if I were to be completely honest; heard she's going crazy," Ricin added blithely. "But some collateral damage is always inevitable, right?" Ricin fastened his eyes on James's, daring him to react.

Not everything requires a reaction, Wang Gu's words echoed—James struggled to control his rage but let the memory of Wang Gu's advice suffuse him with calm—

and if you choose to react, make sure you're not just creating waves. James remained looking Ricin in the eye but focused on slowing his breathing; sharpening his anger like a sword, a weapon to be wielded at a better time.

"Anyway," Ricin said. "I need to get going. Make sure you get some rest, James, your surgery is up next."

James watched Ricin disappear around the corner before he went back into John's room.

John's eyes were closed, Matthew's wide open, waiting for James to say something.

"I promise you," James whispered to Matthew, "I will figure something out and get you both out of here."

Matthew sighed heavily and sank deeper in his chair. James sat down on the other armchair next to the window where Logan was still standing square.

A silence fell upon the room. John was fast asleep, his countenance peaceful. Matthew began dozing off and soon lay his head on his crossed hands, on the edge of John's bed.

James leaned back in his chair and tried to get some rest, but thoughts kept startling him awake.

Restless hours went by and the clock struck two in the morning.

John and Matthew were still asleep and James quietly got to his feet and left the room.

Ramon was still posted near the door and James went to him.

"May I go up to the roof?" James whispered. "Just for a few minutes—I need some air. Please."

Ramon peered at him, then cleared his throat calmly.

"You know you are not allowed."

“Where do you want me to go? I just need some fresh air, please.”

Ramon exchanged looks with the other two guards that were standing close by and then nodded to one of them.

“Come on,” Ramon said, and began walking toward the elevator.

James followed him up to the gray metal door of the roof. Ramon was about to open the door with his electronic key card, but paused.

“Don't make me regret this,” Ramon said, looking him straight in the eye.

“I won't,” James replied, his head giving a slight shake.

They stepped out into the moonlight and the chill, crisp air filled James's lungs. He went over to the stone fence and rested his elbows on it, gazing at the tranquil view of distant flickering lights. Those lights were among the few positive memories he had in Ricin's building. Watching the night sky and lights with Edgar was the only highlight of too many months.

All was very quiet and he could hear himself breathing. His hushed breaths resembled the sound of waves crashing gently onto shore. Ramon came next to him and looked out into the distance.

“What a view, right?” Ramon said, and inhaled deeply.

James nodded, his eyes following the remote taillights of a motorcycle.

“Why do you do it? Why work for Ricin?” James asked. He had known Ramon as a guard for several years. Ramon followed orders perfectly yet he had never seen him lift a hand on anyone unless he was told to—unlike most of the other guards.

"Well, Ricin pays really well. And there are no strings attached. I can stop working any day I want to and as long as I keep my mouth shut, I can live my life," Ramon replied, his eyes still resting in the distance.

"Don't you care that what you do…is not right?"

Ramon turned to him, a glaze in his eyes.

"It pays for my daughter's medical treatment."

Ramon turned away; their conversation punctuated by a long pause.

"How old is she?" James asked.

"Seven. She's got a rare condition. The treatment helps her," Ramon replied, struggling to keep his composure.

"Hope she gets better," James said.

Ramon gave a tight nod, his lips pursed into an attempt of a smile.

Everyone was fighting their own battle; everyone had their own demon to deal with, James thought.

James looked up at the bright moon. The dark indigo sky—cloudless—stars glittering across its vastness.

"Thanks…for this," James said.

"You're welcome."

James sat down, resting his back against the cold stone. A light breeze rustled the leaves and disrupted the loud hush. He let his eyelids close, listening to the melody of night, and fell asleep in the arms of nature while she hummed to him a lullaby.

CHAPTER ELEVEN

A chatter of whispers woke James up. Ramon and Edgar's words muffled as they kept their distance from him. He was still on the rooftop, the skies painted by the break of dawn. His back and neck were stiff—sleeping in a sitting position was a mistake. He stood up and swiped the dirt off his trousers. The humid air fogged the distance, camouflaging all but the canopy of nearby trees.

"Good morning," Edgar told him. "Had a good rest? It is rather too cold out here though, right?"

"Always better than in a cage," James answered, still half asleep.

James's head felt heavy—he needed to get more rest.

"We should head downstairs; get some breakfast," Edgar said, and turned to Ramon, "Want a coffee before you leave?"

"Thanks just the same, but I better head home. Belle would be waiting for me; I believe we're supposed to build a fortress with cushions in the living room today. She said the dragons are on their way; we better get prepa—"

A flap of wings grabbed James's attention, and his reflexes tripped—not in the usual way. It was a warning; an inevitable one. His vision blurred before he caught sight of a tall building right in front of him. Two figures were at the edge of the roof, and one fell over. The shriek of a female voice pierced his ears, startling him back to Ricin's rooftop.

"You—okay?" Edgar asked him. "You look a bit off."

James was out of breath, his head spinning.

"I'm—I'm fine," James replied, not sure what had just happened. "I'm still tired," he concluded; it must have been part of a nightmare his sleepy brain was still processing—yet it had never happened before, and why did it feel so real?

"Let's have breakfast," Edgar replied.

***

A lingering smell of coffee filled the kitchen. Near the dishwasher, a clutter of dirty mugs. Edgar put the kettle on and began loading the dishwasher.

"Tea, coffee?" Edgar asked James.

"No, thanks," he replied, taking out the carton of coconut milk from the fridge.

James poured himself a glass and sat down at the table, one side of his neck painful to move.

"Croissant?" Edgar asked, placing a box in front of him. "Just bought; they're still warm."

James opened the lid. The smell of sweetened pastry tempted him awake and he took one filled with custard cream.

Edgar sat down, his mug filled too close to the brim. "Your surgery is scheduled for—"

“Edgar!” Wayne panted as he rushed into the kitchen, “it's John; he's having problems breathing and is in pain.”

James and Edgar dashed out of the kitchen after Wayne.

The door to John's room was wide open. Several infirmary personnel were attending to John, everyone focused and working quick; John looked very poorly. Edgar rushed in, wasting no time to give instructions.

Matthew was pacing at one end of the corridor and James hurried to him.

“What happened?” James asked.

“I don't know,” Matthew replied, his voice trembling. “He was fine, then he just couldn't breathe and said his chest hurt.”

“They are well equipped here, Matt; he's in good medical hands. Edgar—”

“Good medical hands?” Matthew snapped. “Are you even listening to yourself? These people shot him!”

“Matt, Edgar is one of the best medical consultants in the world. I know; I’m sure, he’ll do everything he can.”

Matthew's eyes were glazed, his jaw tense.

“I cannot lose him,” Matthew said, shaking his head, fighting back tears. “And he was shot because of me.”

“It's not your fault,” James replied.

One of the infirmary staff ran out of the room. Edgar could be heard giving further directions—his voice steady and sure.

Matthew rubbed his hand across his mouth. James had never seen him so ill at ease.

“Matt I’m so sorry I dragged you into this,” James said. “I never thought I'd actually get caught; I wouldn't have come anywhere near you or your family.”

“Don't,” Matthew replied, looking away. “Not right now. I don't want your apologies right now.” Matthew began pacing again. “Mom is going to—I don't even wanna think what she's going through right now; she hasn't heard anything from us in weeks.”

Matthew looked at James again and paused, expecting him to say something.

“I could ask Edgar,” James began, spitting out the first thought that came to his mind, “maybe he could arrange a call.”

“A call?” Matthew snapped, eyes lined with anger. “To say what exactly? Hi, mom, your dad got shot and I’m a hostage because Andrew—who you invited over for family dinners—turns out is a mutant freak who is being controlled by a psycho? That ought to make everything just better, right? Huh? Right?” he asked, inching closer to James's face, rage vibrating through his pores. “Oh and I don't know when or even if I’m ever getting out of here alive so go ahead mom, live your happy life.”

Matthew's pulse was racing, his face flushed with fury.

“I’m sorry,” James whispered.

“I don't want your apologies!” Matthew yelled through grit teeth, pushing James violently.

James remained standing still. Matthew's hands in tight fists.

“A call? Seriously?” Matthew repeated, pushing James forcefully again.

James simply stood there, allowing Matthew to let out his wrath on him; maybe that was exactly what he deserved after dragging them into this mess.

"My dad's heart condition," Matthew continued, and pressed his lips tightly together and shook his head. "This is definitely not helping."

James's eyes fell to the ground. He had destroyed a family; even if John and Matthew made it out alive, the mental torment would forever haunt them.

"If Grandpa dies—" Matthew's anger battled his tears to defeat, and he glared at James. "You should have known better."

Matthew looked at James with disgust. His words echoing in James's ears.

"You knew exactly—"

"I wish I never existed," James cut in, his voice hushed, almost unaware that he uttered that thought out loud; the same thought that often creeped out of dark, deadly shadows.

A silence followed James stared blankly.

"James, I'm—" Matthew sighed heavily. "I'm sorry. I didn't mean—I'm just…" A tear escaped the corner of his eye. "I'm afraid I'm about to lose everyone in my life."

"I know."

"I'm sorry," Matthew repeated. "I don't know what I'm doing or saying anymore."

"I don't blame you. I should have known—"

"No," Matthew said, and hugged him tightly. "No matter what, you're my brother, and I'm thankful for that."

Edgar's voice shifted their attention, "John. John. Stay with me, John."

Matthew quickly let go of James and they both rushed to the room.

"Grandpa?" Matthew called in terror.

John lay lifeless, several wires snaking from his chest.

"Get him out of here, now," Edgar told Logan.

Logan grabbed Matthew by the arm and forced him out of the room.

James remained staring at John's body; John wasn't breathing.

"James, you too; get out," Edgar ordered, keeping his focus on what he was doing.

Every hand in the room was rushing against time and James stepped out into the corridor.

The door of the room was shut and a heavy silence echoed. Matthew slumped against the wall, his expression pale and hopeless. Seconds kept ticking by, James failing to come up with what he should say to Matthew.

A shuffle of feet caught their attention. It was Ricin, walking toward them. His gait unruffled.

"How's the old man doing?" Ricin asked, stopping right next to them.

Matthew bounced off the wall toward Ricin, a glare fixed on his face. James grabbed onto his shoulder and pulled him back.

"You piece of—" Matthew yelled, but James pulled him back further. "Let go of me," Matthew told James, enraged. "I'm not afraid of this psychopath!" Matthew continued, looking fiercely at Ricin.

"You keep causing problems, Matthew," Ricin said, his tone calm. "Don't you for a second think that I need you alive," he added in a grave manner.

"Go ahead then," Matthew replied, struggling in James's grasp. "Kill me too. That's the only thing you're good at. You hide behind guns, you coward! You think you can rule by terror but you are just a deranged bastard."

Logan cocked his gun, ready for Ricin's orders. James, fully alert, ready to take a bullet himself if need be.

Matthew and Ricin exchanged looks. James grabbed onto Matthew even tighter.

"Solely out of respect for James," Ricin told Matthew, "I'll let this one go—for now."

Ricin glanced at James before giving Matthew one last glower, then resumed walking down the corridor.

James let go of Matthew, relief instantly replaced by frustration.

"What the hell were you thinking?" James told Matthew. "You keep underestimating what Ricin is capable of."

"Oh no, I know exactly the type of man Ricin is," Matthew replied. "And I'd rather die than bow down."

CHAPTER TWELVE

Matthew slid his back against the wall of the corridor until he was sitting on the floor. Logan kept a close eye on him.

Anxiety kept James on his feet. He had to figure out a way to get Matthew out of there; Ricin could kill him any day if he maintained this attitude.

They waited for someone to come out of John's room. James expected the worst. The door finally opened and Edgar stepped out.

“John's stable,” Edgar said.

Matthew sighed heavily and let his head bang against the wall behind him, his eyes shut tight.

“He suffered a heart attack but he's stable now,” Edgar explained. “He needs plenty of rest.”

Matthew got to his feet, ignoring Edgar as he walked past him to the room.

“Thanks,” James told Edgar, knowing that Edgar had done everything to bring John back.

Edgar nodded and took a deep breath, he too, relieved.

James spent the rest of the day next to Matthew and John. John looked weak and slept through most of the afternoon hours but seemed to be doing much better in the evening.

"You still want to get that tattoo done? Of a wolf's face," John asked Matthew as they ate dinner around John's bed.

"Yeah," Matthew replied, and took another forkful of rice.

"Have you decided where you want to do it?" James asked.

"Still not sure; definitely on the left—forearm or side torso," Matthew replied.

"Both would look cool," James remarked, and finished his plate.

"Do you like tattoos? Want to get any done?" John asked James.

"Yeah, I like them. Never really thought about getting one though; they're quite expensive."

"Indeed. But worth all the money," John said, smiling down at the tattoo on his forearm.

"What does that stand for, LEAD?" James asked, reading the letters of John's tattoo.

"This tattoo has quite the story behind it," John replied. "And two meanings, in every sense of the way. Originally, I had done it to honor my father, Vince. Although I never had the opportunity to really meet him —I was only a few months old when he died—my mother always had good things to say about him and always aspired that I become the man he was. My father used to work in the lead industry. Mama used to say he was a very hardworking man, always making sure we could afford all we needed and more. Yet, he never let work become more of a priority than his own family.

Ironically enough, it was the lead industry that took him away from us; he was involved in an accident at the workplace—he never made it out alive."

John looked down at the wrinkled tattoo and gently ran his fingers over it.

"*Family will always come before work*, mama often used to hear him say, yet work had to take him away from us. Irony is truly the mother of life," John continued. "So I got this tattoo made; lead, symbolizing the chemical element in memory of my father—it was my way of accepting and making peace with the fact that I never got to know him…Not ironic enough? I happened to make a tattoo which also spells to lead; to guide. One Saturday night, I was having a nice, cold beer with some friends at our usual pub. Out of nowhere, comes the most beautiful girl I had ever seen; pale skin, dark hair, brown, almond eyes, and the most gorgeous smile. I was certain she would not notice me but somehow, this tattoo caught her eye and she came up to me, perfectly poised, '*Hey leader*,' she said, '*you must have some fine qualities to deserve that tattoo*.' I was dumbfounded; I couldn't utter a single word," John said, smiling as he relived that moment. "After quite an impolite span of silence, I finally managed to say, '*You're right*'—and those words are like music to women's ears…and that's how I met Martha; the love of my life."

"She was a great grandma," Matthew said. "Remember she used to buy those fruit drops by the box and carry some in her purse wherever she went?"

"Of course," John replied. "She was a diabetic; when we lost Edward, it took a toll on her, and soon afterwards she was diagnosed with diabetes," John told James.

"Do you miss her?" Matthew asked. "You had been married for forty-seven years, right?"

"Forty-seven blessed years," John replied, bobbing his head in reminiscence. "I do miss her every day, but I have no regrets. I treated her like a queen and loved her dearly; and she knew it."

They all went quiet, the hands of the clock in the room loud. Matthew soon fell asleep on his armchair. John too began dozing off on the bed.

James slid down in his chair and rested his head on the padded back. His surgery was due in the morning, but if anything, he was worried about Matthew.

James had fallen asleep and it was light footsteps that woke him hours later. It was still dark outside and Edgar was in the room.

"Sorry, didn't mean to wake you," Edgar whispered to James.

James sat up in the chair, his eyelids heavy.

"What are those for?" he asked in a hushed tone, seeing Edgar put two pills on the bedside table.

"Pain medication for John."

Edgar walked quietly out of the room. Matthew and John were still fast asleep, Matthew resting his head on John's bed.

James quickly stood up and hurried after Edgar.

"Edgar," he called beyond a whisper, "Ricin said that —"

Was he really okay with doing this? He couldn't even seem to say it out loud.

Edgar kept looking at him, patiently waiting.

"Ricin said he would let them go, if I kill some agent. They have a better chance out there than in here so—"

“And you believed him?” Edgar said, raising his eyebrows in disappointment.

“Ricin has always been a man of his word; he takes great pride in that,” he replied, perplexed.

“He is,” Edgar said with a firm nod. “But not when it comes to you. He’ll do anything to get you right where he wants you to be; you’re his exception to everything.”

Edgar kept his voice down, his eyes rebuking.

“Drink only clear fluids this morning,” Edgar added coldly. “We’ll be changing your tracer today.”

Edgar walked away, his pace steady. James's mind in overdrive.

“Hey,” Matthew called from behind him. “Morning. You okay? You look a bit—”

“Matt, promise me,” James said, “that you won't do anything stupid again.”

Matthew looked away and sighed.

“Matt, I know Ricin—he won't kill you, but he’ll make you wish he did instead. Promise me.”

Matthew looked at him, his eyes defiant.

“Knowing Ricin, if you push it again, he’ll bring your mother in here and hurt her just to get to you,” James added.

“Okay,” Matthew replied, and sniffed in irritation. “But I better be out of here soon because I feel like I’m going insane.”

“I’m working on it.”

Matthew and John were given breakfast; some toast with butter and cheese. James only drank apple juice, his nerves on edge.

“If the tracer you have right now is causing problems,” John told him, “it's good that they are replacing it.”

James nodded, his mind focused on their safety rather than his.

"One day," Matthew said, munching on his toast, pointing his index finger straight at James, "you are going to tell your story to a beautiful girl and she will fall deeper for all your scars; figurative scars. The way your body heals does not scar; amazing."

"Right," James chuckled, giving a slight shake of the head.

"No seriously; you will," Matthew said. "I know it. You're a package; the type of guy girls helplessly fall for."

"I'm on the most wanted list; a maniac. Doubt that's remotely attractive."

"That's what the public thinks you are right now," John said. "But the truth will always prevail."

Ramon came for James and he was taken to the operating room for the surgery. Almost like a bad deja-vu, he woke up to the same soreness in his chest. He was alone on the bed in his cell, bars open wide, but this time, it didn't really matter.

Later in the afternoon, Matthew and John were brought back to the room outside his cell and two beds were placed for them.

Days lit on and off periodically. James recovered from the surgery, and John's bullet wound got better too; he was now able to move his shoulder again. They were not allowed out of the room and had to stay in there for over two weeks, conversations the only thing that helped the clock move time forward.

"I was her only child," John said, all three of them sitting on the floor outside the cell, two guards posted by the door of the room. “I was her everything. She raised me on her own with the help of my grandmother. Two peas in a pod.”

“James,” Garth called as he stood in the doorway, “Ricin wants to see you.”

They had not seen Ricin since the day of James's surgery. James stood up and followed Garth to the kitchen.

“James,” Ricin said, sitting at the kitchen table, mug in hand, “would you like a snack or something?”

“No, thanks,” James replied.

“Grab a chair,” Ricin continued.

James sat down on a chair facing Ricin. Garth switched on the kettle.

“How are you?” Ricin asked, and before James could answer, he continued, “Edgar has informed me that your body has fully recovered, so you can get back to business,” Ricin said, and sipped from his mug. “Remember I used to take you to watch fights? Well, you’re old enough to participate now.”

Most of those fights he had been forced to watch, had become some of his childhood nightmares. Contestants always ended up badly hurt, some even dragged out unconscious with their insides hanging out.

“Those fights run huge sums of money and you’ll be surprised who's behind some of the highest biddings. Amateurs enjoy watching animals fight; some even chickens,” Ricin scoffed. “Real men; we take pleasure in witnessing human strength, even if pushed to its utmost edge. As has always been, only a number of my men—and now also John and Matthew—know you are a mutant. My people know better than to open their mouths, so; you will have to play the part. And I will let you know which matches to win or lose, just to keep it realistic."

Participating in brutal fights was not one of his aspirations, but what choice did he have? At least he could make sure his opponents were not killed or critically injured.

"We leave in exactly one hour," Ricin said, looking down at his watch.

***

"At least the president is not involved," Matthew said, while James splashed cold water onto his face from the washbasin in the cell.

"Do the other contestants participate on their own free will?" John asked.

"Some of them," James replied, and gulped down a small bottle of water. "Others—they might owe someone money and it's the only way they can pay off the debt. The highest bidder always has the choice to decide if the participants fight with bare hands, brass knuckles or a blade…not every fighter makes it out of there alive."

"And I always wondered how some could enjoy animal fighting," John said, snickering at himself.

James was soon on the way to the place where the fights were being held. Logan sat beside him at the back, Garth was behind the wheel, Ricin in the front passenger seat. More cars with Ricin's security personnel trailed behind them.

"As I already told you, James," Ricin said before they stepped out of the car. "Play the act; I expect you to have your own blood on your face when the matches are over. And you win both matches today, understood? Both."

The building they entered had long been abandoned. Weeds were growing out of every crevice, the walls screaming words that had been spray-painted on them. James followed them to the back of the building, to an enormous room where an empty pool lay in the center. The room had a high ceiling, yet the air was humid and stuffy. Groups of people were already gathered around the pool, sitting on wooden chairs, awaiting the start of the event. Spotlights were focused on the bottom of the empty pit, illuminating blood stains that colored its faint walls.

Logan remained with Ricin and his other security guards, while Garth took James to another room.

"We wait here, until your turn's up," Garth said, closing the door behind them.

The room was tiled from wall to wall, holed where showerheads had once been. A broken washbasin lay on the floor in one corner of the room, where cockroaches had crawled to their death.

The small broken window let in some fresh air, masking the smell of bleach that lurked in the building. The crowd started whistling and cheering; the matches were about to start.

"Ladies and gentlemen!" a booming voice began through a microphone.

James made his way to the window, choosing to hear the howling of the wind, calling to the vast seas.

"You're up," Garth called to him, minutes later. "Whoever wins gets to move on to the final match; you know who that's going to be, right?"

James was taken back to the large room and next to the man holding the mike.

"Our next contestant; James!" the man said, grabbing James's arm and raising it in the air. "Betting starts now. Place your bets; be part of the game!" the man said, letting go of James's wrist.

All eyes in the room were on James, a low mumble bounced through the crowd. Ricin was sitting at the front, his head high, his gaze full of expectation. Ricin gave him a firm nod and the crowd went grave silent.

"Go down," Garth told him, signalling to the stairs leading to the bottom of the pool.

James began descending. His opponent was already down there, blood oozing from cuts on his face, hands in tight fists, ready for his next round.

"Third match for today!" the presenter said. "Winner of the previous match and all-time champion, Gaha McCoy, fighting the newbie; James. Odds seem slim for the latter but you never know now, you never know! Opponents you must fight until one of you is down for more than ten seconds. Bare hands, knuckles, or blade? Betting stops now. Let's see what the highest bidder chose: drum roll please; bare hands it is! Good or bad for the newbie? We're about to find out. Contestants you are to start fighting at the sound of the bell; no weapons are allowed for this match. Good luck!"

Gaha raised his fists close to his chin in deadly focus. James raised his hands, pretending to get ready to fight.

Ding ding ding! Gaha pounced forward, his right fist powerfully attempting to punch James in the face.

James relied on his reflexes, avoiding every pummel, hoping to tire out Gaha and be able to end the match sooner.

“Doing good, James!” the man said through the mike. “Doing good!”

Too good for Ricin, James thought, and let Gaha punch him in the stomach.

“Oh, spoke too soon. Gaha takes the lead yet again,” the speaker echoed.

Gaha sniffed loudly, his eyes pinned on James, beads of blood and sweat rolling down his forehead. Gaha threw another punch and James let him hit him, slashing his eyebrow.

“Looks like our newbie might be heading downhill. Second strike that hits James; Gaha still looking good.”

James stepped forward; that was enough; show was over. He punched Gaha in his abdomen, slowing him down.

“Ohhhhh, didn't see that one coming. This has just got interesting,” the presenter shouted eagerly.

Gaha got infuriated and James let him punch his stomach once again. But then, James threw a powerful punch, knocking Gaha to the ground.

“Wow! That was some blow,” the man said through the mike.

Gaha lay on the floor, disoriented, struggling to get back to his feet.

“And we might have a new winner; a new champion. This is such a turnaround of events! Gaha McCoy seems unable to get back up. Clock is ticking, Gaha! And three, two, one—Gaha McCoy is out! We have a new winner; James!”

An uproar swept over the crowd; most bets had definitely been against James. Ricin sat square, a self-satisfied smirk plastered on his face, and he gave James a nod of approval.

Gaha had to be carried out of the pool and Garth came down next to James.

"You did well," Garth said, handing him a small bottle of water.

James drank and wiped the blood trickling down his eyebrow, on his sleeve.

"Now remember, James," Garth said, stepping closer to him, his face stern with warning, "you win the next one too and make sure you put on a show; the both of you."

"Both of you?" James repeated, but Garth took the bottle from his hand and walked out of the pool.

"The fourth and final match for today!" the boom of the announcer's voice echoed.

James could hear the crowd mumbling—his opponent was walking toward the presenter. He looked up but was unable to see who it was from the bottom of the pool.

"We have another newbie; Dunderhead! So many exciting surprises happening today. Place your bids now before time ends. And let's all give a warm welcome to our next contestant; he looks shy doesn't he?" the announcer mocked.

James's eyes kept fixated on the top of the stairs, waiting to see who he was about to fight.

Logan appeared at the staircase, a stabbing smirk drawn on his face. He was holding firmly onto the elbow of his next opponent; Matthew.

CHAPTER THIRTEEN

"Dunderhead will be fighting previous match winner, James!" the commentator shouted.

James turned to Ricin, fury boiling his blood. Ricin—composed—sneered at Matthew.

Logan pushed Matthew, forcing him to go down the steps of the pool.

"Who will be taking home the champion's title today? We're about to find out ladies and gentleman."

"What the hell is going on?" James asked Matthew as he came down the last step.

"Ricin told me to ask you," Matthew said, his voice unsteady, "do you remember what his favorite saying is?"

"What?"

"His favorite saying—"

"*Revenge is a dish best served cold,*" James snapped.

"Yeah that one—he said this is for me insulting him the other day."

James turned to Ricin again, his breath heavy, his body pulsed with anger. Ricin glared back, a gleam in his eye.

"Is it true that if we don't fight, they start shooting at us?" Matthew asked.

"Yeah," James replied, facing Matthew again, his mind racing ahead of him.

"Bidding stops now! Bare hands, knuckles, or blade. Let's see what will satisfy the highest bidder: drum roll… *blades* it is!"

"Blades?" Matthew gasped. "Ricin told me he'll be the highest bidder."

"Of course he is," James replied, focusing on how this match was best to be played out.

"Good or bad? We're about to find out. Contestants you are to start fighting at the sound of the bell; the only weapons allowed for this match are blades."

Two combat knives were thrown into the pool, they clattered by their feet.

"I'm not going to fight you," Matthew said. "They told me you're supposed to win anyway."

"You have to, Matt; we both have to put on a show."

James grabbed both knives and handed one to Matthew.

"Take it," James said, seeing that Matthew did not budge.

"James, I can't—"

"Take it!" he repeated, aggressive.

Matthew took the blade from his hand and stepped back.

Ding ding ding! The crowd went hush, the fresh blood splattered on the walls of the pool, screaming at them.

"Matt, come at me."

"I can't do this," Matthew replied in a state of panic.

"Matt, you're down here because of me. I dragged your whole family into this. Your grandfather was shot!

Your mom is going crazy—because of me! Come on. Hit me."

Matthew stepped forward, blade trembling in hand, his face ashen.

"That's not going to work, James; that's not on you."

A booing sound from the crowd caught James's attention and he quickly stepped forward and punched Matthew in the stomach.

"Another disappointed person in the audience and they start shooting at us," he told Matthew.

Matthew winced in pain, bent over, hugging his stomach.

"Come on, Matt; hit me!"

Matthew straightened his posture and they both took a fighting stance.

Matthew threw a punch at his face and he avoided it perfectly. Matthew tried hitting him again with his fist several times and he kept avoiding every strike.

He punched Matthew again in his abdomen, just enough to put on a scene. He pretended to strike with the blade, making sure Matthew moved in time.

"Going well for both so far; going well for both," the man said through the mike. "But will the highest bidder be satisfied? Blades are not really being used."

That was a warning; weapons of choice had to be the primary tools of the fight.

Matthew came at him. He avoided Matthew's fist, promptly scraping Matthew's forearm with the blade, just enough for the voracious eyes to feast on some of Matthew's blood.

The presenter boomed, "And now it's on."

Matthew pressed down on his arm, blood slowly dripped from the wound.

"Use your blade, Matt," James said.

Matthew attempted to strike him with the blade and James swerved away But then, Matthew struck again and he allowed Matthew's blade to stab his side.

"What are you doing?" Matthew said, horrified. "I thought you were going to move."

"Ending the show," James replied, teeth clenched in pain.

"Oh!" the presenter remarked. "That doesn't look good for James. Such a turnaround of events!"

Matthew's blade had stabbed him deep, maybe even deeper than James thought it would.

"That looks really bad, James," Matthew said, looking aghast at the blood pouring out of James's side, rapidly soaking his sweater.

Ricin stood up; his face grave. James could end this match; the audience had seen enough blood.

James attempted to step forward but the pain in his abdomen was severe. He looked up, his vision close to a blur, then his eyes caught a familiar face among the audience; Wang Gu? The last time he had seen Wang Gu was before his twelfth birthday, before Ricin decided James knew everything there was to know about each form of martial art. But Ricin had said Wang Gu was killed; making sure all that Wang Gu knew about Ricin and his organization died with him.

"James?" Matthew called.

Ricin's glare was still on James, his lips pressed tight.

James had to win this fight before he collapsed; Ricin had a lot of money on it. He turned to Matthew, holding his hand down firmly on the wound, attempting to slow down the bleeding.

"Don't get up," he whispered to Matthew, and punched Matthew in the face, toppling him to the ground.

"Wow!" the announcer called out. "What just happened? James is stabbed but Matthew looks unconscious right now. Matthew—clock is ticking. Do we have a winner? And three, two, one; Matthew's out! James takes the win again! Today's champion; James! Will we see him for another match? We'll find out next time, folks."

James fell to his knees, blood drenching his clothes. Matthew sat up and quickly crawled toward him.

"James?" Matthew said. "How can I help?"

But Logan pulled Matthew away and forced him to the stairs.

"What the hell, James?" Garth said, vexed, as he grabbed him by the arm, pulling him up to his feet.

Garth forced him to move forward. He was lightheaded, around him steadily fading away; he had lost too much blood. Garth pulled him toward the stairs and they were about to go up the first step, but everything went silent.

***

James opened his eyes and quickly shut them again. The recessed light fixtures in the ceiling were too bright. His eyes adjusted and he looked around him. He was back at Ricin's headquarters in the infirmary, a drip attached to his arm, his wound stitched up.

"You're lucky he didn't hit your intestines," Edgar said, coming up from behind the bed.

"Where's Matthew? Is he okay? And John?"

"They're fine," Edgar replied shortly.

"How long was I out?" he asked, sitting up.

"A couple of hours. Fights were this morning; it's seven thirty-five right now. You have to be more careful, James; you're a mutant, not immortal."

Edgar removed the cannula from James's arm. James stood up, the pain in his side uncomfortable.

"The wound is quite deep," Edgar said, "so it will take some time to heal. But you'll be fine with just some medication for the pain every six hours."

James remained silent. His mind replaying the moment he was stabbed and how his strength drained out with the blood. Then he remembered the face he had seen in the crowd.

"I saw Wang Gu today, at the fights," he said, curious to see what Edgar would say. "He was in the audience."

"That's not possible; Wang Gu's dead," Edgar promptly replied, avoiding his gaze.

"I know what I saw."

"And I know how the brain works when the body has just been stabbed and is losing a lot of blood," Edgar said, forcing a patient smile.

"What on Earth were you thinking, James?" Ricin said, as he came through the doorway.

"You wanted to see a fight; you wanted blood; you got that," he replied.

"I never said get yourself almost killed."

Ricin sounded irritated yet still concerned.

"You should have been more specific then," he replied indifferently when he saw Ricin still waiting for a response.

"Don't try to be wise with me, son," Ricin rebuked.

“I am following orders perfectly; Matthew shouldn't have been involved,” James said, frustrated.

“Yes, I agree,” Ricin replied. “But something had to be done to put Matthew in his place, don't you think? With the mouth he has, he wouldn't be able to hold down a job. Something annoys him at a workplace and he blows up like that,” Ricin added, shaking his head in disapproval. “Discipline and respect to authority are a must if one is to thrive in life. Didn't I teach you that?”

James remained quiet. Ever since he could remember, discipline and respect were Ricin's holy grail.

“He might thank me one day when his own family would be depending on his income and he has to suck up to a boss,” Ricin continued.

James sighed silently. He was sure Matthew could have learned that in a safer way, but he kept his thoughts to himself.

“I know what I’m doing, son,” Ricin said with a calm smile. “I know you weren't going to hurt him. If I wanted that, I would have simply ordered some guards to beat him up in here. And when I shot at him, I aimed so that the bullet would only cause a minor injury, it was John that jumped right in front of the barrel.”

James looked up at Ricin, from what he could tell, Ricin was telling the truth.

“Anyway, be careful next time, will you?” Ricin added. “Also, I wanted to ask you if you would like to join me for a business meeting tomorrow morning—if you’re feeling up for it,” Ricin said, glancing at James's stabbed side.

There was only one other time James had been asked to accompany Ricin for a business meeting, and he wished he hadn't heard half the stuff that had been discussed.

Ricin stared hard at him, waiting for an answer.

“Sure,” James said, wanting to remain in Ricin's loop.

“Perfect,” Ricin replied. “Meeting is at seven-fifteen sharp, on the third floor. Be near the elevator at ten past —and don't keep me waiting.”

James gave a slight nod and Ricin left the room.

Wayne escorted James back to the cell. The building was abnormally quiet, the walls whispering back to their footsteps.

James had barely set foot inside the room outside the cell, when Matthew leaped to his feet.

“James, I’m so sorry,” Matthew said, chasing his words, “I thought you'd move out of the way. I—”

“It's not your fault,” James replied.

“How are you?” John asked, closing the water bottle in his hand.

“I’ll be fine,” James said.

“Those fights are damn ridiculous,” Matthew said. “You shouldn't be taking part in them; to hell with Ricin. If he wants the money, he should get in the pool himself —”

“I said I’ll be fine,” James repeated sternly, glancing up at the security cameras, reminding Matthew to watch his mouth.

They were given some vegetable soup with sourdough bread and ate while exchanging their views about skydiving. To James's surprise, John had skydived three times in his life while Matthew said he could never do it.

They all went to bed early. James's night was restless, no position seemed to comfort the ache in his side, the pain medication seeming useless.

"James—James, wake up," a voice called as a hand shook his shoulder.

It was Garth again.

"What?" James asked, still half asleep.

"I thought you said you were going to get up twenty minutes ago. It's seven o'clock now," Garth replied. "Ricin will be waiting for you in ten minutes."

He had fallen asleep again after Garth had woken him up at six-forty.

"Just give me a sec; I'll be there," James said, sitting up in bed.

Matthew was still asleep, John lying in bed awake. James washed his face and grabbed a red apple from the breakfast fruit bowl on the floor.

Garth was waiting for him in the corridor, texting on his cell phone. They went up to the third floor and Ricin was already standing by the elevator when it opened.

"Aren't you punctual," Ricin said, looking at his watch. "Precisely seven-ten."

James followed Ricin and Garth into a large room. There was a long mustard sofa facing three armchairs in the middle of the room. Behind the sofa, a snooker table. Along one of the walls, an alcohol cabinet. Two of the windows were ajar. The pecan drapes swayed with the chill breeze. A tall man was looking outside the middle window, a glass in his hand. Four of Ricin's guards were posted at each corner of the room, all alert, one chewing gum nervously.

"Lewis," Ricin called, as the three of them walked in.

The man turned around. He was in his late fifties, his goatee rather pointed at the chin.

"Ricin," Lewis greeted. "I hope you don't mind," he continued, raising the glass in his hand. "I helped myself to some spirit."

"Not at all," Ricin replied with a formal smile. "They're not just there for display. Garth; you already know," Ricin told Lewis. "And this is my son, James."

"Ah," Lewis replied, his grin at James. "I've heard so much about you. Pleasure to meet you," Lewis said, holding out his hand.

James took his hand and shook it.

"Come, let us sit down," Ricin said. "I'm eager to hear your proposition."

Lewis and Ricin sat down on the sofa, Garth and James on the armchairs.

"So," Ricin began, "tell me about this multimillion dollar project of yours."

Lewis put down the glass on the coffee table beside him.

"Well, as I already told you on the phone," Lewis began, overconfident, "the demand for this type of business is ever increasing and too few are the facilities that accommodate such a demand, thus the multimillion income. Have you heard of La Gaitoz?" Lewis asked, his gray eyes peering through a sharp squint.

"Of course," Ricin replied.

"Well, imagine that on a much larger scale with different outlets in various regions," Lewis said with a poised smile.

"Hmm," Ricin voiced, and his mouth became a hard line.

James had never heard of La Gaitoz and had no idea what kind of business Lewis was talking about.

"I can take care of all the supply, both flesh and drugs," Lewis said. "I already have all the connections established as well as potential locations, all I need is your finical investment to get it started. Profits will definitely start to be reaped within the first three months. You know how I do business, Ricin."

Ricin paused, then leaned back on the sofa, lost in thought. Garth's eyes kept shifting from Lewis to Ricin, clearly aware of what they were talking about.

"What ages do you have in mind?" Ricin asked.

"All ages, various nationalities," Lewis keenly replied. "I can also supply newborns."

"Newborns?" Ricin repeated, faking his surprise.

"Well, pedophiles come in all forms. Who are we to discriminate?" Lewis said.

From what James gathered, the business deal was about investing in pedophile brothels; he should not have expected anything less disturbing.

"We can also expand your drug empire into these facilities; it's a win-win," Lewis said, and picked the glass off the table.

"And why should I partner with you?" Ricin asked.

"Well, I am the only one who's got all the connections to make this happen, and fast."

Ricin bobbed his head in thought.

"You know," Ricin began, leaning forward and resting his elbows on his knees, "when it comes to business, I don't really bat an eye about who takes the fall at the other end—business is business—but—" Ricin paused.

“James,” he then said, “what's your opinion on the matter?”

James swallowed hard, his opinion wasn't going to be approved.

“Tell us, James,” Ricin prompted. “I already know what you are going to say, so go ahead, son.”

“I don't think it's right,” James said, his voice low.

“And you know what, Lewis?” Ricin asked, waiting for Lewis to turn his head to him. “I agree.”

“Oh, Ricin, come on,” Lewis mocked. “Since when do you refuse a multimillion dollar deal? So what if some worthless kids get caught up in it; they’re street rats anyway; it's not like the authorities will be looking for them. In fact, we’ll be doing the locals a favor by cleaning up their streets.”

“Lewis, Lewis,” Ricin repeated.

Garth straightened his posture, ready for Ricin's order.

“Three things I hate most in life,” Ricin said, “a lazy man, a traitor, and a child abuser.”

“You got to be kidding,” Lewis laughed in derision. “Since when do you care—”

“Do you know what abuse does to a child's brain? Any form of abuse for that matter,” Ricin said, getting to his feet.

“They end up crackheads?” Lewis replied, shrugging his shoulders.

“No,” Ricin replied in the most serious tone, and quickly reached for the handgun in his belt pocket and shot a bullet through Lewis's head.

Blood splattered on the sofa and table, the glass shattered as it hit the floor. Lewis slumped back on the sofa, his eyes wide, between them a steady, red trickle.

“Dispose of this pig, Garth, and clean the damn mess,” Ricin said.

“Yes, sir,” Garth replied, getting to his feet.

James remained seated, the blood on the upholstery merging with that of when he had shot the president.

“Do you think my decision was fair?” Ricin asked James. “That single bullet saved the life of so many innocent children. Wouldn't you have done the same?”

James stood up, his palms sweating.

“Yes,” he told Ricin, and for the first time, he meant it.

***

A guard escorted James back to the cell. John was telling Matthew about the day he had adopted a dog named Rico—a border collie mix that turned out to be the most intelligent dog he ever had. Matthew kept fidgeting with the empty, plastic bottle in his hand, twisting it hard and pressing down on the deformed plastic, frustration yelling in his every move. James sat down next to him on the edge of the bed and tried to listen to what John was saying, but Matthew's despair kept stealing his peace of mind.

Edgar came in the early afternoon to change the dressing on James's wound. James lay down on the bed after that and without knowing, he had fallen asleep.

“James?” he heard Matthew calling. “James wake up.”

Matthew shook him awake. James was out of breath, sweat dampening his forehead.

“You’re okay; it was just a nightmare,” Matthew told him.

James took a deep breath and rubbed his eyes. All he could remember from the dream was the sound of gunshots, people collapsing, and his own hands dripping blood that wasn't his.

“Some nightmare, huh?” Matthew said. “I just had to wake you.”

“Yeah, thanks,” James replied.

He got out of bed and took a cold shower. He was about to step out of the shower room but paused when he overheard Matthew's words.

“I gave up on ever seeing mom again. He's just going to keep us here until he starts that war, making sure James will do as he pleases. After that—we already know too much; he's not just going to let us go.”

“You can't lose hope, Matt,” John told him. “You will see Katy again. We have to hold on to hope—hope is what keeps us alive.”

They fell silent. James shut his eyes hard, the guilt overwhelming. He stepped out and took a bottle of water from the packs in the corner.

A muffled voice was heard speaking through Ramon's earpiece.

“James, Ricin wants to see you in his office,” Ramon said when the voice stopped.

In his office? James had never been in that room before, nor did he want to—Ricin's office was the sanctuary—the only room in the building that was said to be un-surveilled; the room in which no one was allowed unless Ricin was there with them.

James stood up, his heart palpitating, the walls holding their breath in anticipation.

CHAPTER FOURTEEN

James followed Ramon into the elevator and they went up to the sixth floor.

"Go in," Ramon said, stopping right next to a double wooden door, and took his post by the wall.

A lump lodged in James's throat. He turned the door handle and opened the door.

"James, come in," Ricin said from behind his desk, "and close the door behind you. Have a seat," Ricin continued, pointing to the chair in front of him. There was no one else in the room. Just Ricin.

The office was sizeable. Dim lighting bounced off the red, vintage wallpaper. Mounted on each wall, were several heads of wild animals. Above the fireplace, a large oil painting of a nude woman.

A framed drawing—centered between two windows with charcoal drapes—caught James's eye. It was a pencil drawing of a great white shark; one James drew when he was younger.

"Do you still draw?" Ricin asked, noticing his gaze.

"Yes."

"You should; you already had great talent back then, I can only imagine what you are capable of drawing now."

One of the windows was ajar and the drapes began struggling to keep in place.

"I kept all of your drawings. But that one," Ricin said, pointing to the framed picture, "is my favorite. Sit."

James sat down, ill at ease, not knowing what to expect.

"Care for a drink?" Ricin asked, grabbing the whiskey bottle on the tray beside him.

Ricin was a strategic person, following tight schedules. This was definitely not part of his agenda. James shook his head, his chest uncomfortably heavy.

"Normally people say *no thank you*, James," Ricin said, pouring himself a drink.

Ricin took his glass and moistened his lips.

"The meeting this morning," Ricin began, as the wind whistled nervously through the chimney, "set me thinking—where did I go wrong with you?" Ricin paused to sip his drink, staring at nothing in particular. "I did everything I could for you—I provided all you needed, I trained you to be the best—I taught you what discipline is all about because I truly believe that without discipline, one accomplishes nothing. Yet, here we are," Ricin sighed.

Ricin raised the glass to his lips and paused.

"This morning," Ricin said, and gulped down the rest of his drink in anger, "has brought back many memories that I have tried hard to suppress for too many years."

Ricin kept looking him in the eye. There was a pain in Ricin's voice he had never heard before.

“I have never told anyone, except—except a girl who used to be my fiancée,” Ricin said, and grit his teeth. “My mother died giving birth to me. My father, blamed her death on me—he beat the hell out of me nearly every day. I used to get so scared when I heard his car park in the driveway, wondering if he was drunk and was going to beat me up. My brother was only a year and a half older than me and he was even skinnier, so he never did anything but hide in the closet while my father let out his rage on me. There was this one time—I was eight years old and I was really sick—I didn't manage to get to the toilet on time and threw up all over the carpet in the corridor—I really thought he was going to kill me that day. He hit me so hard I couldn't walk properly for two whole weeks. I never felt so worthless in my life. And he never even apologized.”

Ricin's stare trained on the desk though it was clear he wasn't seeing it. His gaze was turned inward on his childhood and the remembrance of abuse. The features of his face contorted into anger and resentment.

“The beatings continued as I grew older,” Ricin said, looking up at him again. “But at the age of eleven I took off and never turned back. I lived on the streets for five months then started working for a drug dealer who took me in, gave me shelter and food. I made my way up in the business, taught myself how to thrive in this world—I had become so much and yet, my father's face still haunted me. So—I went back home one day, made sure he was alone, and gave him what he deserved. That day, I became Ricin, and my childhood nightmares all died with him.”

Edgar once told James that Ricin took up the name of the same potent poison he had used to murder his own father. And that no one knew why Ricin had done it—until now.

"This morning got me thinking about my own flaws as a father to you. I admit, I'm strict at times, punishing if you will, but I had to learn the hard way in my own life and maybe I don't know how to teach it differently."

James kept looking at Ricin. He understood where Ricin was coming from and why he had done most of the things to him when he was younger.

"I know our views clash—your conscience is way too soft," Ricin said with a patient smile. "But life never gave me the chance to grow a conscience—it was always; do what my father said to avoid a beating whether I agreed with him or not …The last thing I want, is for you to see him in me."

Ricin lowered his countenance as though ashamed and sighed heavily.

"James, I—I think you already know I don't really do well with apologies but—I called you in here because I wanted to tell you that I'm sorry, for all those times I thought a punishment—or hurting you—was the only way to teach you to get things right."

Ricin kept looking him in the eye. James had never thought Ricin would feel guilty for what he had put him through, let alone apologize.

James was stunned and couldn't voice a single word. He kept looking straight at Ricin, somewhat of an understanding resonated between them.

"As a way of expressing the truth behind my apology, I decided that Matthew can leave, right now."

"What?" James uttered in disbelief.

"Matthew can go home," Ricin repeated. "And John—I will let him go if you bring one of the two pieces I need. And about this biological warfare I keep threatening everyone with; it's just that; a threat. Keeps me in a position of power because everyone knows I am well capable of doing it if I wanted to. Obtaining one of the two pieces left will reinforce that."

"Why should I believe you?" James asked in a low voice, recalling that Edgar had told him Ricin would do anything to get him where he wanted him to be.

"I'm not the devil people make me out to be, James," Ricin replied, pouring himself another drink. "I do love power and control, but it is only because they mask one's vulnerability perfectly," Ricin said, and took a sip. "That file you got, Z.T. stands for Zero Tolerance; it contains classified information about operations which only the president and a few other members of the government know about and agreed upon doing, solely for their benefit; regardless of the substantial collateral damage they caused. It is my insurance for your safety. If word that a mutant even exists gets out there, countries will fight to own you to be studied on. File Z.T., is my insurance that if the most powerful man in this world, in terms of legal authority, gets his hands on you, I will have leverage to get you back, and keep you safe. I say safe because let's face it; you are a threat to society; you can take over the world if you wanted to. A threat like that, would not make any president comfortable and a permanent solution would seem more than redeemable… No one in power is ever really innocent, collateral damage is always part and parcel to get and remain at the top; remember that."

Ricin rested his elbows on the desk and swirled the drink in his hand.

"I can show you the documents if you want proof," Ricin added.

"No," James replied. "I believe you."

James didn't want to, but Ricin letting Matthew go made him credible.

Ricin smiled at him. It was a genuine smile.

"You know I always wanted to treat you as my own son, nothing less. And what I had once told you still stands; all that is mine, will someday be yours."

Ricin had been James's definition of evil. Was Ricin more complicated than James thought? He started to think he miscalculated Ricin.

"What do you say? Clean slate?" Ricin said, holding out his hand to James as a sign of truce. "I want you to still live here; I'll set up a nice room for you. You carry out some jobs and fights; no one has to get killed; no jobs will involve civilians, or the president for that matter."

Ricin kept his hand stretched out; patient, expecting. Finally, with trepidation, James lifted his hand and shook Ricin's.

"Oh, son," Ricin said, getting to his feet and coming round the table toward him. "Come here," Ricin said, both his hands stretched out for an embrace.

James stood up and let Ricin hug him. Ricin tapped strongly on his back, then let go of him.

"I still remember hugging you when you were no taller than my thighs," Ricin said with a warm smile. "Good old days," Ricin added to himself, and sighed loudly as though relieved. “You’re sure you don't want a drink?” Ricin asked, lifting his glass off the table. “In moderation, it's good for the heart.”

“No, thanks,” James replied.

“James, about what I told you,” Ricin said, looking at him squarely, “I need you to keep it between us, understood?”

James nodded and Ricin tapped on his shoulder, “Good,” Ricin said, and finished his drink.

James and Ricin left the office and they both went to the cell. John and Matthew looked tense.

“Matthew,” Ricin said, “James and I just had a conversation and it was decided that you are free to go, right now.”

“What's he talking about? What's going on?” Matthew asked James, squinting in suspicion.

“You’re free to go, Matthew,” Ricin repeated. “And John will be leaving here soon, too.”

“I’m not leaving without my grandfather,” Matthew objected.

“Matt, John will be out of here very soon,” James told him. “But you leave today; now.”

“May I ask,” John said, looking at James intently, “what agreement did you both get to?”

“James and I decided to wipe the slate clean between us. Isn't that right, son?” Ricin asked, turning to James.

James nodded; a clean slate wasn't exactly how he would define their agreement, but he had to take any opportunity to get Matthew and John out of there and make sure they remained safe.

John and Matthew kept staring at James, clearly perplexed and unsettled.

“So, do you want to leave or not?” Ricin asked Matthew in a rather impatient tone.

“Go home, Matt,” John said, turning to Matthew and tapping on his shoulder.

“I’m not leaving you.”

“Matt, I said go,” John said, his face solemn. “I’ll be okay. And tell Katy…that I love her.”

“You will tell her yourself; when you get out of here,” Matthew replied. “Right, James?” Matthew added, turning to him.

“Yeah,” he replied, forcing a smile, grasping onto the tiny thread of hope.

“Before you leave,” Ricin said to Matthew, “whatever you think you know about everything that is going on inside this building, make sure you keep your mouth shut about it; not even your parents can know; and no one can know about James. Are we clear? I don't need to elaborate on consequences if you don't now, do I?”

“Right,” Matthew replied, glancing at James as though reminding him who he had supposedly wiped the slate clean with.

Matthew was sedated, as was done when he and John were brought to the building, keeping the location of the headquarters hidden from them.

James remained with John in the room outside the cell, John unusually quiet. They were given some pumpkin soup for dinner and were eating in silence.

“I’m happy Matthew went home,” James said, when he finished his portion. “You’ll get to leave soon too.”

John looked up at him but remained quiet.

"You should get some rest," John said, wiping his plate clean with a piece of bread. "You need to sleep and get a clear head."

It was late and James was mentally drained. He took John's advice and went to bed.

"Good morning," Ricin said as he came to the room, early the next day.

James had just opened his eyes, and sat up. John was already awake, sitting on the edge of the bed, eating a banana.

"I just had your bedroom ordered for express delivery; should be here in a week," Ricin said to James. "And this, is Matthew's reunion with his parents."

Ricin turned his tablet toward them and a footage began playing. Katy fell to her knees at the door as soon as she saw Matthew standing right in front of her. And started sobbing uncontrollably, grabbing onto Matthew, not wanting to let him go. Paul, too, kept wiping his eyes, holding his hand against the door frame as though he could not hold himself up—in shock.

The footage ended. John kept staring at the tablet, his smile serene yet a glaze of sorrow in his eyes.

"I need to get back to work," Ricin said, "but I'll see you for lunch. One p.m. in the kitchen?" he told James.

James gave a slight nod and Ricin left.

"You okay?" James asked John as he got out of bed.

"Yes," John replied, his eyes still to the floor. "I'm glad Matthew is back home."

John cleared his throat.

"Did you sleep well?" John asked.

"Yeah," James said, grabbing a bottle of water. "You?"

"Not really," John replied. "If I am to be honest, I don't know what to make out of last night."

"What do you mean?"

"I'm not sure if I should be worried about you," John replied, looking him in the eye.

"What's there to worry about? Matthew's home and you'll soon be going too. All's good," he replied, and avoided John's persistent gaze.

"It is?" John asked, his tone patient. "Ricin is still the same person, no?"

"Things took a good turn and I'm just going to focus on that."

John inhaled deeply, bobbing his head in comprehension. Edgar walked through the door, carrying a flask.

"Tea with honey," Edgar said, giving the flask to John. Ever since John suffered the heart attack, Edgar brought a flask for John every morning.

"Thanks, Edgar," John replied. "I appreciate it."

"Welcome," Edgar quickly said, and turned to James. "Matthew's home—and Ricin said you two wiped the slate clean; isn't that something—rather odd."

An awkward pause followed. Edgar and John were both staring at James.

"Your point?" James asked.

"Nothing, I just—I'm glad Matthew's home," Edgar replied, and cleared his throat. "I'll see you later—for lunch—with Ricin. You're welcome to join too, John; Ricin told me to tell you that."

Edgar left and the guards changed duty.

"You're sure you don't want a cup?" John asked James, pouring himself some more tea.

“No, I’m good, thanks,” he replied, munching on a green apple. “Will you be coming for lunch?”

“No,” John replied, and sipped his tea. “It's true what they say that one should keep friends close and enemies closer—but not too close; you might easily get mixed up whose side you’re actually on.”

“I could ask Ricin if we could go for a walk along the river,” James said, purposely ignoring John's comment. “As long as Garth joins us, it should be okay.”

“Hmmm,” John voiced in thought. “We can't really go that far though; the police are looking for you.”

James finished his apple and threw the core in the bin. He sat back down next to John on the edge of the bed and leaned back on his hands.

“Tell me something, son,” John said, turning aside to look at him, “what changed?”

James hesitated, then took a deep breath.

“Perspective,” he replied, staring into thin air.

“About?”

“Everything—maybe I was wrong,” James said in a hushed tone, questioning everything the more he thought about it.

“Son, look at me,” John said, and James looked up at him. “Whatever Ricin told you doesn't alter facts; punishing you the way he did throughout your whole life, killing people, keeping hostages and all the other crimes, can never be right. Don't let him get to you like that.”

“He does the wrong things—but maybe it's for the right reasons,” James replied.

“What about that biological war he wants to start? What good reason is there?”

“He's not going to.”

"You're not that gullible, are you?" John asked.

"I cannot think that far, John. I don't want to," James sighed. "Right now, good things are happening, that's all that matters."

John fell silent and continued sipping his tea. Logan was posted by the door, his eyes pinned on the both of them.

"When I was young," John said, looking up at the ceiling as though trying to remember the exact details, "about a year older than you. I had this friend who lived across the street; he was a decent friend, came from a good family. Our mothers were friends too and occasionally, we were invited for barbecues at their house. He started hanging out with some older kids from the neighborhood; they were the kind that went looking for trouble. He kept insisting that I should join—that I was missing out on a lot of fun. I'm glad I never did…A few months later a shooting took place. These kids had gone to rob a liquor store and the owner pulled a gun on them. He was with them that day. Shots were fired and he and the other guys got away unharmed. But unlike what they had thought, they weren't the only ones in the store. Later that day, two police officers showed up at his doorstep to tell him that his own mother had been in that store—a bullet they fired had hit her; she didn't make it… His father had been ill and died several years before—his mom was all he had left and he would do anything for her; he was a good son. Yet she had to die because of a robbery he was partaking in. That is what he had to live with the rest of his life. Some people are sinkholes, they'll just drag you down with them—be careful who you mix with."

CHAPTER FIFTEEN

"The jobs I'll be doing now," James told John, "won't involve any civilians, or the president; people won't get hurt."

"Ricin is a sinkhole, James; you of all people should know better."

"John—just stop!" James snapped. "Matthew's back home; he can get on with his life and I can make sure of that. I've made up my mind. So just—leave me alone!"

James stormed out of the room and a guard hurried after him. It was Ramon. James paused.

"I'm just going up to the roof," James said.

"Sure," Ramon replied with a nod.

Ramon followed James upstairs. James had barely stepped in front of the roof door when he heard it unlock. He was being watched from the surveillance room.

James eagerly pushed the door open and went out into the bright sunlight.

The air was cold but the gracious sun reached out to him with her warmth. He went to the stone fence and sat down, resting his back against it. All was blue over his head, the sweet chirps of birds inducing a calm. A jet began dividing the sky with a white trail, heading toward the bank of dark clouds that steadily approached. He closed his eyes, choosing to enjoy the pleasant rays while they lasted.

Ramon had remained by the roof door, but footsteps were approaching James.

“Looks like a downpour is coming,” Ramon said as he stopped right next to him. “The weather report was right.”

“How's your daughter doing?” James asked, keeping his face up to the sun.

“Belle's better. Much better, thanks. She is responding well to the treatment. There's hope.”

“Glad to hear.”

“Her birthday is in a few days; we’re throwing a surprise party for her—unicorn themed; she just loves them so much,” Ramon added with a chuckle.

He glanced up at Ramon and smiled. Serene hours went by and James had nearly fallen asleep when a muffled voice through Ramon's earpiece drew his attention.

“Ricin wants to see you; here are visitors,” Ramon told him.

James went downstairs with Ramon. Cackles could be heard echoing through the corridors. A particular rasping voice murmuring in between.

“James, son, there you are!” Ricin said as soon as James turned round the corner. “I would like you to meet a cousin of mine, Vice, and his son, Gavin. You had met them once before but you were still very young.”

A bony man, and a well-built boy—a few years older than James—stood beside Ricin.

“So, this is him, huh?” Vice asked with the rasping voice. Vice slumped down to have a closer look at James. His cheekbones protruded, his eyes—hollow pits.

“This is him?” Gavin sneered, eyebrows raised in disappointment, his blue-green eyes vibrant. “I thought you said he was physically strong.”

“Looks can be very deceiving, boy,” Ricin replied.

“We’ll soon see,” Gavin said, his gaze fastened on James. “I’m going to participate in one of those fights against you. I know, I know; supposedly mutant and all, but we are going to be using blades and no one beats me with that.”

James remained silent, aloof.

“I like your spirit, Gavin,” Ricin remarked. “Just as ambitious as your father.”

“So when is he sealing the deal with Mane?” Vice asked, turning to Ricin.

“I’m still waiting for the call. But I’m sure it will be very soon now.”

“I'd wish you luck, James,” Vice said, his eyes crawling out of their pits to look at him, “Mane is quite the animal type—but I’m sure you don't need it.”

They were talking about an upcoming job—hopefully the one he needed to get done and over with to get John out of there.

“He doesn't know anything yet,” Ricin said. “He doesn't need to; when it's time, he gets the information and just does the task.”

“That much of a pro, huh?” Vice remarked.

“He's still got to prove himself, father,” Gavin said. “Being back at Ricin's doesn't mean he intends to stay. Do you?” Gavin asked, turning to James with a smirk.

"Our differences are in the past," James replied, putting a grin on Ricin's face.

"We'll see about that," Gavin replied, squinting hard at James. "Really looking forward to fighting you, mutant."

Vice looked at his watch; a wordless croak escaped his throat in response. "We need to get going, Ricin," Vice said, pulling up the collar of his jacket, burying his neck into it. "I cannot be late for my meeting."

"I'll see you in a minute for lunch," Ricin said to James, and walked away with Vice and Gavin.

James began walking back to the cell to apologize to John—John meant well but couldn't see the whole picture—but James kept going and turned left toward the kitchen. He preferred to avoid any further confrontation before lunch.

The aroma of charred vegetables filled the air. Edgar was sitting at the kitchen table, scrolling through his phone. A woman, preparing their meals.

"Hey, James," Edgar said, putting his phone away. "Gina, this is James. James, Gina."

"Oh, hi," Gina replied, glancing at James while stirring a pan. Her hair was tied up in a neat bun, her black clothes paired with bright purple sneakers. "Pleased to finally meet you, James; heard so many nice things about you," she continued with an Italian accent.

"Hi," he replied. "Food smells really good."

"Oh thanks, sweet. Food will be ready in a minute. Please, have a seat."

James sat down at the table, opposite Edgar.

"The stab wound ain't bothering you, right?" Edgar asked.

"No; it's much better already."

"Good," Edgar replied. "I'll have a look at it after lunch."

Ricin walked into the kitchen and came to the table.

"Glad we're having lunch together," Ricin said, taking a chair near Edgar. "The chef is just great; she's been working here for over a year now. She enhances flavors like no one else does. Right, Gina?"

"Food is art; and I love art," Gina replied, wiping off the edge of a plate. "Mia nonna taught me the best recipes in the world."

She brought over three plates and began putting them down on the table.

"Medium rare steak for you, sir," she said, putting down a big cut of meat in front of Ricin. "And two roasted vegetable salads with brown rice."

She put down the salad plates in front of Edgar and James, and topped all their glasses with more water.

"Buon appetito," she said cheerfully. "Hope you like."

"Thanks," both Edgar and James replied.

Ricin cut through his steak and tasted it.

"Oh, this is perfect, Gina!" Ricin remarked, chewing the piece of meat. "Well done, as always."

"Glad you like it, sir," she replied. "I'll leave you to eat in peace, then I clean later," she said, and hung her apron by the fridge and left the kitchen.

They began eating in silence. The pitter-patter of light rain steady against the windowpanes. James kept his eyes down to his plate. Eating with both Ricin and Edgar had only been the norm before he turned ten.

"You still prefer to eat rabbit food?" Ricin asked him. "If you want to be a lion, you got to eat like one," Ricin said, sweeping some residual blood off the plate with a piece of steak.

"I choose not to eat meat too," Edgar said. "I never thought of myself as a rabbit though."

Ricin released a hearty laugh and picked up his glass, "Edgar Thomson, my man," Ricin said, "you—are a species of your own." Ricin raised his glass of water in cheers to Edgar, and Edgar gave a small noise of amusement.

"Well, that I'll go with," Edgar replied, picking up his own glass and tilting it toward Ricin.

They went silent again, distant thunder clapping closer.

"This rice salad is really good, right?" Edgar asked, looking at James, waiting for him to say something.

"It is," he replied in a low voice, and cleared his throat.

"Remember that time when we wanted to see who could peel potatoes the fastest?" Edgar asked. "How old were you—seven?"

"Oh, the mess we had made," Ricin remarked with a smile. "Garth had used a potato peeler, right?"

"He did," Edgar replied. "His butterfingers didn't do him any good though; peel, roll, peel, whoop; another one onto the floor," Edgar laughed, reenacting the scene, imitating Garth as potatoes kept slipping out of his hands.

James smiled, remembering the exact same scene; they had laughed hard that day; one of the very few days that had been good.

"You remember, right?" Edgar asked him.

"You had won," James told Edgar.

"Beat me by two potatoes!" Ricin laughed.

“I did, didn't I?” Edgar said, and they continued eating, a light, rather pleasant aura resonating between them.

“As we agreed yesterday, James,” Ricin said, when all of them had finished eating, “I need you to get one of the final two pieces and John can leave too.”

James nodded and reached out for his glass of water.

“This job is not that complicated but all of the highly trained people that tried, ended up dead,” Ricin said with a heavy sigh. “There is this brilliant scientist, Professor Benjamin, who has managed to create the antidote for a deadly pathogen. The genius part of it is that the effects of the disease are only reversed for a number of days and an infected person would need regular shots making them dependent on this antidote. There is no cure for this bacterium and if untreated—it's fatal. I need you to get the formula for the antidote which he keeps solely on paper in a safe to avoid digital hacking.”

James swallowed hard, avoiding Ricin's gaze, thoughts racing ahead of him.

“What will happen to the professor once I get that formula?” he asked, knowing Ricin would want to be the only one to know it.

“Well, you worry about your part, I worry about mine,” Ricin replied with a confident smile.

That meant the professor and all those that worked for him were bound to be killed.

“No one is going to die, James,” Edgar said, as though reading his thoughts. “Not even the professor; we’re going to get him arrested for fraud.”

“Which, may I add, he is guilty of,” Ricin said. “I’ll just make sure the professor and all those that might have had info on the formula, do not dare reveal one element of it."

No one killed—that was very different from Ricin's usual way of doing business and tying loose ends; maybe things were really taking a good turn after all.

"So, when are you up for it?" Ricin asked, leaning back in his chair.

"I want John to leave as soon as possible, so anytime; even today."

"Is it okay because of the stab wound?" Ricin asked, turning to Edgar.

Edgar hesitated then said, "Should be fine."

"Great," Ricin replied, getting to his feet. "I'll talk to Garth, see what we need to have in place and all, and you can get going."

***

James went back to the cell. John was sitting on the bed, eating some rice.

"Tonight, you will be able to leave too," he told John as he sat down beside him.

"How so?"

"I'm just going to get a formula for an antidote Ricin wants, and you can leave."

"A formula?"

"Yeah."

"Seems rather important for Ricin to have, seeing that he would only let me go once it's in his hands."

"It's only a formula; one of two pieces I have to get."

John remained quiet and continued eating.

"John, I wanted to apologize for—raising my voice at you before," James said. "I know you mean well, but I know what I'm doing."

“Do you?” John asked with a patient smile.

“I hope so,” James replied with a nervous titter, and lay down across the bed, his feet dangling from the side.

“You’re smart son; I do trust that. It's Ricin I don't trust,” John said. “Just be careful, okay?” John added, turning sideways to look him in the eye.

“Yeah,” James replied, and inhaled slowly to soothe his surge of anxiety.

John finished his food and they chatted away an hour. John told him about one time he snuck into Martha's house through her bedroom window, and had to hide from her father in the wardrobe for what seemed to be like a suffocating eternity for John.

Garth came for James and took him to discuss details with Ricin for his next job.

“This is Benjamin's building,” Ricin told James as they sat around the teak table, looking at the blueprint of the place.

Edgar and Garth were also seated. Edgar kept fidgeting with the pen in his hand. It was rather odd to see Edgar so tense.

“The safe is right here—in the room adjacent to the laboratory,” Garth pitched in, tapping on a particular area of a room.

The building had three floors, square in shape, with two internal yards, one slightly bigger than the other. Garth pointed out the two fastest ways to get to the laboratory and the quickest exits once he got to the safe. Four security guards were normally stationed on each floor, two with the elevator and the other two near the stairs. The room the safe was located in, had motion sensors, which he had to deactivate along with the security cameras, from the surveillance room on the second floor. If the alarm was tripped, all the doors would go on lockdown.

“Remember these?” Garth asked James, showing him a red cuboid.

“Small explosives,” he replied, also remembering the distinct burning scent they left behind.

“Right. Do you remember how to activate these in particular?” Garth asked again.

“Yeah; safety pin then lever.”

“Exactly; you’ll be using one of these to break open the safe. Trying to crack the safe code would take too long regardless your great skills at that,” Garth said. “Any questions?”

“The other people that tried this mission—were they killed by his security team?” James asked.

“No,” Ricin replied, leaning forward in his chair, locking his hands on the table. “I was coming to that. Once a break-in is detected, the building goes on lockdown. Having the intruders isolated in a particular area, a certain frequency is emitted that causes their spines to vibrate and shatter; it's amazing what the power of resonance can do.”

James kept staring at Ricin, appalled.

“But don't worry,” Ricin quickly continued, “you’ll be given extra explosives like they were, but unlike them, your body can bear much more giving you enough time to jump out of a window or blow down a door to get out. In any case, you’re faster and more sharp; they’ll probably only realize you were there, after you’re gone.”

One thing Ricin did always do, was believe in James and his capabilities, sometimes even more than James himself did.

"If for some reason the alarm does go off, you get out of there, even without the formula, understood?" Ricin stated.

James gave a firm nod; he could do this—John could soon go home.

"Right then," Ricin said. "You should get going."

***

James was on his way to Benjamin's Corporation. He was in the front passenger seat, Garth behind the wheel, Logan at the back.

"This is going to be a piece of cake for you," Garth said as they were approaching the building. "We'll be back at Ricin's in no time."

Garth parked the car. The skies were weeping heavily, flashes of lightning illuminating the dark road ahead.

James zipped up his jacket and put on the hood. A huge bolt of lightning streaked across the black sky, followed by a powerful roar.

"It's like hell is coming upon Earth," Garth murmured.

James froze. *May you never allow yourself to be Ricin's means to bring hell upon Earth,* Wang Gu's words echoed loudly in his head. But this job was only one of the two pieces Ricin needed…or was there really no other piece?

CHAPTER SIXTEEN

"What's the other piece Ricin needs to start the biological war?" James asked Garth.

"What?" Garth replied, the thudding of rain drumming on the car.

"The other piece Ricin needs, what is—"

"I heard what you said," Garth interrupted. "Now is not the time, James. You need to focus on this job right now. Got it?"

John could go home after this, James reminded himself—and nodded to Garth.

"Good," Garth replied, and took the backpack from Logan's hand. "You've got six explosives, extra bullets, glass cutter, wire cutter, and a torch in here. And I put the electronic key card here," Garth said, his finger on the small velcroed pocket on the strap of the bag.

James took the bag and closed the zipper. All the lights of the building were off, except for two adjacent windows on the top floor.

"That's the laboratory, right? People still working this late?" James asked.

"No, no one's there. The lights of the lab are always kept on for security purposes," Garth replied. "Here," Garth added, giving him a gun and earpiece.

James secured the gun in his waistband and put the aural device in his ear. Garth then attached the mini camera to the front of his jacket.

"Remember," Garth said, "if the alarm goes off, you get out of there as fast as you can with or without the formula, okay?"

"Yeah."

"Good luck, James, you got this," Ricin said in his ear.

James got out of the car and hurried toward the building through the downpour. His clothes and shoes were waterproof and he splashed his way to the alley Garth had parked close to.

A gurgle from the gutters bounced off the walls and added to the rhythm of water sloshing on the cobblestones.

No sign of life was in sight. He climbed up the alley wall—pulling himself by ledges—to the rooftop.

He kept a fast pace, jumping from rooftop to rooftop, cautious not to slip on the wet stone. He leaped onto Benjamin's building and went to the smaller interior yard.

The window to the surveillance room on the second floor was cracked open, just like Garth had said it would be—the janitor had come through.

He climbed down to the second floor, pushed the window wide open, and leaped inside—ready for the two guards that were on duty that night.

Both men in the room reached down for their firearm, but James was quick to punch them out senseless. He went to the keyboard attached to the monitors the guards were watching and shut down the surveillance.

"Garth, which ones?" he asked, hacked into the system's motion sensors operation. There were more than expected.

"That's probably a trick loop in the system," Garth replied. "Deactivate the first five in red."

James did as instructed. His fingers clacked anxiously at the keys; a trick loop could easily trip the alarm.

"Now what?" James asked, active motion sensors still detected in the building.

"Try the next two—the ones in orange," Garth replied.

James began deactivating the orange coded ones but the system abruptly shut down and a red box with a fifteen-second countdown began on the screen. The intrusion was detected and the alarm was seconds from going off.

"James, reroute," Garth said with a lilt of panic.

James's fingers raced against the clock on the monitor, beads of sweat dampened his forehead. He hit in the last command just as the clock turned zero, and held his breath.

"Great job," Ricin sighed in relief as the monitor redirected James to the page he was on before the countdown initiated.

James exhaled heavily, unzipping his jacket to let in some air.

"Should I try hacking the alarm instead?" he asked.

"No, any attempt at that would notify Benjamin directly," Garth replied. "Wait a sec; let me check something quick."

The two guards were still unconscious on the floor, a loud hush echoed in the building.

"James, reactivate the red ones and then deactivate all of them at the same time; should override the glitch," Garth said.

He followed Garth's instructions and it worked; all the motion sensors were deactivated.

"Good!" Ricin said. "Keep moving."

James quietly opened the door of the surveillance room. The corridors were dimly lit; the faint glint of the moon complimenting the dipped wall lights. He hurried to the stairs, not allowing his presence to be noticed. Two guards were standing on each side of the staircase, one paying attention to his phone. He took them by surprise, knocking them out before they had any time to alert the others.

He made his way up to the third floor; no guards were posted at the top of that staircase. He went to the door of the lab and entered using the electronic key card. All the lights were on, soft squeaks came from the glass containers on a side bench.

He hurried across the lab, keeping away from the windows, and went to the room at the back where the safe was.

"Fourth cupboard from your right, James," Ricin reminded him.

He went to the fourth cupboard in which there was to be the safe embedded in the wall. He opened it—a blaring alarm went off.

"What the—" Garth muttered.

"How did that happen? What did I do?" James asked, agitated.

“He must have installed an independent motion sensor with the cupboard door. It wasn't there before; no one on the inside told us about it,” Garth replied, chasing his words.

“James, get out of there. Now!” Ricin ordered.

But without that formula John was not going home. He quickly swung around his backpack from his shoulders and took out an explosive.

“What are you doing, James? Get out,” Garth yelled.

James pulled out the pin and hit the lever as he stuck the cuboid with the door of the safe, and moved back.

“James, you don't have enough time!” Ricin said, his tone full of apprehension. “Get out of there now! You won't hear the frequency. Move!”

But he knew it was about to begin as his reflexes heightened, warning him of the harm that was about to happen to him.

The explosive blew up, slamming open the door of the safe.

“James! Get yourself out of that room right now,” Ricin yelled louder.

James snatched the box file and headed to the metal door—the only exit in that room. He was nearly there when an acute pain struck his back. His legs felt heavy and he dragged his feet, forcing himself to move.

He pushed at the door with his shoulders, but he lacked his normal strength. The pain in his back kept intensifying and he quickly reached for another explosive.

“Geez, James,” Garth said, his nerves choking his voice.

The explosive blew the door lock off and he quickly jumped out of the room, throwing himself onto the laboratory floor.

His spine was sore but nowhere near shattering; he made it.

"James; talk. Can you stand?" Garth asked.

"Yeah, I'll be fine, just a bit unsteady," he replied.

He got on his knees and put the file into the backpack.

"Get to the window before they start resonance in the lab, James," Ricin said.

He got up, a heaviness numbing his limbs. He was making his way to the closest window when he had to duck down behind a bench, to avoid bullets.

He was still a few meters away from the window; too weak to make a run for it, too unsteady to fight. There were several men in the room with him, their footsteps thudding closer to where he was.

He could use an explosive as a distraction; he could yell bomb and throw one, inactivated, simply to make them take cover while he hurried to the window to get out. But as he was reaching down in his bag, a small gas canister was thrown close to his feet and a yellow-green gas began hissing out.

It was toxic; his reflexes tripped as he was about to inhale, and he held his breath.

"James, get out of there," Ricin said, "that looks like chlorine gas."

He kept holding his breath and stood up with his hands in the air, pretending to surrender; hoping they wouldn't shoot.

Seven men were in the room, all wearing gas masks, their aim pinned on him. Two of them hurried toward him, the others maintaining their perfect shot. He moved away from the gas can, unable to hold his breath much longer. His hands still in the air, his eyes starting to burn.

The two guards came at him; one grabbing his bag, the other attempting to punch him in the stomach. He grabbed the fist, shoving the guard away. He could not lose that file; John had to go home.

The guard was still pulling at his bag, the other coming at him again. Drowning in a sea of green, he grabbed his gun and popped two bullets off—one each into the men's thighs—with rapid precision.

He could not hold his breath any longer and helplessly inhaled. A flame burnt down his lungs and he began coughing, blindly running toward the window, the green mist fogging their clear shots.

He reached out for the window lock, opened it, and pulled himself up and swung over the ledge. He dropped down, brushing against the wall, and grabbed onto the last ledge just in time.

He jumped onto the ground, unable to catch his breath, his throat on fire. He lifted his face to the rain hoping it would soothe the sting in his eyes. Logan rushed to him, grabbed him by the arm and helped him to the car. Bullets swooshed close to their heads—the heavy rain distorted the aim from the laboratory windows.

The back door of the SUV was wide open. James climbed in and slumped in the back seat. Logan got in after him and slammed the door shut.

“Go. Go. Go!” Logan shouted, and Garth revved off.

James couldn't stop coughing, his breath was a loud wheeze.

"Why did you have to do that?" Garth snapped, his foot down on the accelerator.

James focused on his breathing, trying to keep calm and ease his tense airway.

They were back at Ricin's and he was rushed to the infirmary.

An oxygen mask was put over his face.

"Deep breaths, James," Edgar said, while several other of the medical team began attaching wires and tubes to his body.

James inhaled as deep as he could, struggling to suppress his persistent cough. His back was still sore, his throat and eyes irritated.

"You keep holding this up—and you're going to end up dead," Edgar told him.

"I do appreciate that you got the file, son," Ricin said, "but I did tell you to get out of there if at any point the alarm went off."

"I'll heal," he replied, breath starting to ease through him again. "And John can leave."

"Of course," Ricin replied, and forced a smile.

James remained on the hospital bed, breathing through the mask. His body felt weary and he soon fell asleep.

***

When James woke up, the sun was shining through the window, the sound of birds harmonizing the air.

He was feeling much better, the mask had been removed from his face, and he sat up.

"Morning," Edgar said from across the room, swivelling on a stool to face him. "How are you?"

"Better," he replied. "What time is it? Did John arrive home?"

Edgar paused and clicked the pen in his hand.

“No. He's still here.”

“Still here?” James's anger began mounting; that was not the deal.

“Ricin wanted to send him home,” Edgar said, “but—”

“Where are they? Ricin and John.”

“John's still in the room outside the cell. You should go talk to him,” Edgar said, and a muffled ringtone went off in his pocket.

James took off. He still hadn't fully recovered; his spine radiated sharp pains with every footstep, his throat still sore. He pushed aside his discomfort and headed to the cell.

“John?” James called perplexed.

John was sitting on the edge of the bed, a hot drink in one hand, the flask in the other.

“How are you?” John began. “Heard—”

“John, you can leave; I got the formula; that was the deal! Ricin—”

“James, son, calm down,” John interrupted, his tone firm yet tranquil, his eyes lined with determination. “Ricin did let me go—*I* wanted to stay.”

CHAPTER SEVENTEEN

James's head spun. This had to be just another nightmare he'd soon wake up from.

"I don't—" James said, his voice weak. "Wha—Why —"

"I want to stay, James," John repeated.

"No, John, you can't," James said, shaking his head. "You have to leave; you need to leave, right now! Go back to Katy, and Matthew, and Paul."

Silence. John's expression unchanged.

"John, please," James pleaded. "You're making a huge mistake."

"No, James," John replied. "I know what I'm doing—I want to stay."

"What about Katy and Ma—"

"One day, they'll understand," John said.

"One day they'll—" James murmured in disbelief. "I just got poisoned by chlorine gas and nearly fractured my spine just to make sure you get out of here," James snapped.

"I didn't ask you to do that; I was actually against getting that formula in the first place—so, you did nothing for me; you only did it for yourself, to ease your guilt that I am here. Besides, I'm safe here now, no? Ricin got what he wanted; you're his puppet now."

John's gaze locked with James's. A tense aura resonated between them. James's frustration brewed, yet his eyes began to glaze, overwhelmed by the flood of emotions.

"What choice do I have?" James said, his voice defeated. "Do you want Matthew back in here, or Katy? I'm doing what's best for everyone."

James turned away and entered the shower room. He remained with his clothes on, turned on the cold water, and just sat under the showerhead. His clothes soaked up and he let the chill numb his every pain. He felt the touch of the ocean, those icy currents that had rocked him to sleep so many nights. He closed his eyes and let the rush of water above his head, merge with waves smashing into shores.

***

"James?" Edgar said, a light tap on his shoulder. "You okay?"

James had dozed off. The water was no longer running. His clothes still drenched.

"Yeah I'm…fine. Just tired of everything."

"Hey, come on; get up," Edgar said, pulling at his arm. "Dry yourself up and we're going for a walk. I'll be waiting in the corridor," Edgar added, and stepped out of the shower room.

James let his head bang against the tiles behind him. He was doing his best for everyone else, regardless of where that left him, yet still, it didn't seem to be enough. He had to change John's mind; John had to leave—the sooner the better—even though things seemed to take a good turn, James knew Ricin was still as unpredictable as he had always been.

He got up and changed his clothes.

Edgar was waiting for him in the room outside the cell, talking to Logan.

"John, want to join? We're going for a walk," James asked, hoping that getting him out of the building would make him miss home.

John looked at Edgar as though asking for permission and Edgar gave him a slight nod.

The three of them headed out of the building and Garth followed them. Ever since James could remember, whenever he left Ricin's building, Garth had to accompany him. Ricin had always insisted it was for protection as one could never be too careful, but now that James was much older, Garth accompanying him only meant he was Ricin's eyes and ears.

They began walking toward the burble of the river.

"Did you see that?" Edgar asked in a hush voice.

The smell of damp soil instilled a pleasant sense of life.

"Yeah," James replied, his eyes still resting across the narrow part of the river where a rabbit had just hopped by.

Spring was about to boom through every vegetation, insects already paving their way to start the harvest.

"They seemed to have established again," Edgar said. "These last two years, I barely saw any."

Edgar led the way through the bushes and they came to the open area where the river bent.

“It's beautiful out here,” John remarked, gazing around him. “I have never been in this area.”

Feathered spirits set a tranquil tone of tweets, the gentle breeze accompanied them with a light rustle.

“We used to come here regularly,” Edgar replied. “And we used to jog up that steep hill and back, remember?” he added to James, reminiscing.

“Yeah—part of the training program,” James replied, and stepped toward the water. He remembered some of those jogs more than others—especially those at five in the morning in pelting rain, when he would have much rather remained asleep.

Garth came next to him. Edgar and John talked by the large rocks, John rested against one.

“The old man is dumb,” Garth remarked, kicking a stone into the water.

“No one asked for your opinion,” James replied, keeping his eyes on a small fish that was swimming upstream.

“It's not an opinion—it's a fact,” Garth sniggered. “Or maybe he's done with life and figures here at Ricin's things could end very quickly.”

“You feel like going for a swim?” James asked, picking up an elongated, flat pebble from the ground.

“Come again? The water's freezing—”

“So watch your mouth or I’ll push you in,” James said, his gaze on the clear stream. He ran his thumb over the smooth surface of the rock in his hand, then threw it forcefully along the surface of the water. It skipped eight times and disappeared beneath the last ripple.

“Is that so?” Garth replied. “Love to see you try.”

James turned his face to Garth, his eyebrows raised.

“I’m just kidding, alright?” Garth said. “But you know what? I’ve been building more muscle,” Garth continued, flexing his right arm. “And I'd love a friendly take on you. What do you say?”

Garth stared at him and waited for his response.

“You serious?” James snickered. “And you think John is dumb?”

“Okay—now it's on,” Garth said, taking off his jacket.

“You want to get beaten—right here? Right now?” James asked, confused.

“Who said I’m going to let you beat me—I say it will be close to a draw. Come on,” Garth said, throwing the jacket on the ground and moving away from the water to the open space.

Edgar and John were both looking at them. Edgar smirking at Garth's foolishness.

“And what are you going to tell Ricin when we get back? That I beat you up?” James asked Garth.

“Oh come on; it's just some guys testing each other's strengths. Edgar's here—he knows it's not hostile. So come on!”

Garth took a fighting stance. Edgar and John both quiet.

“Garth, you’ll just get hurt; there's no point,” James told him.

“We’re doing this,” Garth said as his fists blocked his chin, ready to fight. “So, are you stepping forward or am I going to have to make you?”

“Fine,” James acquiesced.

James moved toward Garth and stood still. Garth came at him aggressively but James swerved out of the way and pushed Garth onto the ground.

“Are we done?” James asked.

“Hey, just let me grab onto you at least,” Garth said, getting to his feet again. “If you simply keep dodging me, we cannot compare strengths—tell you what; you just stand and I try to topple you over, okay?”

Edgar crossed his arms over his chest, ready to burst out laughing.

James let Garth grab onto both of his shoulders and Garth tried to wrestle him to the ground. Without any effort, James barely jerked. Garth then tried to off balance James using his feet as well, but without any success.

“Is that all you got, Garth?” James bantered.

Beads of sweat were rolling down Garth's face, his breathing heavy.

“Maybe I could ask Ricin to infuse a mutant gene into my DNA,” Garth said, his elbow now around James's neck, his foot trying to move James's leg. “Is that even possible, Edgar?”

“Even if it were—no,” Edgar replied.

“Okay, okay,” Garth sighed, and stepped back. He lifted his hands on his waist, catching his breath, “You win…mutant.”

Edgar sniggered loudly.

“How did it even cross your mind that you could ever stand a chance, Garth?” Edgar asked.

“Don't know—in my head, James is still the young boy I used to guard, I guess,” Garth replied. “Lesson definitely learned,” he added in a mutter. “We’re cool, right?” Garth asked, turning to James, his hand stretched out as a sign of truce. “Didn't hurt you or anything?”

Garth clearly wanted James to say that he did, to validate his own strength.

“No,” James replied, taking Garth's hand. “And my back is still not a hundred percent—just saying.”

“Right,” Garth replied with a sigh of defeat, and picked up his jacket, smacking off any dirt.

They all engaged in a light conversation about the weather and the river, then headed back to Ricin's headquarters.

James joined Ricin and Edgar for lunch. John ate alone in the room outside the cell.

The afternoon ticked by. John took a nap. James lay on his bed and read through one of the science magazines Edgar had brought for him. The science behind life never ceased to amaze James.

It was nearly seven in the evening. A guard would soon bring their meals.

“Hey, John, do you want to have dinner in the kitchen?” James asked. “There won’t be anyone at this time.”

“Is that okay with Ricin?” John replied.

“Why not? Come on.”

James had to remind John what a kitchen felt like; what home felt like—maybe that would do it.

“This is a nice kitchen,” John said as they walked through the doorway.

“It is,” James replied. “No herbs growing on the windowsill though. Those fresh herbs Katy used in her dishes really made the difference, right?”

“They surely did,” John said, still looking around the room.

James opened the fridge and took out a container labelled with their names.

"I loved cooking," John said, smiling at the wooden spoons and spatulas in their holder on the countertop. "Desserts were my specialty; Martha had always said I made the best apple pies and sweet pastries."

"No reason to give it up if you like doing it," James replied. "You should help Katy open that bakery; give her a hand. I'm sure you'll make a great team."

James removed the lid of the container and opened the microwave.

"Do you need any help with something?" John asked.

"No, have a seat," he replied. "I'll just warm up this mushroom soup."

John sat down at the kitchen table. He pulled the flower vase toward him and inhaled deeply, his nose buried in the pink roses.

"Ahhh that smell," John remarked. "There is nothing like the smell of roses. It was my mother's favorite too."

James put down two plates of soup and a loaf of crusty bread on the table.

"This looks delicious, thanks," John said, picking up the spoon.

"I don't know anything about real cooking," James said as they both began eating. "I'd love to learn someday."

"No better time than the present; I can teach you."

"That would be fun. Matthew had said he wanted to learn one day too. He should; remember when Katy had to rush out and he continued cooking that sauce?"

"Oh my," John said. "Glue is the word that describes that goo he had made."

They laughed at the memory, then fell silent, the clink of their spoons chiming with the hands of the clock until their plates were empty.

"John," James said, carefully choosing his words, "Matthew needs you, Katy still needs you—John you still —"

"I know what you're trying to do, son," John interrupted, his smile patient. "As much as I miss them, I know where my place is right now."

"John, I'm fine. And there is a line I would never cross, even if I was forced to; I can't."

"I'm not doubting your morals—I'm worried about Ricin and his manipulative determination," John said, and leaned closer toward him. "Son, Ricin craves power and will never stop," John whispered carefully. "You have to find a way to stop him and his organization."

"That's not possible," James whispered back. "Even if Ricin is out of the picture, many will jump at the opportunity to take his place."

John straightened his posture and filled his chest.

"Anything is possible; limitations are only real in the mind," John said, his tone back to normal.

"Hey," Edgar said as he walked briskly into the kitchen. "When you're finished with dinner, James, come to the infirmary; I need to run some tests—to make sure everything is healing okay."

"Sure," James replied passively.

Edgar took a yogurt drink from the fridge and came to the table.

"So—you're not changing your mind?" Edgar asked John, standing right next to him.

"No," John replied, looking Edgar in the eye.

Edgar hesitated.

"Like I told you this morning, John," Edgar said, "leave. Nothing's worse than being in the wrong place, at the wrong time."

Edgar left the kitchen, his words echoing debilitating chills.

James looked at John, waiting for him to say something.

"Edgar makes me wonder," John said. "There is something more to him than just working for Ricin… maybe he hopes to take his place one day."

"Edgar prefers working in the shadows and pulling strings from there," James replied. "Being in the spotlight like Ricin is definitely not his ambition."

James stood up and took the plates off the table.

"Or so it may seem," John remarked to himself.

"Hey, want to play?" James asked, finding the old pack of cards in the same drawer they had always been.

"Sure." John's face lit up. "Do you know any card tricks?"

"No—not really. I knew just a few which I have totally forgot how they went."

John took the pack of cards and began teaching him some tricks. He enjoyed watching John living in the moment, laughing at his failing memory and hands that weren't as steady or swift as they had once been. They spent the rest of the evening going over several card tricks John recalled, and played a few games until John called it a day and let James take the victory.

The next few days were tranquil and pleasant. James joined Ricin and Edgar for lunch and ate dinner with John, conversations light and cheerful at times. Ricin got a bedroom set up for James; the furniture was made of solid wood—light in color. The drapes and bedsheets, matching shades of blue. The bedroom also had an en suite bathroom with a rainfall showerhead. Still, James slept on the bed in his cell, with John sleeping in the room next to him.

John had made up his mind and there was nothing James could say or do to make him leave. James had also managed to persuade Ricin to allow John one call to Katy, hoping that hearing her voice would make him want to go back to her. But John refused, saying those tears wouldn't do anyone any good. Instead, John wrote a letter to them and Edgar promised he would have it delivered for him. When James asked John what he had written to them, John simply replied that it was nothing they wanted to hear but everything he had always taught them to stand for, and that they'll surely understand his decision to stay.

***

"This is how it has to be done now," Garth said to James, after having shown him the new way of hacking into the latest bank systems. "This method does not allow for overrides but it's a shorter process. You think you got it? Do we need to go over it another time?"

James hesitated. The last input of codes was quite elaborate but he managed to memorize it as Garth was showing it to him the second time.

"No, I'm good."

"Perfect," Garth remarked. "I'll prepare another simulation and you can try it on your own tomorrow. Go get yourself ready now; we'll be leaving for the fights in thirty minutes."

It was late in the afternoon. John was still having a nap and James went to his bedroom. He picked up the sketching board and pencil from the desk, and sat down on the bed, resting his back against the wall. He began sketching from where he had left off—the face of a Hawksbill sea turtle—and gave life to its eyes.

Ramon soon came to his room and stood in the doorway.

"Time to go," Ramon said.

"Sure," he replied, getting off the bed. He went to the desk and began flipping through some of his drawings. "This is for Belle," he said, handing Ramon a drawing of a unicorn.

"Oh wow; she's going to love this," Ramon replied with a broad smile. "Thanks, James. I appreciate."

"No problem. How's she doing? How did the surprise party go?" he asked as they walked out of the room.

"Perfect; she had no clue. The smile on her face when she saw all the family and her friends there—priceless."

They entered the elevator and went down to the underground carpark. Garth was already waiting for them in the car, and they got in.

They began heading to the abandoned building where the fights were still being held. The sun was setting, orange-red hues kissing the faint pink that dressed the graceful skies.

"Gavin is an idiot," Garth continued as they drove on.

"Young and naive," Ramon added. "Well, Vice is not exactly the role model to be looking up to."

"You make sure you punch him out for real, James," Garth said. "Match with Gavin; you win. The one after, you lose, just to keep things realistic."

"Got that," he replied.

"And, James," Garth quickly added, "don't—just don't —let yourself get in a bad shape, okay? Highest bidder for both matches will be Ricin's representative so we'll still have control over the use of weapons. The fight you'll lose; bare hands—just play along."

Garth parked the car and they stepped out. A group of men and women dressed in long jackets and trench coats headed inside the building before them, the women's giggles loud and flirtatious.

Garth gave a firm nod to the man who was at the door and they were allowed inside.

"You and Gavin are up first," Garth told James. "You good?"

"Yeah," he replied, his eyes on the crowd, making sure Wang Gu wasn't among them.

"Ladies and gentlemen!" the presenter said. "Let the fights begin. Our previous champion, James, seems to have made a full recovery and is here to fight again."

"Come on, James," Garth called.

James followed Garth toward the staircase of the pool and began descending.

"There he is!" the presenter said. "Previous champion —James, will be fighting Gavin Munich," and grabbed Gavin's hand, raising it in the air. "Start placing your bids now; be part of the game!"

Gavin began coming down the stairs toward him. Vice viewing from a front row seat, his long neck bent like a vulture's.

"Had enough time to practice, James?" Gavin asked.

James remained silent, calm—ready to get this over with.

“Cat got your tongue?” Gavin mocked, stepping closer. “You can give me all you have got, mutant,” Gavin said, ending in a whisper. “I’m more than ready for you; you’re about to get your first face scar, pretty.”

“Blades it is!” the presenter announced, and a rumble ran through the crowd.

Two knives were thrown down in the pool. Gavin quickly grabbed the curved one and began rotating it in his hand.

“This is dope,” Gavin said, carefully feeling the pointed edge of his knife.

James picked up the other blade. The handle was still stained with blood from a previous fight.

Ding! Ding! Ding! Gavin inhaled deeply, nostrils expanded, veins bulging out of his forehead. Securing a powerful stance, Gavin thrust the blade skilfully at James's face.

James dodged perfectly and Gavin tried even harder, forcefully striking the knife at him repetitively. But James kept moving out of the knife's path every time.

“You’re good—I’ll give you that,” Gavin said, his upper lip twitching in irritation. “But I’m just getting started.”

Gavin came at him again without mercy, blade aimed for his face. James grabbed Gavin's fist and twisted his hand until Gavin dropped the blade. Then punched Gavin in his abdomen and pushed him onto the floor.

“Impressive,” Gavin said, getting to his feet. “But Ricin was right about you; you’re soft. You don't have it in you; you’re weak at heart,” Gavin said sniggering, and came at him again.

He avoided Gavin's blade and punched him in the face, lacerating his lip.

“Damn it!” Gavin said, his teeth grit hard as he glared down at the blood he wiped off his lip. “You ruin my face, dimwit, and I’ll make sure you’ll pay.”

“Why? That face all you’ve got to offer to girls?—or whoever you’re into.”

Gavin's face flushed with fury and he began thrusting the blade blindly at James. James avoided each strike perfectly, using his own knife to scrape Gavin's leg, putting on a show for the audience.

“Damn you!” Gavin shouted, his hand pressing down on his wound.

“James takes the lead once again. True champion he is. But will Gavin make a comeback?” the presenter said.

“You might be a freak,” Gavin said, “but I’ll find your weak spot and I’ll make sure I’ll hit it next time.”

Gavin's leg was dripping, his lip starting to swell up. James stepped toward Gavin and with one powerful strike, he knocked him unconscious.

“That was awesome! Gavin, your seconds are ticking away with your victory; so what's it going to be? …and three, two, one. Match is over! Our champion, James, has done it again. Stick around folks; three more rounds to go for the day.”

Gavin was carried out of the pool, Vice's disappointment shrivelling his face even further.

Garth came down into the pool and gave James a bottle of water.

“You did good,” Garth said. “Next contestant looks a bit off; probably high on something. Just play along and we’ll hit the road.”

The guy that came down the stairs to fight him was brawny. His eyes unfocused, his hands constantly in tight fists. James allowed himself to get hit, just enough for the spectators to see, and threw a few punches himself. The last strike hit his head, and he pretended to get knocked out and didn't get up until the other guy took the champion's title.

"You did well, son," Ricin told him, as James walked out of the elevator with Garth and Ramon when they got back. "Have a shower and join us for dinner? We haven't eaten yet; we were waiting for you," Ricin said, glancing at Edgar who was standing right next to him.

James normally ate dinners with John. But it was late anyway, John was probably tired, maybe already asleep.

"Sure," James replied, without further hesitation. "I'll be there in ten minutes."

***

Garth joined them for dinner and James found himself laughing at his jokes.

"Oh Garth," Ricin said, his eyes close to tears with laughter, "since when have you become such a comedian?"

Garth shrugged his shoulders and took a big bite of the chicken leg on his plate. "I've been watching a lot of stand-up comedy lately," Garth said, chewing loudly.

They continued eating and laughing at Garth's stories, Edgar almost choking on his water when Garth told them a restaurant joke.

It had been a long time since James laughed so hard and felt so relaxed—it was a first with Ricin—and the first time James felt like he almost belonged.

CHAPTER EIGHTEEN

"Didn't hear you come in last night," John said the next morning when James walked into the room outside the cell.

"Yeah. It was late; I didn't want to wake you and um—had dinner, then slept in my bedroom," he replied, feeling rather awkward.

James hadn't even come by the cell yesterday after the fights—he didn't want to feel the sting of John's disappointed gaze, moreover, since he had chosen to have dinner with Ricin, Edgar, and Garth.

"You wouldn't have woken me," John replied. "I couldn't sleep—ended up pacing most of the night."

James escaped John's gaze and sat down on the edge of John's bed. John remained standing, his hands joined calmly behind his back.

"How did the fights go?" John asked.

"They're just fights," James replied with a shrug.

"Did you fight that boy—Gavin?"

"Yeah; total moron."

John sat down next to James, silent in thought.

"If you could choose any profession, what would that be?" John asked, taking him by surprise.

James hesitated.

"I always liked sciences," he said, but paused again. Why should he even bother—his job was predetermined.

"You don't see yourself studying or having a job along those lines?" John asked.

"When I was little," James replied, and gave a small laugh, as if to say *I was young and foolish*. "I wanted to become a scientist like Edgar. I used to watch him work in the lab sometimes and was always fascinated. Now, there is no point in studying. Besides, I'm not going to have the time. Ricin is soon flying in the top expert to teach me all there is to know about any type of bomb. It should have been my next training program before I—had left."

"Bombs?" John repeated.

"Yeah—I'll learn how to deactivate them as well."

"Is that something you are interested in?"

"Learning is always learning, right?" he replied, not taking any time to tap into his real feelings about bombs. "Whatever you learn is yours to keep."

"That's true," John replied, bobbing his head. "What I meant to ask was; if you were given the freedom of choice, where would you like to see yourself in five, ten years' time?"

"If I'm not with Ricin," James said, "I'll probably be behind bars or even killed—I'm a mutant; I'm a threat. My future is here."

"I never thought of you as a threat," John replied surprised, and went silent. "Is that—what Ricin's been telling you? That you will be seen as a threat and killed," John asked with a fixed gaze.

"I've already proven to the president that I am," he replied, letting his eyes fall to the floor.

"The president is smart," John said, his voice sure. "He knows someone sent you—and I'm sure the president knows much better than what Ricin is telling you and he will surely do better than see you as a threat."

James pondered for a second on John's words, then sighed heavily.

"It doesn't really matter," James concluded. "With Ricin is where I should be."

James's leg started jiggling in irritation. Every time he thought about his future, a stifling anxiety creeped up on him. He couldn't think that far, nor did he want to—the negative possible outcomes always seemed to outweigh the positive ones.

"James, I just—" John began, and waited for James to look up at him. "I just wanted to tell you, son—ever since I met you; from the first time you came over to Katy's house, I knew you were a good, great kid. You are everything a father would want in a son—don't let anyone turn you into something that you're not."

He stared at John, unable to utter a word, while a sense of shame engulfed his soul.

John smiled at him, his wrinkles a journey of wisdom. John then looked away and cleared his throat as though realizing he had hit something in James.

"I don't think it snowed that much this year, did it?" John remarked, changing the subject.

"I don't think so," James replied in a low voice.

John began telling him about how much his dog, Rico, loved snow. How he would dash out the front door to jump around in inches of snow for endless minutes. And how he would rush back inside when he was done, and have the most peaceful nap on his favourite shag rug, outstretched in front of the fireplace.

They chatted till noon, Ramon occasionally adding to their conversations while he stood post by the door.

"One time, on Christmas Eve," John recalled, "I remember it was a cold, cold night," John said, his eyes lit up in the memory. "Edward was six years old, Katy nearly a year. Edward was convinced he had been a good boy and that Santa was coming down the chimney that night. He had written to him that he wanted a train set and—"

"And Santa brought him a big pile of black soot," Gavin interrupted, barging into the room. "Did Santa ever bring you a present?" he added, looking straight at James. "Since you are such a kindhearted, good boy."

"What are you doing here?" James asked, annoyed.

"I had to get stitched up because of you, dimwit; you're lucky this wasn't my face," Gavin said, pulling up his trouser leg to reveal the butterfly stitches below his knee.

"You knew exactly what you were getting yourself into," James replied.

"Well, I wanted to see for myself—oh, mighty mutant," Gavin mocked, coming closer to James. "Remember I told you, freak, that I will find your weak spot? Well, I might have already," Gavin said, and twisted his tongue sideways and bit down on it.

"Get out," James said, eyeing Gavin fiercely.

“I decide where and when I want to go—unlike yourself,” Gavin replied. “You are a very impressive experiment. Pity you don't possess the drive that I do. You could rule the world if you wanted to, but you are just plain stupid.”

Gavin took a step back, smirk still on his face.

“You do resemble your mother; she was a sweet chick,” Gavin sneered. “Curves in all the right places.”

“I never had a mother,” James replied.

“Oh, they never told you? Oh I’m so sorry you had to find out like this,” Gavin laughed. “Don't worry, mine abandoned me when I was young; yours kind of did the same.”

James's heart began racing, unsure if Gavin was just making it all up.

“And about your weak spot,” Gavin continued. “You might be able to sense danger to yourself, but bet you cannot sense…this—” A gun swiftly appeared in Gavin's hand, aimed at John.

James lunged at Gavin and a bang went off before Gavin hit the ground. John was still standing; the shot had missed. James took the gun and tossed it across the floor while keeping Gavin pinned down firmly.

“Outstanding,” Gavin remarked in nothing other than sheer ridicule, and burst into taunting laughter.

“Shut up,” James shouted, pressing down even harder on Gavin's chest. But a groan caught James's attention, and he looked up.

Ramon fell to his knees, a dark stain on his uniform shirt rapidly growing; the gunshot had hit him.

“No, no, no!” James cried, rushing over to Ramon, grabbing him just in time as he was about to collapse.

“Edgar!” James yelled, holding his hand down on Ramon's wound. “You’re going to be okay. You have to be okay,” he told Ramon frantically as he looked him in the eye.

Ramon fixed a blank gaze on him, as though struggling to hold on to his escaping soul.

“No, please no—Edgar!” Warm blood gushed beneath his fingers, Ramon's body getting heavier in his arms. “Stay with me. Come on; listen to me,” he voiced steadily, giving Ramon a slight shake. “You’re going to make it. You have to make it for Belle.”

Edgar, Ricin, and other guards came rushing into the room, followed by Vice.

“What on Earth—” Ricin said, flustered.

“Edgar, you have to save him,” James cried. “He has a sick daughter...”

Two guards picked up Ramon while Edgar placed his fingers on the wound, freeing James from the task. They rushed Ramon out of the room. The jingle of keys steady with their footsteps.

“What the hell happened?” Ricin asked, furious.

“It was just an accident,” Gavin began, “I came over to talk to James here and was going to rid him of his weak spot, but then this happened instead—whoopsie,” Gavin said, full of indifference.

James was still on his knees, covered in Ramon's blood. His heart beat vigorously, his whole body shook with rage.

Gavin smirked—as though proud of what he had done. James blindly sprung up and dashed to Gavin, punching him violently to the ground. Kneeling over Gavin's body, he began hitting him in the face with his fists. The world fell away and it was only James and his fists smashing into Gavin's head. Right fist into Gavin's nose, crack; left fist into Gavin's nose, splattered blood. Black began to seep into the edges of James's view as his vision tunnelled, and in that moment he existed only to smash in Gavin's skull. James knew he wasn't using his full strength, yet there was a distant part of him that was sure Gavin was dead, and it didn't matter.

Vice grabbed onto James's arm.

"Ricin. Ricin!" Vice called in desperation, trying to get James off Gavin.

Ricin said nothing until James punched Gavin again. "That's enough, James," he said, voice calm.

Gavin lay unconscious, deformed, blood spattered over his face, seeping into his hair and onto the floor.

James stood up and Vice dropped to his knees beside Gavin.

"Gavin. Son!" Vice cried, trying to shake him awake. "Ricin get help; he's my son!"

Ricin gave a brief nod to the guards standing by, and they picked Gavin up from the floor and carried him out of the room. Vice hurried after them, his bony hands trembling in front of his face.

"Ramon has a sick, young daughter. His job pays for her treatment," James said in a low voice, catching Ricin's stare.

"I know," Ricin replied. "I'm not mad at you—Gavin brought it upon himself. Besides, I decide who gets shot in my headquarters. You showed him that you do have it in you. Get yourself cleaned up. I'm proud of you, son."

Ricin left the room and James remained standing there, looking down at the blood on his hands. He had never killed someone before, but he might have killed Gavin now, and he did not feel any thread of remorse about it—people like Gavin did not deserve to breathe.

James turned around; John was standing by the bed, shock setting in.

"You okay, John?" he asked.

"I'm fine," John replied, barely beyond a whisper. "You?"

James stared at John, not really knowing what to answer, a hint of glaze in his eyes; this was what his future looked like; blood shadowing his days.

"Have a shower; get cleaned up," John told him, forcing a smile.

A slow hour went by. Lunch with Edgar and Ricin was cancelled, and guards brought food for him and John. Both had no appetite and the food remained untouched.

James was lying on the bed, John pacing from wall to wall.

"You!" Vice shrilled as he came through the doorway, pointing his index finger straight at James. "You should learn to pick your battles! You better pray my son fully recovers. And mark my words; this is not the last you have seen of me."

Vice stormed out of the room, avoiding any eye contact with Ricin who was standing by the door.

"Don't you worry about any of that, son," Ricin said when Vice had left. "Vice is just upset, which is reasonably fit right now—you broke Gavin's jaw, caused multiple fractures in his skull and surely cost him one eye. However, I'm sure he knows that initiating a battle with me or you, is simply signing his death warrant."

James remained quiet. Vice's yelling still echoed through the corridors.

"Gavin said," James then voiced, and swallowed hard. "He said I have a mother. Is that true?"

The silence—deafening. Ricin's eyes locked with James's.

"A mother," Ricin said, "is not exactly the term I would use to describe her."

CHAPTER NINETEEN

"What?" James whispered, taken aback. For over fifteen years, he was made to believe he was just a science experiment; having a mother made him more human than ever.

"You had a mother," Ricin replied, his head agreeing with his words. "She carried you for nine months, took care of you until you were nearly a year old, then left."

"Left?" he repeated.

"Yes—went for good."

Why would a mother leave her child? Why would she have left him with Ricin knowing what that meant about his fate?

"Where is she now?" James asked.

"She's dead," Ricin replied.

A hurricane of emotions swept James—swirling together were a deep sense of belonging and that of rejection, and abandonment, and loss.

"You didn't miss out on anything," Ricin added.

"Why—why did you never tell me about her? Why did you let me believe I was just a freak of science?" James asked.

“She left James; what was I supposed to do? Tell a young boy his mom couldn't be there for him?”

“I don't believe you,” he replied, not sure if he questioned Ricin's integrity, or didn't want to believe his own mother would abandon him.

“I have proof—you could see for yourself.” Ricin raised his eyebrows.

James's heart missed a beat, his hope shattered into a thousand shards.

“Do you want to see it or not?” Ricin asked with an impatience.

Edgar walked into the room—he had been listening in on their conversation. James stared at the both of them, struggling to hold himself together.

James didn't remember saying anything else, nor following Ricin and Edgar out of the room, but he soon found himself in Ricin's office, sitting on a chair; Edgar beside him, Ricin behind the desk.

“Here it is,” Ricin said, and turned his laptop for James to see. “This happened only a few months ago—before you got that file from the president. I went to pay her a visit in the jail she was in and I have access to recordings. This was it,” Ricin continued, and began playing the footage.

James looked at the screen—a CCTV image. The angle was high and from a corner, the frame held Ricin and the woman who was supposedly James's mother; clear and in color. The room was divided by a long table, halved by plexiglass and partitioned further by slats of wood. Other inmates were in the frame speaking with other people but their conversations could not be heard. The audio started.

“If it is not but the devil himself,” the woman said to Ricin as she picked up the receiver from behind the thick glass of the prison's visiting room.

“That's her; Alina Niclin,” Ricin interrupted.

The woman was thin and pale. James had her chestnut hair and the same dark brown eyes.

“I know the years in here have not done me any good, but I can say the same about yourself,” she told Ricin.

“You look fine,” Ricin replied. “I came to tell you—”

“Tell me what?” she cut in, annoyed. “After all these years…what could you possibly want to tell me?”

“You will soon get to see him,” Ricin replied.

She paused, her eyes wide, then looked away blankly.

“He will soon make news headlines,” Ricin said. “He —”

“This is what you came to tell me?” she snapped, pinning a scowl on Ricin. “After all this time, you show up, to tell me this?” she added with a scoff. She leaned closer to the glass window. “You are such a disgrace, Ricin! And for a second—” she paused, shaking her head as though disappointed in no one other than herself. “To think that maybe you came to apologize for having me locked up for the rest of my life for something you had done—ain't I the fool?”

“You framed her?” James said, pausing the footage. “You lied; you said she had left.”

“You haven't seen all the footage yet,” Ricin replied. “So shall we?” Ricin pressed the play button again.

“I thought you'd be happy to see him,” Ricin told Alina.

"You put me in hell," she replied with detestation. "I'm surprised you even put in the effort to remember my full name to visit."

"You know I only did what had to be done," Ricin said, his voice low. "Nothing out of spite for you."

She sniffed and wiped her cheek swiftly.

"Does he still work for you? That snake in your ear," she asked through clenched teeth.

Was it Edgar she was talking about? Edgar was the one who had the most influence on Ricin's decisions.

"I run everything," Ricin told her. "It was always that way and it will always be."

"Of course—believe what you want to; you were always so delusional," she remarked.

"Watch your mouth!"

"Or what?" she asked. "There is nothing worse you can do to me than what you have already done!"

"Just look out for him on the news," Ricin concluded as he stood up.

"Ricin!" she called, preventing him from hanging up the receiver. "Do you know how I manage to get by each day?" she asked with a rather deranged gaze. "How I manage to get an hour of sleep each night? I constantly repeat to myself—over and over again—you are all dead; all of you. So don't even think that I'll be following any news," she said, and hung up the receiver and walked away.

"See?" Ricin told James, stopping the footage. "Like I said, she was in prison; she didn't want to have anything to do with you anymore. Clearly did not regret not being in your life."

"You framed her?" James repeated. "Why?"

“At that time, it was the best for everyone; even herself,” Ricin replied.

“For everyone? How was—”

“James,” Ricin cut in, “I am not going to go over what happened fourteen years ago. All I will tell you is that a problem had arisen and it had to be dealt with; getting her locked up was best.”

“That's still very different from saying she left like she didn't care about me.”

“Yes but as you heard her say, she then preferred to think of you as dead rather than to see you,” Ricin replied.

“How did she die? What happened to her?”

“A fight broke out in prison among the inmates; she was stabbed.”

James went silent.

“If I have a mother, then I must have a father, right?” he asked. The idea of having a father pulled him into a deeper emotional trench.

“No,” Ricin replied eagerly. “Care to explain the science of it, Edgar?”

Edgar's gaze paused on Ricin's.

“The ovum was Alina's; your biological mother,” Edgar said, turning to James. “The sperm was artificially created to carry all the dominant genetic mutations.”

James inhaled deeply, too overwhelmed to process everything.

“Any more questions?” Ricin asked, tapping his fingers on the desk in an irritated manner.

James shook his head. He had learned enough for one day, besides, his mother was dead; there was nothing he had to build toward.

He went to his room and lay down on the bed. He kept staring at the ceiling, forcing his mind to suppress any thoughts—the feelings attached to them were all too real—too painful.

The clock kept on ticking. His mind mostly blank. A gentle knock on his bedroom door redirected his focus.

"Come in," he called.

It was John. John wasn't allowed in Ricin's office and had remained in the room outside the cell.

"You okay?" John asked.

"Not really," he replied, gaze still ceiling-ward. "I saw—I saw her on a video—Ricin framed her and she was imprisoned, that's why she had left."

"I see," John said. "It wasn't her choice then."

"Yeah but I heard her say—she actually told Ricin, she preferred to think of me as dead, rather than get to see me," he said, and sat up and swung his feet onto the floor. "It shouldn't really matter," he added with a frustrated shrug. "She's dead anyway."

John came next to him and sat down on the edge of the bed.

"Being framed and sent to prison for something you haven't done takes a toll on anyone," John said. "I'm sure that is what got in the way of her feeling like a mother—she would have been proud of you."

"Would she?" James asked, highly doubting that.

"Well, *I* am," John replied with a smile. "I see beneath whom Ricin forces you to be; I see beneath the choices you make out of fear. I'm proud of who you are, and may you be more of yourself and less of what others want you to be."

He looked up at John; the closest to a father figure he ever had in his life; the person who cared about James's emotional well-being.

"Thanks," James said.

John gave a firm nod, then tapped on James's knee.

"Hey, what do you say we head to the kitchen and cook dinner?" John said. "I could teach you some basic cooking techniques and how to make the best dessert of course."

John dressed his voice with enthusiasm and James couldn't let him down. They went to the kitchen and decided on cooking pasta with red sauce and vegetables, and an apple pie for dessert. They began preparing the sauce and John explained the basic types of sauces and which herbs paired best with each of them.

"When it comes to baking desserts, you have to respect ratios," John said as he sifted some flour into a mixing bowl. "Every ingredient has to be added in proportion, otherwise it's ruined."

James watched John prepare the dough for the apple pie, surprised by the amount of butter that was actually in it.

The food smelled and tasted just like Katy's cooking and the apple pie was perfectly crisp. They cleaned their plates and were walking back to the room outside the cell, when a commotion started in the building. Through the mutterings and exchanges of the guards, James was able to figure out Ramon had died. Belle had lost her father and might soon lose her life.

The next two days dragged. The time ticked through molasses if it budged at all. A constant fall of rain thudded the windows. The knowledge of James's mother and her last words to Ricin kept haunting James in his sleep, her face imprinted forever in his mind.

***

James failed again the same hacking simulation he had been practicing from early morning.

"If this was the real thing, the alarm would be ringing in everyone's ears right now—again!" Garth told James.

James paused, staring at the digital clock at the top corner of the screen.

"Your head's not here today," Garth said annoyed, snatching the keyboard from beneath his hands to restart the program. "You keep repeating the same mistakes. Start again."

The keyboard was back beneath James's fingers, the cursor blinking impatiently for his commands.

"Is it slash four dash or slash—"

"Are you kidding?!" Garth said, losing his temper. "This is the fifth time you're writing this today! What the hell, James?"

The screen in front of him was full of codes, his mind completely blank.

"I need to use the bathroom," James said, getting to his feet, but Garth grabbed him by the arm.

"Sit—down!" Garth ordered. "You finish this; you get it right at one go—then we're done."

James sighed forcefully and sat back down. He positioned his fingers on the keyboard, his mind still void.

"Slash four colon," Garth said impatiently.

James began typing, inputting codes only to delete and rewrite most of them. He finally managed to get through the whole program, Garth still looked displeased.

"You took more than double the time you should have," Garth said. "The reason you are trained to do this, is because you are normally the fastest at getting through a program—I don't know what's up with you but you better get it together; fast."

James kept looking down at the letters on the keyboard, just wanting to go to his room and be alone.

"Dismissed," Garth said. "But you better bring your A-game tomorrow morning," he added, pointing his index finger steadily at James.

James left the room. Garth's words simply rolled off his shoulders. He headed straight to his bedroom, hoping to get some sleep and forget everything for a little while.

John was there, standing next to his desk, looking carefully at one of his drawings.

"Hey," John said as James walked in. "Is this her? Is this your mom?"

"Yeah—from what I could remember from the footage."

"She's pretty," John said. "You okay? I came by because I didn't see you for breakfast."

"Yeah, I was with Garth going over some stupid hacking processes," he replied, taking off his shoes.

James sat down on the swivel chair at his desk and began fidgeting with a pencil. His leg jiggled.

"Do you want to talk about what's on your mind?" John asked.

"There's nothing to talk about—my mom's dead and I never knew her."

"It's hard growing up without a parent," John said. "I never got the chance to know my father—I never let that stop me from being a good dad myself, even though I had no footsteps to follow. You know, life has its own way of putting the right people in our lives exactly when and for how long we need them. I know it hurts and I know it's hard, but whoever is not in your life was never meant to be."

John left his room, allowing him to rest. He kept turning over in bed, unable to fall asleep. Edgar soon came by, his persistence getting James out of bed and joining them for lunch.

***

James barely touched his plate, detached from the conversations Ricin and Edgar were having. An emptiness shrouding his thoughts.

"Hey, do you want to go for a ride?" Edgar asked James. Ricin paused with his fork midair. "I need to get some supplies; you can come along for the car ride if you like."

"Some fresh air will do you good," Ricin said. "Heard you did more than poorly in the simulations this morning," he continued, pulling at the meat on the chicken bone. "Why is that? Something the matter?"

"I'm fine—just didn't get enough sleep," he lied.

"Well, make sure you do get enough sleep before your next task is up," Ricin replied, chewing impatiently. "Garth is free this afternoon, Edgar; he can come with."

"Good," Edgar said. "We'll leave in an hour."

They got into Edgar's car. James sat in the front passenger seat, Garth at the back.

Edgar drove into town. James was given a navy blue cap and told to wear glasses if they were pulled over. They drove into a small parking area and Edgar turned off the engine.

"I'll be back in ten minutes; just need to grab a few things from the hardware store," Edgar said, and got out of the car. Garth remained with James.

A group of teenage boys and girls were gathered in front of the confectionary adjacent to the store, their laughter boisterous, two of them hugging and talking chest to chest.

One of the girls turned her face to the wind, allowing the breeze to push her caramel-brown hair aside. She bit into the doughnut in her hand, her dimpled smile echoing the simple pleasures of life.

"You still like the ones with custard cream filling, right?" Edgar asked James as he got into the car with a large doughnut box in his hands. "I got you some of those and some cronuts too; the chocolate ones are really good; you got to try them."

Edgar opened the box and gave it to James.

"Garth, you want one?" Edgar asked, taking a cronut.

"No, I'm good—wouldn't want my early gym session to go down the drain for a greasy piece of dough."

"More for us," Edgar laughed, and bit into the cronut and started the car.

James ate one of the custard filled doughnuts. They tasted the same as those Edgar used to buy on Sunday mornings.

"I thought you said one stop," Garth said as Edgar took the highway.

"Just a detour—nice weather for a trip to the beach, right?" Edgar asked, glancing over at James.

"The beach?" Garth snapped, leaning forward, coming closer to Edgar. "Ricin wouldn't allow that."

"Well, he doesn't really need to know now, does he, Garth?" Edgar replied, his eyes on the road.

"He'll know; he'll be following James's heart tracer and I will get in deep trouble if—"

"Oh, Garth," Edgar sighed loudly. "I'll tell Ricin myself that I held a gun to your head while we drove over to the beach, okay? No trouble for you; I'll deal with Ricin myself."

"Are you crazy?" Garth replied, furious. "The sea is how he got away the last time."

"I said we're going to the beach, Garth," Edgar replied, his tone overly solemn. "And I need not repeat myself."

Garth hesitated, then leaned back in his seat and remained silent.

It wasn't long before James caught the shimmer of crests, glistening across the vast ocean. Edgar pulled over near the fence, the golden sand only a few meters in front of them.

"Looks like we're alone," Edgar said, glancing around. "Come on, James," he added, getting out of the car, and James followed.

The light breeze carried salty air and the sound of crashing waves. Edgar made his way to the sand and James stepped behind him. Garth, too, got out of the car and slammed the car door shut.

The sand crumbled beneath their shoes while a crab scuttled sideways to the water.

"Look at the size of this," Edgar said, picking up a cuttlefish bone. "That was a big one."

They walked closer to the sea and James's eyes rested on the ocean, his body craving its cold touch. Garth caught up with them, a scowl furrowing his brow.

"I can trust you to take a dive, right?" Edgar asked James, taking him by surprise.

Garth gaped at Edgar, then let out a loud scoff.

"Yeah," James replied, nodding repetitively to Edgar, a rush of exhilaration sweeping over him.

"Go ahead," Edgar said with a calm smile.

James quickly took off his sweater and trousers, leaving only his boxers.

Small waves were foaming the shore, dancing with small pebbles. The damp sand sank beneath his feet and the icy waters touched his toes, sending a numbing chill up his spine. Without any hesitation, he continued walking into the waves until they crashed into his thighs. With one strong leap, he dived into the murky waters and all around him went completely quiet.

He remained submerged, frigid water filling his lungs. He swam out to the ocean for tens of minutes without stopping or looking back while freedom drugged his veins. After one last stroke, he let go, surrendering to the current to take him wherever it pleased.

A euphoric tranquility came upon him and as though the life he lived on land was that of someone else and he could just stop following it. His eyes closed, giving in to the heavy drowsiness of the cradling current, and he almost fell asleep. His reflexes shook him awake, warning him of the strands of a propelling jellyfish, and he swerved away. He swam toward the surface and pushed his head out of the water, expelling the liquid in his lungs and breathing in air.

He was far out, the beach he had left from only a few centimeters in length. He floated on his back as he looked up at the cloudless sky. Then began swimming back to shore.

Edgar was strolling along the beach. Garth looking to the ocean with his hands on his hips, posture tense. James continued to shore and when he arrived, Edgar gave him a large towel.

"Is it cold?" Edgar asked.

"It's perfect," he replied, throwing the towel over his back, the serenity of the sea lingering within in.

"We'll come again soon," Edgar said with a warm smile.

James looked out to the sea again—he couldn't wait.

CHAPTER TWENTY

The ocean filled the void land created. Now, James had something to look forward to; his next dive.

He was having dinner with John in the kitchen, a relaxed atmosphere between them.

"This is really good," James said to John, savoring the peppery taste of basil that complimented the tang of the eggplant and bell peppers.

"Glad you like it," John replied. "This pasta sauce was Martha's favorite."

"Katy used to do something similar in the oven, right?"

"Yes, nearly the same recipe but heavier on the cheese and cream," John replied, and smiled. "Glad you went for that swim—you look alive again."

"Yeah, I could live there forever. I always imagined I'd live in a beach house one day. There's something about the ocean—all that power harnessed in a peaceful grace."

"What made you come back to land? After that year in the sea," John asked, picking up his glass of water.

"It was lonely," he replied. "Nights were too dark…If it wasn't for that plane crash though, I don't know where I would have been right now."

"Plane crash?"

"Yeah, I was on this deserted island. It was already dark. A plane was flying overhead. All of a sudden, it caught fire and came crashing down into the water, close to the island. I swam out to it—I couldn't really see a thing, everything was just black. The plane sunk to the bottom—a lot of stuff was floating around. I tried to look for any survivors and heard splashing. There was this man, Kenan, struggling to keep afloat, and I took him to shore. His leg was badly injured; he lost too much blood. I did what I could but—he didn't make it. The next morning, dead bodies kept washing onto shore."

"Sorry you've been through that too," John said.

James took a deep breath and shrugged.

"I made it alive; they are the ones that didn't. They had families waiting for them. Seeing them all dead—their life over—I didn't want to end up dead alone; live a whole life by myself, so I came to land. Maybe that was a mistake."

"No one deserves to be alone," John replied. "You made no mistake."

They finished their plates and John took out the lemon tart he had prepared for dessert. A light drizzle tapped on the windows, just enough to smudge the glass.

"What do you prefer?" James asked John as they ate the tart. "Countryside or ocean?"

"Me? I love the sea, but I'm more drawn to the smell of soil and wet grass. I used to wake up early just to watch the sun rise on the fields. Isn't that something to see?" John said, staring blankly, watching the sun rise. "It's as though the majestic sun reaches out of the skies and kisses each of the crops good morning. The rich smell of moist soil breathes life into your body. The chirping of birds; the most delightful melody. Then, a sweet scent begins drifting in the air as petals stretch to greet the bright sunlight, ready for another day. Out of nowhere, fuzzy bees and flossy butterflies start fluttering their way around, falling for the most attractive, colorful blossoms to drink from the heavenly nectar and fulfil mother nature's promise. That is how each beautiful day begins."

"My beautiful mornings," Ricin said as he walked into the kitchen, "begin with additional cash in my bank accounts. The larger the figures, the more beautiful the morning is," he continued, and took out a glass from the cupboard. "By the way, James, Vice and Gavin just left. Gavin made it—with a deformed jaw, an eye less and still isn't walking; something wrong with his spine from when you knocked him to the ground—but apart from that and all the prominent scars on his face; he made it. Just thought you should know."

James didn't respond—he cared little for Gavin's well-being—maybe even should have beat him harder.

"Tomorrow you'll be doing another job," Ricin said, pausing to sip apple juice. "And this won't be just another mission; Mane is tremendously impulsive and bonkers at times. The worst thing someone can do to him is lie; that is exactly what you are going to do," Ricin said, and finished his glass. "But don't you worry about any of it; I always make sure things go my way. Will be briefing you before the task tomorrow morning."

Ricin left his glass on the countertop, and left the room.

"Here we go again," John mumbled to himself, and got to his feet and took the empty plates off the table.

"I'm sure it won't be as bad as getting that file from the president, or fighting Matthew," James said, trying to make fun of the situation.

"Not as bad—but what if worse?" John said, looking at James intently. "That's the thing with Ricin; some people are like fire; hang around them long enough, you will get burned."

***

The next morning, Ricin placed a photograph in front of James.

"This is Mane," Ricin said.

The man in the picture was brawny and bald. His eyebrows too bushy. A mad look in his eyes, like he was witnessing an apocalypse coming upon him, and enjoying it.

"You are going to give him a case, supposedly containing a pure compound which he thinks he is purchasing from me. For obvious reasons, I don't share my toys," Ricin smirked. "But I am willing to get paid a huge sum of money for a less pure compound which will only suit him till I see fit. No doubt, he will test the chemical but hopefully, the impurity will go undetected. The meeting is going to take place in two hours. Under the bridge."

"What happens if the impurity is detected?" James asked.

Garth laughed, "Boom," he said.

Ricin cleared his throat, his fingers locked on the teak table. "Well, if that happens," Ricin said, "grab the money and flee the scene as fast as you can before I blow up the place."

"You're going to blow up the bridge?" James asked, shocked. "Innocent people will be there."

"I don't intend to," Ricin replied. "But if Mane finds out that I'm giving him less than what we agreed upon, he will start a war—I won't waste any energy or resources on that lunatic."

"You had said no civilians will be involved," James protested.

"The impurity won't be detected," Edgar reassured, leaning forward in his chair, resting his elbows on the table. "I made sure of that," Edgar added confidently, looking James in the eye. "The exchange will go as planned."

James trusted Edgar's expertise so if Edgar said the impurity won't go detected, it won't.

"Okay," James said with a small measure of relief.

"If not—the show will definitely be spectacular," Garth said, a glint of mischief in his eyes as he bit on the toothpick between his lips.

"Right," Ricin concluded. "Garth will drive you; usual routine. You leave now."

James headed out with Garth and Wayne and within two hours, they were at the bridge. No one was there yet and they remained waiting in the car. The sound of vehicles passed over their heads and ruffled James's composure.

"This mission is very important to Ricin," Garth told him. "Pull yourself together and focus."

James's palms sweated with nerves—Edgar couldn't be wrong.

“Here they come,” Wayne remarked from the back seat of the car. “Looks like he upgraded vehicles.”

Two black SUVs pulled up several meters away from them. The engines were both turned off but no one stepped out of the cars.

James's earpiece and mini camera were already in place and he took the briefcase from Garth's hand.

“If everything goes right, you get back in the car,” Garth told him. “If not, I’ll start driving away while you grab the money and catch up, okay?”

James kept looking at the two vehicles. The windows were tinted and he couldn't see how many people were inside.

“Okay?” Garth repeated as he shoved James's shoulder.

“Yeah,” he replied. “Do I get out or do we wait for them?”

“His guy normally steps out first, then you go, then Mane,” Garth replied, squinting at the cars in front of them.

“James act normal—look relaxed,” Ricin said in his ear. “Mane might appear insane but he is not to be underestimated.”

A burly woman stepped out of the car, a gun on each side of her waist belt.

“Go,” Garth told James.

James got out of the vehicle with the briefcase in his hand and one of the cars began honking.

“What's going on?” James asked. There was no reply.

The woman stood next to the SUV and kept her eyes fastened on James. A man stepped out of the same vehicle whose horn was still going—Mane was definitely crazy; why would he keep blowing the horn to attract unwanted attention?

The man was tall, fit, and he walked right up to James with a determined stride. The horn finally stopped when the man came next to him.

"Mane won't do business with a kid," the man said with a hostile glare.

"Introduce yourself," Ricin told him.

"I'm Ricin's—son, James."

The man's glare disappeared. His gaze now that of awe—the man knew he was a mutant.

"I'm Zakari," the man said, and turned his head round toward Mane's vehicles and gave a firm nod.

The woman opened the front passenger door of the car. A bald man stepped out, looking fiercely mad; that must be Mane.

"What's this?" Mane asked Zakari as he came next to them, his walk with a slight limp.

"This is James," Zakari replied.

"Oh! I see," Mane replied, turning to James with a wide grin. "You are Ricin's mutant, huh? Interesting," Mane continued, limping closer toward James. "I've heard about you; very impressive, yeeeeessss."

Mane hobbled even closer to James until he was face to face with him.

"So, tell me, how does Ricin treat you?" Mane asked, slowly tilting his head sideways, still up close to James's face.

“I have the chemical,” James replied, stepping back; wanting to get the deed over with.

“Not so well I see,” Mane remarked with a smirk, and went around him, ogling him from head to toe. “You know, you’re pretty. I can take you in, raise you as my own if you like. How much will he take for you?” Mane asked, raising his hand to caress James's face.

James quickly moved his face away and watched Mane carefully.

“I’m not for sale,” he replied. “I have the chem—”

“No?” Mane said, his smile sly. “So, how do I get my hands on you? Hmmmm? Would be so nice to wake up to your pretty face.”

Mane stood there, grinning, eyes wide.

“Do you want the chemical or not?” James asked, losing his patience.

“Ask him to see the money first,” Ricin instructed.

“Do you have the money?”

“In such a rush I see; is Ricin keeping you that busy?” Mane asked, his deranged gaze still pinned on him.

“Are we making the deal or not?” James repeated.

“Chill child; of course we are. Why would I have come all the way here? Although, I must admit, seeing you in person is such an unexpected, pleasant surprise,” Mane replied, and started laughing, shrugging his shoulders excessively in an absurd manner.

“Bring over the money!” Mane told Zakari. “Handsome here has other things to attend to it seems.”

Zakari went to one of the cars. Mane ogled James, a creepy smile etched into his face.

“Do open it and show this pretty boy that we mean business,” Mane told him.

Zakari opened the metallic case and grabbed some bundles of cash, showing James there was more beneath the first row.

"Nice," Ricin remarked. "He would know better than to give me fake money or a bill short."

"This is the chemical then," James said, trying to sound assertive, and opened his briefcase.

"Is it?" Mane asked, looking closely at the burgundy liquid in the sealed tubes. "You wouldn't mind me testing one out now, would you? You know—just to make sure it is the real deal and not some raspberry flavored liquor."

"Go with it, James," Ricin said.

James nodded, trying to convey a confident and care-free demeanor.

Zakari had a small machine already in hand and he took one of the test tubes and opened it.

"This device was just custom made for me—highly sophisticated piece," Mane said, as Zakari poured some of the liquid in the device. "I don't rely on commercial junk."

James's pulse pounded, his chest tightened—the impurity might as well be detected.

"Let us see," Mane voiced with excitement as Zakari pressed the button on the device.

Percentage purity bars began loading one after the other, then the loading began to slow down. The vehicles passing on the bridge above their heads, worried James and he swallowed hard.

"You look tense," Mane said, his countenance suddenly grave. "Why is that?"

"No, I'm not tense; just impatient; I really hate waiting," James quickly replied, trying to sound annoyed.

“KEEP IT TOGETHER, James,” Ricin scolded fiercely.

Mane paused with a sharp squint on James, then his doltish grin reappeared.

“Of course—who enjoys waiting?” Mane replied.

James feigned a smile, his stomach in knots.

There was a lengthy, frozen hush. Everyone watched the strokes on the machine light up, one by one. The screen on the device then lit orange and a loud beeping sound went off.

CHAPTER TWENTY-ONE

"Pure," Mane remarked, beaming with bulging eyes as though they were about to pop out of his face.

James could breathe again and he sighed silently.

"Okay then," James said, "I give you the chemical and you give me the money."

"Of course, handsome," Mane replied, signalling to Zakari to give him their briefcase.

The exchange was done. Mane gazed at James, lost in a trance. James turned around and walked away.

"Well done," Ricin said. "Well done!"

James got into the car with the metallic briefcase.

"That went well," Garth said as he began to turn the car around.

"What's up with Mane?" James asked. "How can he be in such a position of power?"

"Mane's got brains," Wayne replied. "He just comes across as crazy but beneath that foolish act—"

"It's not an act," Garth said. "He's got a mental condition. None the less, he's a genius."

Whatever Mane was, James hoped he'd never have to cross paths with him again.

***

It was half past one in the afternoon when they arrived back at Ricin's headquarters, and James went to the kitchen to have lunch with Ricin and Edgar.

"Plates will be ready in a minute," Gina said, as she grabbed the pan off the stove.

"No need to rush, Gina," Ricin said. "We're in no particular hurry; today's job was done thanks to James here," Ricin said, his fist nudging James in the shoulder. "You did great, son."

James remained silent, his eyes on the water in his glass, forcing himself to escape the reality of what could have happened if the impurity was detected.

Gina placed their plates in front of them and they began eating. Ricin and Edgar started talking about the latest equipment they had received for the lab and how the new drug was selling out faster than candy.

James put his fork down and poured himself another glass of water. The taste of chili overpowered the whole rice dish, his mouth on fire. He took some more sips but the burning sensation got even worse.

"You still don't like hot spices, do you?" Edgar asked him.

"Not really," he replied, wiping his runny nose in a napkin. "It's okay," he added with a sniff.

"You should have said so; Gina would have made a separate dish for you," Ricin said.

"It's okay," he repeated, his eye tearing, his tongue and lips in flames.

"Here," Edgar said, getting to his feet, and opened the fridge. "Have some milk; it helps with the heat. Water makes it worse—spreads the capsaicin."

James poured himself a glass of coconut milk and it gradually soothed the burn.

"Did you enjoy the swim?" Ricin asked him, moving his empty plate aside.

"Yeah," he replied. "Cannot wait for the next."

"Thing is," Ricin voiced, fidgeting with the water bottle cap, "the search for you isn't over, if anything, your face has reached other countries too—most wanted with a generous reward. So that trip to the beach had to be a one-off—even car rides; we should be very careful," he added, glancing at Edgar.

"Nobody saw me—"

"Bet that is what you thought before I got you back," Ricin said with a raised eyebrow at James.

James escaped Ricin's gaze, the air instantly tense.

"I knew where you were hiding out days before I got to you—until we got everything set up—I had eyes on you for days—but you never realized that, did you?"

James remained quiet, his face lowered to the table.

"It's okay," Ricin said. "I forgave you for that—but my point is that we can never be too careful."

Dives were the only thing James was counting on to help get him through the days. All the rest was just negative and dull.

"It's funny really, looking back," Ricin continued. "We got to know where you were because a security camera in a grocery store picked up some details of your face. You managed to keep hidden perfectly for so long and even after that, eyes on the ground were the only thing that could pick up on where you were. You were helping an old woman who couldn't reach a box of oats from the top shelf," Ricin added with a chuckle.

That was it? That was the moment? He had always kept his head down, his cap low, everywhere he went but that time, he remembered, an old woman asked him to grab a cereal box for her. He noticed the camera when he reached for the box but figured his cap shadowed his face and his jacket was zipped up beyond his jawline—his face couldn't have been identified. So he'd thought.

"Maybe I could take him up north, beneath the cliffs—shores are quite deserted up there," Edgar suggested.

"No, better not," Ricin replied. "Better safe than sorry."

Lunch was soon over and James went to the cell. John was standing right next to Wayne, a dismal look on his face.

"Ricin gives the orders, John," Wayne said. "I just follow them."

"Right. Of course," John replied.

"Everything okay?" James asked John.

"Yes, yes, all good," John replied with a smile. "Are we preparing dinner together today?"

"Yeah," he replied, trying to sound positive. "I have to go over some programming stuff with Garth first; he said I have to be there in half an hour but after that, I'm free."

James was heading up the corridor to meet Garth when Edgar came round the corner.

"Edgar," James said, "I was thinking maybe we could go at night, to the beach; no one will see me then."

"He didn't really approve of me taking you the other day, but I'll talk to him," Edgar replied, and was about to continue on his way.

"I can't just live my whole life inside this building," James said.

“I know,” Edgar agreed. “I cannot promise you anything—Ricin has the final say, but I’ll try. I need to get going; something urgent came up.”

Edgar hurried down the corridor and James went to the small room in which he practiced programming simulations. The room smelt of coffee and cologne. Garth was already waiting for him, and James sat down.

A long two and a half hours went by and Garth was getting on James's last nerve.

“Keep up the pace,” Garth repeated. “If something goes down, you have to be able to go through these without even needing to think. Start again.”

“Again?” James said. “I just went through the whole process seven times already.”

“I didn't ask—I said start again.”

James looked at the long program in front of him, his frustration mounting

“I’m done,” he said, quickly getting to his feet.

Garth was about to seize his arm but James grabbed Garth's hand instead and pressed down hard on it.

“I said I’m done,” he repeated, and pushed Garth's hand away and walked out of the room.

“You better show some respect if you know what's good for you,” Garth said, rushing after him.

James continued walking.

“Don't forget your buddy, John, is still here in the building,” Garth added.

James made an abrupt turn toward Garth. “What did you say?”

“You better show some respect for authority,” Garth replied.

“Or what?” James said, closing in on Garth's face, challenging him with eye contact. “Or what, Garth?”

“There will be consequences,” Garth replied, smug.

“If you dare touch John; I’ll kill you,” James said through a clenched jaw.

“Then what?” Garth asked. “There will just be more consequences.”

Frustration took over James and he punched Garth in the face, slamming his head against the wall. Garth lost balance and fell forward to his knees.

“What the hell, James?” Garth spat, grabbing the back of his head.

“You mess with me or people I care about and there will be consequences for you too,” he said to Garth, who was still on his knees.

Logan came running down the corridor, gun in hand, cord in the other.

“Let him be, Logan,” Garth said, pushing against the wall to get back to his feet. “I’m not afraid to take a hit. But then again, I’m sure not everyone feels the same way,” Garth said, maintaining eye contact with James.

James exchanged glowers with Garth, then walked away. He went straight to his bedroom and shut the door. There was no lock.

He lay on his bed, rage getting the best of him. He reached for the sketchpad and pencil on the desk, and began drawing on a blank page. He got lost amid the coral reefs, detailing crevices, reliving among the tiny creatures of the ocean.

A strong knock at the door pulled him back to reality hours later. It was Wayne, who escorted him to Ricin's office.

Garth was sitting at the desk, holding an icepack against his cheek.

"Have a seat, James," Ricin said, his elbows on the table, hands locked together.

He sat down, avoiding Garth's stare.

"Care to explain?" Ricin asked James, pointing to Garth.

"He should have watched his mouth," James replied.

"James, you caused Garth a slight concussion. I will not tolerate this behavior," Ricin said. "We're a team in here—we do get on each other's nerves sometimes but we don't go punching each other, understood?"

Ricin waited for his reply, lips pursed.

"Yeah," James replied, struggling not to roll his eyes.

"Good. Garth also said that you're not practicing enough," Ricin continued. "Tomorrow—hopefully Garth will feel better—you will spend all day going over whatever Garth needs you to practice; no stopping for lunch; no unnecessary bathroom breaks."

"I'm not a kid anymore," James grumbled.

"Well, stop acting like one then," Ricin replied. "You need to focus on sharpening your skills—keep improving, because if you fail to prepare, you are preparing to fail."

"Fail at what exactly?" James asked.

Ricin paused, scowling at James.

"You prepare for whatever I need you to be prepared for because I do not fail and I'll make sure that you won't either."

A tense hush took over the room, Ricin looked hard at James.

"Whole day of practice tomorrow," Ricin concluded. "After that, I was going to invite you to join me for a short trip—a late dinner out of town with a good friend of mine and we'll spend the night there, come back the next day, late morning. Everything's done privately; place is a penthouse suite above his own casino, so you need not worry about the police. Sound good?"

"Yeah," he replied with reluctance only acquiescing because he had the trip to look forward to.

"Great. Now get out."

James got up and walked out of the office. Garth remained in the room with Ricin. He went to the kitchen and found John kneading dough.

"Hey, you okay?" John asked.

"I'm…" James paused, "existing," he finished with a heavy sigh.

"Right. Existing," John repeated with a smile. "You know? Life is too short to merely exist; one day we're here, the next we're gone. Brave are those who have the courage to live before they die."

John began wrapping the dough in a piece of cling film, careful to make sure it was all covered.

"Want something to drink?" James asked John as he took out a glass from the cupboard.

"No thanks, just had some tea."

James poured himself a glass of water and drank half of it. He began swirling the glass, looking down at the whirling liquid.

"You are reminding me of the half-empty or half-full glass perspective," John said, washing his hands in the kitchen sink. "You know, where different people are shown a normal shaped glass which is filled up to the middle and asked if it is half-empty or half-full. Well, the way I see it; it does not matter which one it is but rather, what one is capable of doing with the amount that one has. The person who sees the half-empty glass might be able to utilize that water more efficiently than the person who sees the half-full glass."

"And what if one doesn't have a choice on how to use that water?" James asked, looking up at John.

"As long as there is life, there is always a choice."

James remained quiet, thoughts stabbing his mind—trapped between worlds.

"Son," John said, grabbing him by the shoulders, looking him in the eyes, "every pain has a purpose as it does an end. You just have to hold on; things will get better."

"Do you really believe that?"

"Of course son, that's how life is," John replied, his face full of wrinkled wisdom. "Hold on, things will get better, they always do."

CHAPTER TWENTY-TWO

James spent the next day practicing simulations with Garth. Time dragged on. Garth unusually quiet. His cheek was bruised and he only drank water, unlike his normal black coffee.

Five hours into practice, Garth brought James an avocado quinoa salad, and they continued till six in the evening.

"You did well today," Garth said, turning off the monitor. "Get dressed; we'll be leaving in half an hour."

James stood up, his eyes itching, his back stiff. He took a shower and wore the light blue shirt and navy blue suit that were prepared for him. Garth and Logan were accompanying them as security, they too wore suits. Ricin, a black tuxedo with a silk, maroon tie.

They flew with one of Ricin's helicopters and landed on the helipad of the place, an hour later. Two security personnel greeted them and escorted them down to the top floor.

The elevator door opened and the musty smell of cigars filled James's nostrils.

“Ricin!” a tall man in a brown tuxedo called in greeting, as he walked over to them.

“Walter, my man,” Ricin replied, shaking his hand and tapping strongly on his shoulder. “How have you been?”

“Great,” Walter grinned. “And no doubt you have been doing the same. Glad you could join us.”

“Wouldn't miss it,” Ricin said. “Walter, I would like you to meet James,” Ricin added, moving aside for James to step forward.

“Pleasure to finally meet you, James,” Walter said, reaching out his hand.

“Nice to meet you too, sir,” James replied with a hand shake.

“Please, come join us,” Walter said, and they followed him to a large dining room.

Upon entering the room, the clamor of chatter diminished from a thrum to a silent thrall; all eyes turned to Ricin, then to James.

A waiter came up to them with a tray of drinks and James picked out a glass of water.

Curiosity quelled, chatter re-established itself as conversations resumed.

A crystal chandelier hung from the tray ceiling, right above the long table. At one far end of the room, a large fireplace, its wood consumed by low flames. There were six abstract paintings on the walls, their dark hues complementing the tone in the room.

Several people were seated along the table, others standing, all engaged in talk.

Ricin and Walter spoke; heads close, voices indistinct. Garth and Logan took their positions at opposite ends of the room, Garth looking rather exhausted. James paused in front of one of the paintings, aware that most eyes in the room were still on him. Inside the rustic frame, a splatter of frost blue danced with purple flames above a signature in red with the name 'Ivy.'

"James," Ricin called to him, "I want you to meet some friends of mine."

James stepped toward Ricin and the two stout men standing next to him.

"James, this is Lorenzo," Ricin said, gesturing to the man with the moustache. "And this is Fernando, and his lovely lady, Michelle."

Michelle gave James a polite smile, her red lips popped against the black fur scarf around her shoulders.

James reciprocated with a slight nod, and shook hands with the men.

"Impressive work you do for Ricin, James," Lorenzo said. "Ricin and I might be partnering on some business in the near future, would be nice to have you working for me too."

James cleared his throat, aware of Ricin's encouraging expression.

"Pleasure would be mine, sir," James replied, meeting Ricin's expectations.

Lorenzo bobbed his head, pleased with his reply.

"Please, let's all have a seat," Walter said, his voice raised for all to hear.

Walter sat down at the head of the table, Ricin beside him on one side, two empty seats on the other.

"James," Ricin said, pointing to the chair adjacent to the empty one opposite to him.

James sat down on the chair Ricin pointed to. An old man was sitting on his left, talking loudly to the others across the table.

"It's James, right?" the man asked, turning to him.

"Yes."

"I'm Raphael," the man said, pushing back a white strand of hair that fell on his forehead. "How is business with Ricin going?"

"Good," James replied, reaching for his glass of water.

"That new drug Ricin has going is sweeping across countries—impressive," Raphael continued.

James nodded politely and drank some water.

"What exactly do you do for Ricin?" Raphael asked, his eyes squinting sharply at him.

"Whatever he needs me to get done," James replied uncomfortably, hoping he wouldn't have to answer any further questions about his job.

"Such as?"

"Hi, Daddy!" a voice called, shifting both their attention.

The young woman gave Walter a kiss on the cheek. Her jade, sequinned dress glistened with every movement.

"Sweetheart, you remember Ricin," Walter told her.

She smiled politely. "Of course."

"And this is James," Walter added.

"Hi, I'm Cassidy," she told him with a bright smile. "Everyone calls me Casey."

"Pleased to meet you," James replied.

"Have a seat, darling," Walter said, pointing to the empty chair between James and himself.

Cassidy sat down and turned to James, her blonde, wavy hair falling perfectly just above her bare shoulders.

"So you're the famous James, huh?" she said, reaching for the bottle of red wine on the table.

"Famous is not exactly what I would call it," he replied, escaping her green eyes.

"You prefer most wanted?" she asked, her brutal honesty taking him by surprise.

"I'd prefer neither—if I had to choose."

"Don't worry, I'm not judging. Everyone in here is guilty of something, myself included—the things I pretend I don't know about my dad's business," she said, and shrug her shoulders. She drank some wine, pausing to savour each sip. "So tell me, how old are you? Eighteen?"

"Soon turning sixteen."

"No way!" she replied, gaping at him. "You look more mature than that."

"Sixteen at the end of the month," he repeated, nodding.

"I'll soon be seventeen but hey, what's in a number, right?" she said, and sipped more wine.

All the guests were seated and various dishes of food were placed in the middle, along the whole table.

"Please, everyone," Walter said, "help yourselves and enjoy."

Everyone began eating, a chatter roaring in the room.

"You don't like meat?" Cassidy asked, looking down at James's plate.

"I choose not to eat it," he replied.

"Same!" she said elated. "Finally! Someone who won't make fun of my eating choices," she added beaming.

"My dad doesn't get it—and I gave up on trying to explain."

She poured herself another glass of wine and swirled it close to her face.

"Ahh that smell," she said. "This wine is really good—on the sweet side yet not too much. Did you have some?"

"No."

"Here taste it; it's really good," she said, handing him her own glass.

He didn't want to disappoint her and took a sip.

"It's good, right?" she said.

"Yeah it is; very fruity."

"So—where's your hideout?" she asked, raising her eyebrows at him in a playful manner.

"Ricin's place," he replied, and poured himself more water. "You live around here?"

"A few blocks away. But I really hope we move soon."

"Why so?"

"Neighbors suck. They're old people—always finding something to complain about."

"Where would you rather live?" he asked.

"Up north—somewhere cool by the sea," she replied. "Hey; I know I'm not supposed to say anything," she said, leaning closer toward him, her voice a hushed whisper, "but are the rumors true? Are you really what they say you are?"

"And what is that?" he asked, looking into her vibrant eyes which were begging to know.

"You know—mutated genes—you can breathe under water, etcetera etcetera," she said, pausing for his reply. "Oh, come on tell me—I won't say anything," she continued, placing her hand just above his knee. "Pleeease," she added, forcing a cute smile.

"Something like that," he replied, and grabbed his glass.

She kept gazing at him, then looked away with a giggle.

"That is awesome," she said, her face down to her plate.

He remained quiet and looked at Ricin. Ricin and Walter were still engrossed in their own discussion, unaware of what Cassidy and himself were talking about. He wasn't sure if Ricin would approve of him revealing who he really was, not that he wanted to.

They continued eating, exchanging casual conversations. She occasionally leaned onto him, bumping her shoulder against his while giggling at what they were saying, her eyes full of life and joy.

"Fresh parsley, really?" she asked. "For me it's anything that has nutmeg in it; if it's there and I cannot taste it, it's fine, but if the taste stands out, I just cannot eat whatever it is."

She poured more wine and handed him the glass.

"Want some more?" she asked.

"No, I'm good. Thanks."

"Hey, is it just me or is it becoming too stuffy in here?" she asked, grabbing her napkin and fanning herself. "I need some air, want to join me? Want to see the wine room? It's always cooler in there."

She kept looking at him with wide eyes, blinking twice at a time.

"Sure," he replied.

“Daddy, we’re going to step out of the room for a bit; get some air,” she said, turning to Walter.

“Sure, hon,” Walter replied. “Be back for dessert; I ordered your favorite.”

“Thanks, Daddy,” she said, getting to her feet.

James furtively looked at Ricin, waiting for his approval, and Ricin gave him a slight nod.

***

“Voila! The wine room,” she said, opening her arms wide as she walked into the room.

Bottles of wine were neatly stacked against each wall. At one corner, a glass cabinet with several other bottles inside. There was no one else in the room, not even security cameras in sight.

“It is cooler in here,” he remarked.

“It is, right?” she said loudly, going over to the glass cabinet, almost missing a step. “See these bottles right here? Some of them are worth thousands. Can you believe that?”

He stepped toward the cabinet, most of the labels he recognized.

“We should open one,” she said, smacking her lips, scanning the row of bottles on the third shelf. She reached for the glass knob and pulled at the cabinet door. “Darn! It’s locked.”

She turned to him with expectation, “You can open it, right?—Like pick the lock or…gently break it.”

“I don’t think I should do that,” he replied.

She smiled at him in an impish, mocking manner.

“Ricin wants you on your best behaviour today, right?” she said, staring into his eyes. She clicked her tongue, “I love breaking rules—makes life fun.”

She held his eyes and took a step closer to him, their faces almost touching, her pink lips slightly apart. Her perfume was delicately sweet, her skin, a radiant bloom.

"You know what else is fun?" she asked, her voice sultry.

She leaned in closer, her warm body against his, and she kissed his lips. His heart began pounding. Her tender lips brushed against his mouth. And he kissed her; gentle, just long enough to inhale her breath.

Her eyes smiled at him, a strand of hair fell perfectly onto her cheek. She slowly slid her hands up to the back of his neck and they kissed again, their tongues tenderly twirling together, a playful back and forth. Her fingers slowly began descending against his chest, down to the buckle of his belt. She paused, her soft breaths heavy through her lips. Then gently, she pulled at the buckle, and he caught her hand.

"I can't," he whispered, and swallowed hard.

"You can't, or you don't want to?" she asked softly, her smile full of lust.

He remained silent, the flutter of her emerald eyes hushing his words.

"Come on," she whispered, pulling her hand out of his, touching his belt again. "Let's have some fun."

She leaned in and kissed his neck tenderly, undoing the buckle.

"Casey, we should stop," he whispered, gently grabbing her hand again. "You had too much to drink."

"I did not," she quickly replied, taking a step back from him. "It's just wine; I'm good."

"Casey, I—"

"Whatever," she cut in. "You don't need to explain; I'm good."

She quickly turned away and began heading toward the door, then paused.

"You coming?" she asked, turning her head to him.

He followed her out of the wine room and into the elevator. She kept pressing down on the button that held the elevator door open, glancing impatiently at the open door.

"This stupid thing won't shut," she said, repeatedly pushing the same button.

"You're pressing the wrong one," he told her, pointing to the number she was supposed to press.

"Oh, right," she replied, and burst into uncontrollable laughter. "Imagine I kept holding that button for minutes —waiting for it to close," she laughed.

She was still giggling at herself when they entered the dining room and the loud discourse shadowed her laughter. Several different desserts were being placed all along the table, a sweet scent filled the air.

"Just in time," she told him as they got back in their seats.

Ricin was still talking to Walter and gave James an awkward glance.

"My favorite," Cassidy told James, as she helped herself to a slice of lemon meringue that was placed in front of them. "What are you having?"

"I don't think I'll have dessert—I'm full."

"Oh—trust me, they're really good," she said. "Can you pass the wine, please?"

He purposely reached for the bottle of water and poured her a glass.

"You need to drink some of this," he told her.

"Awwww you're so sweet and caring," she said, leaning onto his shoulder, and took some water.

She began eating her piece of pie, savoring the meringue first before digging into the yellow custard.

"You got to try this," she said, heaping her fork with a piece of pie.

She held it to his mouth, forcing him to take it. It was overly sweet with an occasional burst of sour acidity.

"You like?" she asked.

"It's good," he lied, "lemony."

"Lemony?" she laughed. "Is that even a word? Lemony," she repeated to herself, laughing heartily.

Dinner ended with a toast from Walter, thanking everyone for coming, proposing another dinner in the coming weeks.

Sometime later, everyone began leaving the room. Ricin, Walter, and Lorenzo concluded their conversations.

"Goodnight, James," Cassidy said, her lips in a soft smile, her eyes merry, and she gave him a kiss on the cheek.

"Goodnight," he said, and watched her walk out of the room with Walter.

Ricin and James were shown to a spacious room with four beds.

"I'll cover the first half," Logan told Garth, and stood by the door inside the room, facing the window.

Garth lay down on one of the beds, his shoes still on, his hand on the gun in his belt.

"You enjoyed it?" Ricin asked James as he pulled at his tie to take it off.

"Yeah," he replied.

"Good," Ricin said with a smile and nod.

They both went to bed. James fell asleep, Cassidy's smile and luscious lips the last thing he thought of.

The creak and soft slam of a door woke James up the next morning, and he sat up in bed. Ricin and Logan were not in the room, Garth slouched on the edge of a bed, holding his head in his hand.

"You okay?" James asked.

"Not really, James," Garth sighed. "Been with a persistent headache ever since you punched me."

James got out of bed and put on his shoes.

"I'm sorry about that," he said, forcing his words. "Can I get you some pain medication or something?"

"No, I've just taken."

"You should get checked out again."

Garth got to his feet and glared at James.

"Edgar said this might happen—so thank you," Garth said, and turned away and went to the window. "You've got breakfast," he added, his back still toward James.

There was a breakfast tray on the bedside table and James uncovered it. The croissant was still warm and had blueberry jam inside. The orange juice was fresh and sweet.

Ricin and Logan returned to the room and they all soon headed out to leave. James wondered if Cassidy was still in the building, but thought it was pointless to ask—besides, they had already said their goodbyes, wrapped in last night's goodnights.

As they stood by the elevator, Walter shook Ricin's hand, "It was so good to see you again, Ricin," he said.

A breeze caught James's attention and he looked out through the open terrace door. There she was, resting her elbows on the stone fence, looking out at the city view.

“Please excuse me, I’ll be right back,” James said in a rush, and went out onto the terrace.

“Hey,” he called, walking toward Cassidy.

“Morning,” she replied, turning to him with a faint smile.

“Did you sleep well?” he asked.

“Mhm,” she replied, her eyes resting on the gray view again.

“About yesterday,” he said, picking up on her distant attitude, “I hope you were not offended or anything like that.”

“No. No, not at all,” she said, turning to face him. “If anything, you’re a gentleman—many would have taken the advantage. I was rather tipsy, so…Besides, if I got pregnant at this age, my dad would kill me…Coming to think of it, probably he’ll have second thoughts if it were yours,” she added with a smile.

“Right,” he replied with a stifled laugh, his eyes falling to the floor.

A silence followed. A soft wind lifted the loose strands of her hair and they tussled in the breeze.

“We’re going to head back,” he said. “I don't have a cell phone so—”

“I know,” she replied. “I already asked Ricin for your number. Didn't know if you were going to show up this morning,” she continued, then escaped his gaze, “Ricin also said that you’ll be too busy to afford any distractions.”

His face grew solemn, a deep well of frustration awakened.

"In any case," she continued, handing him a small piece of pink paper, "I still wanted to give you this."

He took the paper. There was her number written on it and three small kisses at the bottom.

"Call me," she added, her smile sweet and inviting.

"I will," he replied, and nodded in goodbye. He turned and as he began to head back, he heard her take a step toward him.

"James," she called, keeping her voice down.

He turned to see worry deepen lines on her forehead.

"I heard Ricin mention Edgar Thomson's name," she whispered. "Be careful around him."

"You know Edgar?" he asked in surprise.

"Not really—but he was the one who framed my uncle for the murder of his own family. My uncle loved his family; he had three beautiful, young daughters. Rumor is Edgar got them killed, then framed my uncle. The irony about that is, Edgar and my uncle were best of friends. Just watch out for him."

James was soon on the helicopter, heading back with Ricin, Garth, and Logan. The skies were shades of gray and the closer they got to Ricin's building, the more faint Cassidy's laughter resounded, her smile—a dream he had to wake up from and move on.

CHAPTER TWENTY-THREE

At noon sharp, their helicopter landed on Ricin's headquarters. A strong wind had picked up and they all hurried inside.

James took a shower and went to the kitchen. John was there, helping Gina cook, an amicable aura resonating between them.

"Of course; the cinnamon spice pairs so well with baked fruit. I just love it with pears especially," Gina was telling John.

"Oh hey, James," John said. "How did the trip go?"

"It was—good," he replied, resting his elbows on the kitchen counter they were working on.

"Glad it was," John said. "Gina and myself have prepared a special dish and dessert for today."

"Smells really good," James remarked.

"And it tastes even better," John said.

"Ricin told me he won't be having lunch here today," Gina said. "He will be out on business—and Edgar…"

Gina paused, a dismal look on her face.

"What happened?" James asked.

"Edgar had to catch a plane home," Gina replied. "Both his parents were involved in a car accident—they are not doing so well." Tears welled up in her eyes. "I can imagine what he is going through right now…I lost my wife to a car accident two years ago—she spent eight days in intensive care before she died—we were nearly through with the adoption process of our first child."

"I'm so sorry," James said.

"You never move on from certain things that happen, you just have to learn to move forward with that reality," Gina said.

"No truer words ever spoken," John said.

James and John sat down for lunch and Gina joined them. The stuffed artichokes tasted spectacular and the banoffee pie was the perfect amount of sweetness and balance of textures between the crumbly crust, rich filling, and whipped topping.

"This was so good, thanks," James told them, finishing the last piece of his pie.

"Want another slice?" Gina asked him.

"No. Thanks," he replied. "It's delicious but I'm full."

"I had never done banoffee pie with coffee before," John told Gina. "It certainly gives it a pleasant kick."

"It does, right?" Gina replied. "And I have to try that recipe you told me with the peaches and tuna—I can only imagine what an exquisite balance of flavors that will have."

"Peaches and—tuna?" James repeated.

"Hey, don't look disgusted about something you never tried before," Gina told him with a daring smile. "That's prohibited in my world—no exceptions."

“Thousand apologies,” James bantered. “Thankfully, I don't eat meat so—”

“I could always do it with the vegan tuna recipe for you,” Gina said.

“Thanks but I think I prefer to keep peaches for desserts.”

“Suit yourself.” Gina rolled her eyes with a smile. “Hey, Edgar mentioned your birthday is at the end of this month. Any special food or dessert requests for your birthday?”

James fell silent, bitter birthday memories surfacing in his mind.

“No, thanks just the same,” he replied. “And I—don't do birthdays. It’s just another d—”

“What do you mean you don't do birthdays?” Gina said. “Birthdays are special and I’m going to make sure your food is special that day, I promise.”

“Thanks,” he said, trying to sound appreciative.

He could only remember two good birthdays at Ricin's —when he turned seven and Edgar took him for a whole day at the beach beneath the cliffs, and when he was given the watch. Other birthdays were ordinary training days and as he grew older, some fell on punishment days where he wasn't even given any food. Birthdays were days he'd rather skip.

Gina told them about a surprise party she had organized for her mother, and how her cousin had slipped on the rug and toppled over the four tier cake she had spent hours making.

The clock struck three and James helped Gina and John clean the dishes before going to his bedroom. He lay down, his mind drifting from one thought to another. The remembered echo of a giggle, teased his ear and Cassidy's bright smile took over his thoughts.

He reached in the first drawer of his bedside table and took out the pink piece of paper Cassidy had given him. He longed to hear her voice, her laughter, the warmth of her lips against his; just one more time. Ricin wouldn't allow James to call her. And one of the guards would be standing outside his bedroom door, following him everywhere he went. He couldn't just go to a phone.

A thought came to his mind and he leaped out of bed, hoping to catch Gina before she left for the day.

“Hey, Gina,” he called, almost bumping into her in the kitchen doorway.

“Oh, hi, James; I was just leaving,” she replied, keys in hand.

“May I talk to you for a minute,” he said, entering the kitchen, knowing Wayne would remain by the door.

Gina followed him to the furthest end of the room, their backs toward the security cameras in the ceiling.

“What's up?” Gina asked.

“On the trip, I um,” he began nervously, keeping his voice down, “I met this girl.”

Gina's eyes widened, her eyebrows arched in anticipation.

“She gave me her number and I was wondering if I could maybe—borrow your phone?”

Gina gave him a broad smile. “Do you like her?”

“Yeah, I um—she is a very sweet girl,” he replied, awkward.

Gina hesitated, her smile still resting on him.

“You do realize I could get in big trouble for that?” she said.

He swallowed hard, "You're right. I'm—I'm sorry I shouldn't have asked," he replied, near panic.

Gina glanced at the door, then turned back and looked him straight in the eye, "I'm going to leave it in the cupboard. I'll be back for it in twenty minutes, put it behind the cereal boxes." She turned around, not giving him the chance to say anything else, and walked over to the cupboard where they stored bottles of water and reached for one.

"I'll see you tomorrow, James," she said as she headed out of the room, sipping some water.

He went over to the same cupboard and took a bottle of water, grabbing the cell phone and hiding it up his sleeve.

He went to his bedroom and closed the door. He put up his hood and sat on the desk chair, pretending to draw, his back toward the camera in the ceiling.

"Who is this?" Cassidy's voice answered, after the phone had barely rang once.

"Hey, it's James," he replied, his nerves on edge.

"James? Oh my god; I didn't think you were going to call."

"I told you I would," he replied, keeping his voice down. "How are you?"

"I'm fine, I'm good. You?"

"I'm okay."

A hush fell and his heart quickened in apprehension.

"It's nice to hear your voice," he said, unsure if she was actually happy he had called.

"Yeah yours too. Been thinking about you—and the wine room."

"You remember?" he teased.

"I was tipsy not blackout drunk," she said in a playful manner. "Besides, how can I forget?"

"Right—me too."

"So is this your phone? Did Ricin allow you to have one?"

"Um no—I borrowed the chef's phone. Ricin can't know."

"Oh, I see. Your innocent eyes hide a bad boy after all."

"I had to call you."

She giggled, her laughter music to his ears.

"Do you think Ricin would let you see me if I came over to his place?" she asked. James was surprised. His pulse doubled at the thought of seeing her again and he was about to turn round in his chair with excitement, but remembered the security camera in his room.

"I'm sure he won't mind, unless I'm actually doing a job," he replied, unsure of his own words but desperately wanting to see her again.

"I'll talk to Daddy then," she replied, elated. "It shouldn't be a problem; he's happy if I am."

"It would be great to see you again," he said. "Listen, I don't want to but I have to return the phone."

"No problem. I understand," Cassidy replied. "So glad you called."

"Yeah, me too."

"Soooo, you'll call me again?"

"I'll do my best to."

"You better, tiger," she giggled.

"I will. Bye."

"Bye."

He hung up the phone, an unusual tightness in his stomach. He went to the kitchen and left the phone where Gina had told him, pretending to take out the raisins from the same cupboard.

He was helping himself to some, when Wayne entered the room.

"Ricin wants to see you right away," Wayne said.

James went to the room with the teak table. Ricin and Logan were there, Logan sitting square on his chair, his ponytail done tighter than usual.

"James," Ricin said, "a pressing issue came up and I need you to carry out a job this evening. Nothing grand—bug a place—but I need you to get it done today. Logan will drive you."

"Is Garth okay?" James asked.

Garth had always been the one to accompany him on tasks ever since he started doing jobs for Ricin, and never was Garth absent for one.

"Garth had to take a few days off because of your mindless actions. His headache has gotten worse," Ricin replied. "Logan will be joining you for this one."

Logan leaned back in his chair, a smug air about him.

"Remember you bugged a house once, the Sanchez residence?" Ricin asked, not giving James a chance to respond. "Well, today you'll be doing something similar."

That hadn't been so bad, James recalled. He had just gone into a large villa when the owners weren't home and hid small cameras all over the place. This was going to be easy—just break into a house, place the devices, and leave.

"I need eyes and ears inside a house and given the security parameters of this villa, you are the only one who can do the job without causing a scene," Ricin said, and showed him the blueprint of the house and pointed out the security obstacles James would encounter. "That's all you need to know," Ricin said, folding away the blueprint, then paused as though carefully choosing his next words, "Make sure you get the router secured in the basement before you do anything else."

"Okay," James replied, confident this task would go smoothly.

"Good," Ricin said. "You should leave now because it will take about an hour or so to get there. The owners will be back home by eight p.m."

James nodded, and Logan stood up, more chunky rings on his fingers than usual.

Logan and James went down to the underground carpark and got into a gray car. Logan's cologne was acrid and James opened the window.

They headed out and Logan kept his foot down on the gas pedal, swerving perilously on the slippery roads.

A sharp turn was up ahead and Logan hit the brakes savagely. The car skidded, avoiding a parked van by an inch.

"You trying to fulfil a death wish?" James asked Logan.

"Didn't realize you were so spineless," Logan replied. "I'm not even hitting the speed limit."

"Roads are wet," James noted.

"So?" Logan snapped. "What's the worst thing that can happen? I run over a stinking dog or crush open someone's head," Logan sneered, glancing at him.

James didn't respond. Logan revved up the next road and skidded again at the turn.

“Seriously, man,” James said, “you’re gonna get yourself killed.”

“Death doesn't scare me,” Logan replied, eyes on the road.

“No family, huh?” James asked.

“Had one. Had a brother. He was all the family I had. He was a bank security officer—got shot on the job,” Logan said, his tone angry. “The guy that killed him got away with it. Such a just system, right?”

“Is that why you work for Ricin?”

“Hell yeah. With Ricin, if you do your job well, you know he's got your back covered and he will seek revenge for you if something goes wrong. That's the kind of system I like to be part of. You’re lucky, you know?” Logan said with a glance toward James. “When it comes to you, Ricin is even willing to go beyond and do anything.”

Another few minutes of driving and Logan entered a street and slowed the car.

“That's the one,” Logan said, pointing to the tall gates at the entrance of a detached villa.

He drove past it and pulled over on the other side of the road.

“Remember; go in through a basement window to avoid tripping the alarm,” Logan said, giving him the earpiece and mini camera. “And their cameras are out for the next twenty minutes. I’ll be waiting right here.”

Logan reached for the bag on the back seat and opened the zipper. He took out a small mesh bag and gave it to James. “Those are the pieces you have to set in place. You’ve got twenty-five in all. Avoid sticking any under tables as they’ve got young kids who are bound to find them. And this," Logan said, taking out a thick cuboid the length of a large match, "is the router that needs to be placed in the basement—make sure you get this fixed first."

James was about to open the car door but paused and turned to Logan again.

"Who lives here?" he asked.

Logan chuckled, "What difference does it make?"

"I'm just curious."

"The owner is Dominic Miller," Logan said, his smile sly.

"Dominic Miller? Miller, as in the chief of police?" James asked, baffled Dominic was working on strategies to capture him and he was going to walk right into his home.

"Yes, James; the chief of police," Ricin snapped in his ear. "Hurry up before they get back."

James got out of the car. The sun was painting the last rainbow across the sky, more dark clouds swiftly approaching.

He made his way to the tall gate that rose to high pointed stakes. The rest of the area was surrounded by a wall, tapered at the top, with motion sensors ready to alert of any intruder that dared go over it.

"Don't forget the damn dogs in their front yard," Logan said through his earpiece.

James had to be quick—if the dogs started barking once he entered, it would attract too much attention.

He glanced up and down the road, then quickly climbed up the gate and swung over it. Two black dogs began barking ferociously, running toward him with bared teeth.

He moved away from the gate, not wanting to be seen from the road, and stood still, waiting for the dogs to come closer. They stopped a meter away from him, growling, teeth bared, hesitating their next move.

"Easy," he voiced calmly, purposefully evading any eye contact with them. He crouched down slowly, his hands low to the ground.

One of them moved closer, cautiously sniffing at him, still ill at ease. He steadily held out his hand, keeping it low. The same dog began sniffing it, the other maintaining its distance.

"Hey, you," James said gently, slowly reaching out further, patting the dog's shoulder with the back of his fingers.

The other dog stopped growling and began approaching him carefully. He held out his other hand and the latter dog sniffed it, both canines now tranquil.

"Good dogs," he whispered, then stood steadily.

He walked toward the house. The dogs shadowed him.

"Nice," Ricin remarked. "You always had a way with animals."

James went to the basement windows. Both windows were locked shut and he kicked at one of them, denting the window frame at the lock, enabling him to open it.

He slid inside and jumped down to the basement floor. The dogs whimpered, pacing to and fro outside the window, taking turns to try and stick their heads inside.

The basement was dim, the two small windows the only source of light. The room was empty, except for storage boxes on shelving and an elongated workbench in the middle.

James reached down in his pocket and took out the cuboid. The workbench was well-organized—all the tools were gathered according to their function, each bunch in a separate plastic box—the cuboid would definitely be noticed there.

"Hurry up, James," Ricin uttered with impatience.

He went to one of the shelves and studied it closely. There was enough of a gap between the back of the wooden shelves and the wall, for the cuboid to fit without being seen. He uncovered the adhesive layer on the router and made sure it was secured in place behind one of the upper shelves.

"Perfect!" Ricin said. "Now set up the cameras."

He scanned the room to assess the best placements; one could be stuck on the light fixture, another on the framed picture, the third on the shelving on the opposite wall; all angles would be covered. He took out three pin-size cameras and went to the hanging picture. He began carefully fixing the camera at the dark corner of the frame, when the creaking of a door broke the silence and light flooded the room.

James turned, startled.

"I finally get to meet you, huh, James?" Dominic said, descending the last few steps to the basement.

"I thought you said he wasn't going to be home," James mumbled to Ricin.

"I'm sure this is not how you were intending to turn yourself in," Dominic continued, moving closer. "What are you doing here?"

James pictured the exact layout of the room, deciphering the quickest exit. The window he had come in through was behind Dominic and he didn't want to go into the house—Logan had mentioned they had young kids; he didn't want them to witness a scene.

“It's okay, James; I know,” Dominic said, resting one hand on the workbench. “You are forced to carry out jobs, right?”

James waited for Ricin to give his directive.

“He can hear me, right?” Dominic said, signalling to James's earpiece. “Why is James here?” Dominic asked, his voice raised. “I'm sure you don't want me to call this in.”

“James, take out your earpiece and press the red speaker button,” Ricin ordered.

James did as told.

“Hello, Dominic,” Ricin said, “I'd ask what you think of my creation, but we can surely agree his abilities speak for themselves.”

“What do you want?” Dominic asked, enraged.

“I wanted you to take a good look at James. And stay out of his way.”

“You know I cannot do that, Cole.”

Cole? Was that Ricin's real name? And how did Dominic know it?

“I don't think you have a choice,” Ricin said with a snigger. “Having just learned about James's abilities, you do understand he can destroy everything in his path? Moreover, you know, Jessica and Naomi are really pretty girls. How old is Jessica now, ten?”

“Leave my daughters out of this,” Dominic snapped.

“Oh, my bad,” Ricin replied. “Then maybe your lovely wife, Hannah. Is she pregnant again?”

James avoided Dominic's glare, ashamed to just stand there while Ricin threatened his family; threatened the life of his innocent children.

“I will bring you down, Cole, if it's the last thing I do. Your threats mean nothing to me,” Dominic declared, breathing heavily.

“Oh, don't they?” Ricin said. “Then why haven't you issued my arrest warrant yet? I’m sure he would have appreciated that from you.”

“Oh, he will appreciate more than that one day. And I’ll make sure you’ll see his grinning face through mine when I lock you up for the rest of your miserable life.”

“You don't stand a chance; you are just as pathetic as he was,” Ricin snarled.

“Past his flaws, dad was still more of a man than you will ever be.”

“Dad?” James voiced, taken aback.

“If that piece of scum is a man to you, I have nothing but pity for your wife and daughters.”

“He's your brother?” James gasped.

“Yes, James,” Ricin replied. “We share nothing in common though.”

The silence was violent—the chief of police was Ricin's brother.

“Dominic,” Ricin said, his voice fierce, “I’m sure you’ve heard of a certain Gustav Milakovich and Dune Kaiser; your men are onto them; let them be—for now.”

“I don't take orders from you, Cole.”

“You should—if you want Jessica and Naomi to continue making it home from school in one piece.”

A young voice called from the top of the staircase, “Daddy?”

“Honey, don't come down!” Dominic said in panic. “Go back to the living room with mommy and Jessica, sweetheart; I’ll be there in a minute. Close the door, please, hon.”

The door to the basement was shut and Dominic grit his teeth, his scowl fixed on James.

“Was that Naomi? What a darling,” Ricin remarked. “You can leave now, James. Goodbye…brother.”

Dominic stared daggers at James, his fists balled. James walked past him and out of the window he came in through. The two dogs sniffed at his feet until he climbed up the gate and jumped over it.

He got into the car, his thoughts screaming. Ricin couldn't have made the mistake of not knowing his brother would be there. And he didn't finish the task, yet Ricin did not seem bothered. Maybe Ricin wanted James to deliver the message personally about Gustav and Dune.

James sat in the front passenger seat, the engine running, yet the car stationary. Logan stared intensely at Dominic's house, as though waiting. James was about to ask why he wasn't driving, but he was cut off by a loud boom and a fireball exploding into the air. It was Dominic's house; it blew up.

CHAPTER TWENTY-FOUR

The alarm of the parked car in front of them went off. Thick, black smoke rose from behind the wall of Dominic's residence.

"What—what just happened?" James whispered, breath quivering.

"You just finished another job," Logan replied, driving away.

"What?"

"That device," Logan said, "it wasn't a router—that was a bomb."

The reality of what James had done stabbed him. His head reeled, his lungs failed to draw in air, his stomach, one tight knot. What had he just done? What had he let Ricin trick him into doing?

"Pull over," James uttered, groping for the door lock, unable to breathe.

"Come again?" Logan asked.

"I can't…breathe," he struggled to say in a hoarse whisper, opening the door and holding it ajar.

Logan braked hard and the car screeched to a stop on the deserted road. James sprung out, the cold night air clearing his airway. He tried to take a steady, deep breath but the young girl's call began echoing in his ear; *Daddy?* Snippets of the conversation raced through his head—*Is she pregnant again?—Go back to the living room with mommy and Jessica, sweetheart*—They were all inside the house; he killed an entire family.

His stomach churned with a violent twist and he threw up. He stepped back and fell to his knees, his body shaking in shock.

Logan approached, loomed over him, arms akimbo, "You ready?" Logan asked, impatient.

"You knew," he whispered, fighting back tears.

"Oh, for crying out loud," Logan sighed. "Just hurry up and get back in the car when you're done, will you? Or Matthew's house will blow up next."

Logan got into the vehicle and slammed the car door shut. James; on his knees, lacking strength, tears streamed down his face, *What had he just done?*

A gust of wind ran through the bushes with a loud rustle. Branches creaked in despair.

"James!" Logan called, putting down the window. "You're done; get back in!"

James stood up, feet weak, and got into the car. Logan revved off, tapping rhythmically on the steering wheel, unconcerned with his complicity in murder.

***

Back at Ricin's headquarters, James walked down the corridor, Logan next to him. James's mind numbed and his thoughts existed in a hazy ether. His limbs weighted and lethargic.

“Well done, son,” he heard Ricin's voice say.

James paused and looked up. He gave Ricin a vague stare, his conscience crushing him—his thoughts poisoned with pure hate for Ricin.

“You did a great job,” Ricin continued.

A rage sparked within James and he stepped toward Ricin and punched him in the face, knocking him to the ground.

James allowed Logan to pounce on him and pull him away from Ricin—he was too overwhelmed to fight back.

Ricin was helped to his feet, his upper lip bleeding. He came closer toward James, a scowl on his face, his mouth agape, “If you—”

“What did you make me do?” James yelled. “There was a family in there! There were children! I don't want any of this! I never wanted any of this!” Tears welled up in his eyes and he stepped toward Ricin again, but a thick cord was promptly thrown over his head and tightened around his neck.

“You better grow the hell up, James,” Ricin snapped. “You were designed for a purpose; you were created to stand by me and all I stand for. You want to know why I blew up my own brother?” Ricin yelled, up close to his face. “It's because this afternoon, *your* friend, Matthew, went to him and told him everything he knew about my organization. Do you think I can allow a loose end like that? Matthew got the message and I’m sure he’ll think twice before opening his mouth again.”

James stared Ricin in the eye, rage racing through his veins.

"More so, I did it to protect you and your mutant identity."

Ricin glowered at him, demanding appreciation. James spat in his face.

The cord around his neck tightened further and he could not breathe. His arms were locked in the guards' grasp, his feet caught between heavy boots—reality sapping all his strength.

Time stood perilously still as Ricin looked down on him in bitter wrath, allowing more seconds to tick by to choke him.

"Lock him up," Ricin said, and walked away.

It was only until Ricin had turned round the corner that the cord was let loose. James gasped for air, coughing through his breaths.

The guards kept a firm grip on him and forced him to walk back to the cell.

John was asleep on the bed in the room. They forced James to walk past the metal bars and the gate slammed shut behind him.

John was startled awake and sat up. Four guards remained in the room and the electric door closed after Logan stepped out.

"What's going on?" John asked full of concern, as he got out of bed.

James was too ashamed to look John in the eye. He shook his head in despair and slid his back against the wall until he was sitting on the floor.

"What is it?" John asked again.

"You were right," James whispered. "I just didn't want to believe it."

John sat down on the floor. The metal bars separating them.

“Ricin told me—’ James began, and shut his eyes, letting his head bang against the wall behind him. “I thought it was just a router—I thought I was just bugging a place.”

His head hung in shame. The room dead silent.

“There was a whole family in that house—young kids —It was a bomb I planted.”

John was quiet and reached out his hand to hug James's shoulder. James buried his head between his knees, culpability razing his sense of self.

John stayed up with him for hours, his lips silent yet his presence a thousand words of comfort and courage.

That night froze in time for James. It dragged on endlessly, yet he couldn't sleep. He sat on the floor with his back aching—punishment for what he'd done.

He kept staring at the small barred window in his cell that opened into the narrow shaft. It was pitch dark outside, an infinite hollow black reflecting his predestined life.

Morning came for the guards to change duties and to remind James that Dominic's family would not see its light.

John had managed to get some sleep, James was still sitting with his back against the wall. Some fresh fruit was brought for them for breakfast but James lacked any appetite.

The electric door swooshed open and Ricin walked in. He had stitches just above his lip, a prominent bruise on one side of his nose.

"Good morning, James," Ricin said as he stood outside the metal bars.

James ignored him and stared off at nothing in particular.

"I hope yesterday's overreaction was simply in response to the unforeseen aspect of what went down," Ricin said. "I hope you had enough time to get your head together so that we can move forward."

James looked up at Ricin in detestation.

"There is no *we*," James replied. His tone reflected his exhaustion.

"Get up," Ricin ordered, stepping closer to the gate.

James did not budge. Wayne—posted by the door inside the room—placed a hand on the gun in his waistband.

"I said get up!" Ricin repeated.

James stayed on the floor, looking indifferently at Ricin.

Ricin pulled out his gun, aimed it at John's head, then turned back to James. James stood—slowly, teeth grit, frustration and guilt battling within.

"Care to repeat what you just said?" Ricin asked, his aim still on John.

James remained silent, his breathing loud.

"I always get what I want, James," Ricin said. "You should know that by now. So, what's it gonna be? My way—or the hard way?"

James's eyes were locked with Ricin's. John stood tall in front of the barrel.

"I don't need your protection," James said, carefully choosing his words. "That family didn't have to die."

"You don't get it, do you?" Ricin said, lowering his weapon. "Your body is the most advanced thing on this Earth. Nations will fight to have you—to study you. I myself have failed over and over trying to create another embryo like you; thankful for my protection is what you should be."

"I'd rather be killed than be the cause of pain to others," James replied.

Ricin gave a suppressed laugh of disbelief, "Never in a billion years had I thought that the thing I am most proud of, would also be my greatest disappointment," Ricin said, looking down on him. "You're just a disappointment, James; so complex and unique, yet so fragile and vulnerable. Just like a snowflake. You don't even deserve to be called my son—you are just a disappointing snowflake."

A deadly hush fell between them, even the walls were holding their breaths.

"Snowflake," Ricin repeated, and turned around and walked out.

James sat back down on the floor, the hopelessness consuming what was left of him. The safety of John's life hanging by a thread once again.

John came toward the bars of the cell.

"I'm so sorry, John," James said.

"It's not on you, son. You are doing the right thing."

John sat down right next to him, the bars the only thing between them.

"I can't do this anymore," James whispered. "And I don't know how to move forward."

John leaned to him and covered his mouth, “You’ve got to put an end to all this,” John whispered, only for James's ear to hear.

“How? You, Matt—the tracer.”

“I trust that Katy is keeping them somewhere safe; I’m sure of it,” John said with confidence. “The tracer—you have to get that removed by the government—turn yourself in.”

James looked at John, recognizing that was exactly what he had to do to bring all this to an end. But that also meant condemning John to an inhumane death.

“I can't,” James replied, imagining what Ricin would do to John.

“Of course you can,” John replied, his smile tranquil.

“Ricin would—”

“I know,” John cut in, at a peace only wisdom could instil.

James began shaking his head, not wanting to accept those consequences.

“John—”

“I chose my own fate—I chose to be here for you.”

CHAPTER TWENTY-FIVE

James's countenance fell.

"James," John said gently, waiting for him to look up, "I'm glad to have known you," John said, holding James's eyes. "I know you might feel that whoever comes in your life suffers because of Ricin—but I'm still so glad to have met you."

How could John say that? How could someone who spent the last days of his life a hostage, away from his family, taken a bullet—say that?

"Maybe," James began, his mind racing, "there is a way to get you out—"

"Shhhh," John quickly cut in, leaning in tight against the bars. "There is no time. You cannot risk killing more people. To what? To maybe find a way to get me out? I won't let you do that. Listen to me now," John continued in a cautious whisper "When your next mission is up, on your way, you get out of that car and run to the nearest police station—and you don't look back—I've lived my life; it's time to live yours."

James's eyes glazed. John's smile serene.

“I’m not afraid of Ricin; he could only do so much to my body but that won't matter knowing you have a bright future,” John said. “You are a remarkable person and I am truly glad to have known you—and I don't regret that I chose to stay.”

James now understood why John had not left when he had the chance. He could now see that John had recognized the type of man Ricin was and could predict what was yet to come. He could now comprehend what John had done for him—because nothing is more powerful and profound than finding a shoulder when one is consumed by despair.

He had to turn himself in. He had to believe Matthew and his family were somewhere safe. That the authorities knew better than to kill him, unlike what Ricin said they would do.

His mind kept trying to find a way to save John, but all seemed to lead to dead ends.

Without realizing, James had fallen asleep. It was John's voice that woke him up hours later.

“Edgar,” he heard John call once more in a hushed tone, “James is still a boy—this is too—”

“I don't have any time to waste, John,” Edgar said.

“Can't you see you are breaking him?” John cried. “You are pushing him way beyond what he can handle, what anyone can handle for that matter, with all your manipulative schemes and repercussions. James is not your experiment, he is just a human boy with a human heart!”

“Which has an advanced tracer attached to it so we can monitor him, every step of the way, making sure he will adapt to the circumstances he was designed and purposely created to be doing."

"He is just a child," John cried.

"James was never just a child," Edgar objected.

"Your sick minds are plain pitiful," John said. "You think you can play god and mould the boy into something he is not, but his values will undoubtedly stand the test of time. Then again, that is something someone from hell can never understand."

"You don't have any clue who you are dealing with, John," Edgar replied. "Ricin is not from hell; he rules it."

"Did you know?" James said, sitting up, looking straight at Edgar. "Did you know Ricin was going to have me plant a bomb?"

Edgar hesitated, then cleared his throat.

"No, but that's what needed to be done."

"That's what needed to be done?" James repeated, standing, facing Edgar. "Kill innocent children and their pregnant mother because of information you think their father knew? Do you even hear yourself?" he scoffed. "To someone else, I would have asked if their parents made it and are well, but in your case; death will do them the great favor of preventing them from getting to know the monster their son really is."

Edgar stood still, face blank, his eyes as though in battle. Wayne coughed, redirecting Edgar's attention.

"Right," Edgar voiced, forcing a fake smile, and left the room.

Seconds kept crawling. James and John were given some rice for lunch. John told him stories from his past—how awful the wind had been on his wedding day and about the two most beautiful days of his life; when Edward and Katy were born.

James tried to keep his mind focused on what John was saying, but a heaviness in his heart kept pulling him lower and lower.

The electric door opened and Ricin stepped into the room.

“James,” Ricin began in a calm manner, “or should I start calling you Snowflake? It seems to be picking up fast among those who look up to me.”

Ricin's smirk disappeared and he came closer to the cell.

“Tonight you are going to fight again; win both matches,” Ricin told him, then looked over at John. “I’m glad you stayed, old man—James, unless you want John to be chopped up limb by limb and left to bleed to death, do not even dare to try and step out of line again. Are we clear?”

James's head lowered in submission.

“Good! You’ll be leaving with Logan and Wayne in about an hour,” Ricin said, and left.

John's eyes rested heavily on James, then gave him a nod. James promptly shook his head.

“They’re just fights,” James said.

He had to come up with a plan to get John out of there, until then, he could get through the fights. He went to the washbasin in his cell and opened the tap. Cold water gushed out and he splashed it all over his face. The sound of rushing water merged with that of crashing waves rolling onto sandy beaches, and he let the water droplets run down his neck, yearning for the touch of the ocean.

***

Logan and Wayne came to the cell and James followed them to the car. He was taken to a different building this time; an abandoned boxing ring with old benches all around it. Cobwebs hung low from the wooden beams of the ceiling, the paint was peeling off all the walls.

He was taken to a small, empty room while the first two rounds were fought. He stared at the scattered, used needles on the floor, craving any form of high that would numb reality.

His turn was up. The spotlights on the ring limited his vision of the audience. Both matches were fought with brass knuckles and he left the ring a champion, nose bleeding, a gash on his cheekbone.

Logan's grip on his arm was firm as they were walking out of the building with the crowd.

“Hey, tiger,” a female voice called. Cassidy stepped in front of him.

“Casey?” James said, surprised.

“You wouldn't mind me borrowing him for a sec now would you, handsome?” Cassidy said, turning to Logan.

Logan hesitated. Cassidy's eyes fluttered at him, her lips in a soft curl.

“Sure, madame,” Logan replied, letting go of James's arm.

“What are you doing here?” James asked as he followed her to one side of the room, Logan and Wayne close behind.

“I got word that you were fighting tonight and thought I'd come see you,” she said, beaming at him. She quickly reached down in her purse and took out a tissue.

"Here," she said, and gently dabbed his bleeding cheek. "Pity you have to fake getting punched," she whispered with a smile.

A particular white beard, moving with the crowd, caught his attention. The face was shadowed beneath a black hat, but then it lifted and his eyes met Wang Gu's.

"James?" Cassidy called, gently grabbing his face and turning it back to her.

"Yeah um—" he uttered, losing Wang Gu in the crowd.

"You okay? You seem a bit distracted."

"Yeah; sorry, I'm just—"

She leaned in and her lips kissed his, hushing his words.

"Feeling any better?" she asked, her smile sultry. "You must be tired; these fights today and that smooth job yesterday," she added, her hands feeling his chest. "I heard what you did—well done; the authorities don't even have a clue who did it."

"Well done?" he asked, baffled.

"You should be so proud of yourself; got a job like that done and—"

"I'm not proud of what I've done, Casey," he said. "I didn't even know I was planting a bomb; Ricin told me it was just a router. That bomb killed a family."

"Well," Cassidy began, maintaining her cheerful attitude, her hands reaching up behind his neck, "it's a job—some people died; people die every day," she said with a shrug.

He gently removed her hands from around his neck and held them in his, "We're very different you and me," he said.

“Oh come on—you can't be serious? How do you think real money is made in this world? By praying?” she scoffed.

He stared at her, her beauty dimmed by her heart.

“There are more important things in this world than money,” he replied, letting go of her hands.

“Yeah; my mom used to say those exact same words until she was found dead at the bottom of a river, tied to a stone. Money brings power, James, and power, protection and options.”

“James, we need to get moving,” Wayne called firmly.

“Hope you change your mind, tiger—I don't want us to be on opposite sides when the war starts,” Cassidy said, and paused to look him in the eyes before walking away with her bodyguard.

Logan grabbed his arm again and they walked out of the building and got into the car. Cassidy had long drowned in that sinkhole and there was no way he could pull her out. And why would Edgar tell him Wang Gu was dead when he clearly was alive and well?

It was late when they arrived back at Ricin's building and he was allowed a shower before being locked up again. John was already asleep. James lay on the bed in his cell and closed his eyes.

He hadn't even been in bed for five hours when Garth came to his cell.

“James, get up,” Garth repeated, tapping on his shoulder.

“I need to sleep,” he mumbled, turning his head away from Garth, still hugging the pillow.

“Get up, James,” Garth said. Cold water poured onto James's head and dripped down his shoulders.

"Okay, I'm up," he groaned.

"We're heading out for your next job—wash your face, eat something, and get ready. I'll be back for you in fifteen minutes—don't let me come in and find you asleep."

James heard the door swoosh shut. His eyes were still closed and he just wanted to fall asleep again and forget everything for a little while longer.

"James," John called, coming next to him, and sat down on the edge of his bed. "This is it, son," John whispered in his ear.

James sat up, reality slapping him hard in the face once again.

"John—"

"Promise me, son," John said, his face solemn.

James struggled to nod, and John quickly grabbed him and hugged him tightly.

"I'll see you for lunch," John said as he got to his feet, throwing off any suspicion from the guards in the room with them.

James stared at John's smile—a tender smile speaking promises that it would all turn out for the best and that it would all be okay.

James got out of bed and forced himself to drink a glass of almond milk, lacking the will to do anything.

Garth stood in the doorway and an apprehensive chill flushed through James's veins—he did not want to go, or rather, he did not want to leave John behind.

"Good luck, son," John said, his smile warm and calm.

James kept a neutral face.

"Thanks for everything—Grandpa," he whispered, and John tapped gently on his shoulder.

James stood and walked out of the room, his feet heavier than ever. He followed Garth to the third floor and they entered the room with the teak table.

Ricin and Edgar were already seated, Ricin looking impatient.

"Hurry up, grab a seat," Ricin told him.

James sat down. Garth remained on his feet, resting his hands on the back of a chair.

"I need you to focus today, James," Ricin began. "What you will be doing is entering the data center of the bank that practically runs the world—the KJC bank. I need you to start chaos before I obtain the last piece I need to begin the war. Garth will be accompanying you on the job. Logan will have the car ready to drive you back when you're done. What I need you to do from in there—something which cannot be done from anywhere else—is enter the system and upload a virus that cannot be tracked or removed, and link it to the backups."

"The one we practiced all day long," Garth said, his head bobbing.

That virus *would* create chaos; it had a mind of its own and once in a system, it would play around, disrupting all procedures and randomly deleting pieces of information that would cause the entire system to malfunction.

"Garth will be entering the building with a fake pass," Ricin continued, then turned to Garth, "Remember your gun was moved to the middle toilet on the first floor, left wing."

Garth nodded, lips pursed.

"You will get inside from the rooftop," Ricin told James. "The data room is on the fourth floor."

Garth placed the blueprint of the bank in front of James and pointed to the location of the data room.

"What about security guards and cameras?" James asked, knowing he would never actually get to the building.

"Garth is going to start some drama involving a fire; create a distraction—People will be evacuated; security will be focused on handling the matter," Ricin replied.

"Okay," he replied, emotionless.

"Any more questions?" Ricin asked, leaning back in his chair, crossing his hands over his chest. "Good! You should get going then, boys. Get this done before lunchtime."

Garth promptly put the camera and earpiece on the table in front of James.

"Your jewels, Snowflake," Garth laughed, and headed toward the door.

James took the devices and followed Garth, glancing furtively at Ricin and Edgar, trying to convince himself this was the last time he sat with them.

He sank in the front passenger seat, his anguish and guilt growing roots within him—John was about to die. But he had to do it; he couldn't upload that virus and with Garth on the job with him, more people were bound to be killed. He had to turn himself in; he had to grab the first opportunity to run and never look back. And this was it.

CHAPTER TWENTY-SIX

Garth was behind the wheel, Logan in the back seat. Garth sang along to songs on the radio, tapping on the wheel as he drove.

James was quiet, his head against the headrest, looking up at the same blue sky he used to watch every peaceful afternoon on the warm sands of uninhabited islands.

Was this really going to be it? Was he really going to be free from Ricin once and for all?

"So, I heard Walter's girl came to see you at the fights," Garth said, glancing over at James. "Sweet one she is, right?" Garth added with a grin.

"She's not my type," James replied, his voice flat.

"Ohhhhh," Garth voiced in a derisive manner. "Hear that Logan? Snowflake has a type," Garth teased. "You like them dark? More curvy?" Garth asked.

"What happened to Wang Gu?" James asked, wanting to know Garth's version.

"Wang Gu?" Garth repeated. "Well, loose end tied."

"Who had killed him?" James asked, eagerly waiting for the reply.

"Edgar."

"Did you see him do it?"

"No but the picture with the bullet in his forehead—he looked pretty dead to me," Garth replied, his focus on the road. "Why ask?"

James shrugged.

"Saw this Chinese guy at the fights—reminded me of him," he lied. It was definitely Wang Gu he had seen—when their eyes met, they recognized each other.

"Wang Gu had a brother—practically same face," Garth said.

But James had never met Wang Gu's brother—the recognition was rooted in years spent practicing together every day.

Edgar had lied about killing Wang Gu and went as far as to stage his murder.

"You didn't answer my question," Garth said with a snicker. "What kind of chicks do you like?"

"I don't really have a type," he replied.

"Bull! Everybody has a type," Garth said. "Am I right or am I right, Logan?"

"True that," Logan agreed.

Garth kept looking over at James, waiting for him to say something.

"Me," Garth said, swerving the car to overtake another vehicle, "I prefer them with long, black hair—don't really mind the size of breasts—but the behind has to be nice and round if you know what I mean," Garth said with a bite of his lower lip. "Also, I prefer them shortish—you know, easier to handle," Garth laughed. "You gotta have a preference, Snowflake, come on, what is it?"

"I'll know it when I see it," James replied, just to give Garth an answer. But a dimpled smile flashed before his eyes, caramel-brown hair blowing in the wind—the girl he had seen outside the confectionery.

"Right," Garth said, and turned up the volume of the song playing on the radio.

They drove, heading toward the city center. Soon they would be close enough to the police station for him to get out and make a run for it. His anxiety took over, every movement making his dizziness worse. *Promise me, son*, John's words echoed in his head. He shut his eyes and took deep, steady breaths to calm himself.

"James," Garth said, "remember, if an unexpected glitch comes up—"

"I reboot the system without shutting down," he said, finishing Garth's sentence.

"Right on," Garth replied, turning the wheel into a long, wide road.

They were in the city center. This was it; this was his stop. A rush of adrenaline flooded his body. He kept his face ahead, his hand slowly reaching for the seat belt button. Time slowed to a crawl. His heartbeat boomed in his chest, the thump thump speeding up, his breaths loud gusts in his ears. Garth's focus was on driving, Logan looking out of his window. James's hand kept moving toward the seat belt button then paused... *act casual, don't call attention to your movements, hold...hold...*

Now!

He pushed the seat belt release, opened the door, and jumped out. He hit the ground—hard—and rolled several times. Up on his feet, he sprinted away in the opposite direction. The car screeched to a fuming halt. He raced away even faster.

He dumped the earpiece and mini camera from his pocket and ran on, focused on his freedom that finally seemed to be somehow in reach. He dashed up another block, carefully brushing past any people in his way, pushing his topmost speed to another level.

He jumped over some fruit crates a man pushed along his path and made a right turn into the steep, hilled road, keeping a steady pace.

He was two blocks from the station, his feet still racing, when his reflexes heightened. But the warning was different—as though the harm inevitable—and a sharp pain stabbed his chest. He bore the agony, forcing himself to keep going, but with warning, the debilitating ache struck again and he tumbled to the ground.

"No, no, no," he panicked, struggling to get back to his feet, gasping in pain. The new tracer must have the same problem as did the old, interfering with his heart activity.

He managed to get back up, Garth and Logan still out of sight. A woman paced down the hill, coming his way. He began walking toward her, beads of sweat rolling down his face, the agony in his chest intense.

"Please, help me," he called to the woman as he approached her, his voice unable to go beyond a whisper.

She hurried closer, but paused, her expression grave.

"You're that dangerous boy they're looking for!"

"Please, I need—to get to the police station," he told her, unable to catch his breath, but as he took another step, his reflexes heightened again and a more severe pain struck his heart and his knees hit the ground.

"He's right here!" the woman shouted, gesturing to someone behind him. "The police are coming for you! You are going to get what you deserve!" she said, rushing her words.

He glanced behind him—Garth and Logan were running up the hill in their dark uniforms.

"Those are not the police," he cried, turning back to the woman in panic. "Please, I need to get to the station," he repeated as he held onto the wall, unable to pull himself up. "Please—"

He couldn't draw in any more air—his chest paralyzed, the agony unbearable—and he helplessly collapsed, hitting his head hard against the pavement, all going black and silent.

***

There was a beeping sound in the distance. And the more he listened for it, the louder it became. A bright light forced his eyes shut and a familiar smell of frigid steel was in the air. He couldn't remember anything and muffled voices caught his attention.

"We cannot trust him now, Edgar," he heard the voice say. And all came back to him in a flood—the car ride to the bank—the run—his failed escape—he was back at Ricin's.

The beeping quickened in intensity and someone approached him.

"He tried once, he will try again," Ricin's voice continued. "We have to keep him locked up. He can rest in his cell until we figure out how we shall proceed."

“Right,” Edgar replied. “I’ll monitor him for a bit longer, make sure he remains stable. Then I’ll get him transferred.”

He heard footsteps leaving the room and opened his eyes again.

Edgar stood beside him, texting on his phone.

“I can't work for Ricin anymore,” James whispered feebly, grabbing Edgar's attention. “I won't.”

“Hey,” Edgar replied, ignoring what he had just said, “I’m so glad you made it,” he added with a smile of relief, then paused, his teeth grit, his eyes glazed. “I cannot lose you, too,” Edgar whispered.

What was Edgar trying to say? Why was he getting so emotional?

“What happened exactly?” James asked.

“You…um…” Edgar said, and swallowed hard. “When we inserted the new tracer, we added a defibrillator to ensure that if the same problem arose, we would be able to assist your heart—Ricin, he um—he activated the defibrillator to stop you from getting away.”

“I thought it was the new tracer,” he replied. No wonder his warning reflexes kept getting triggered.

“No,” Edgar said. “The new tracer works perfectly well.”

So not only did he have Ricin's tracer in him—he couldn't even get away if he wanted to, let alone turn himself in.

Edgar checked the level of fluid in the drip bag attached to James's arm, then looked down at his watch.

“Edgar,” James called weakly, “I can't work for Ricin anymore; I don't want to and I won't.”

Edgar hesitated, his eyes resting heavily on James's.

"You need to rest right now," Edgar said. "We—"

"He's awake?" Ricin interrupted from behind Edgar, his tone furious. "I thought we agreed that we cannot trust him anymore, Edgar."

"I was about to get him transferred," Edgar replied, "but then decided to let him in on the information that he has a defibrillator and can be stopped there and then whenever you please." It was as though Edgar detached from the person he was a few seconds ago.

Ricin squinted sharply at Edgar then turned to James.

"I never thought it would really come to this," Ricin told him in complete disappointment. "If it weren't for Edgar, you'd be dead, James—I did intend to kill you, because I cannot have a loose end, especially it being you. You were going to turn yourself in, weren't you?"

James remained silent, escaping Ricin's baneful glower.

"Right now, you need to rest," Ricin said, "and if you must know—I only agreed not to kill you because Edgar said we need you alive to be able to get your replicant done."

Replicant? James had never heard of his replication process before, nor did he think it was even possible. And as much as the thought of it being successful terrified him, he was too exhausted to dwell on it.

"Yes," Ricin continued, "works on your replicant are in progress and I am really hoping he will know better. Still, mark my words, James; what you tried to do this morning, you are going to regret for the rest of your life."

Ricin walked out and three more guards entered. James was bone tired—lacking the strength to even raise his head from the pillow—and shut his eyes.

He had fallen asleep and when he woke up, he was in the cell, the gate locked shut. He sat up and John quickly got to his feet.

"I'm so sorry, son," John began, looking at him through the metal bars. "I didn't know you had a defibrillator as well."

"It's not your fault—I didn't know either," he replied. "John—I—"

"Listen to me—whatever happens now, is not your fault," John said, as though reading his thoughts. "Nothing ever was. You just keep this in mind; never failures, only lessons, okay?"

"Get back, John, and be quiet," Wayne ordered. "You know you're not allowed to talk to him anymore."

"Oh no; do allow him," Ricin said as he walked through the open door of the room. "Let him talk—but John, make these words count this time as they are going to be your last."

Ricin signalled to the guards, and Wayne and Logan seized John.

"Ricin, please!" James cried, leaping out of bed. "It was my choice! I wanted to escape!"

"James, it's okay; it's okay, son," John repeated calmly, simply standing in the guards' tight grip.

"It was your stupid decision, James, but I'm sure this old man had you convinced. Besides, your body cannot handle more physical trauma right now, so John will pay the price," Ricin said, and took out a pocket dagger.

"Please, Ricin! Don't! Please! Please!" James cried, grabbing onto the bars of the cell, falling onto his knees —begging.

"You should know better by now, James. You and your actions demand a consequence that you shall never forget."

Ricin stepped toward John, sharp blade firmly in hand.

"Ricin, please! Please! I'll do anything. Please leave John alone!" James shouted, trying to shake the bars he was holding onto in panic.

"This has long been coming to you, old man," Ricin said, looking down on John. "If only you were smarter and left when you had the chance."

John stood there, his head held high, his eyes resting on James—telling him to be strong and endeavor again, and that he did not regret anything.

Ricin took the knife and held it against John's throat.

"No, please, Ricin, please, please," James cried desperately. "Don't! Please! John, I'm sorry! I'm sorry!" he sobbed as he clung onto the metal bars.

Ricin stared at James, his face lacking empathy.

"Remember this perfectly—people will pay the price for your actions."

With one savage slash, Ricin slit John's throat wide open.

"Nooooooooooo!" James screamed.

Blood gushed out of John's throat and the guards let go of him. His frail body collapsed and he gargled and coughed up blood until he went quiet.

James let out a loud cry and turned away from John's lifeless body, sobbing uncontrollably. Tears streamed down his cheeks, his body wracked with sobs and silent screams of sorrow, until his throat hurt and his face felt numb.

John's body was left there. James didn't have the strength to turn around and look at him.

More hours passed and James's eyes could no longer tear. An exhaustion took over him and he lay down on the floor. His eyelids getting heavier until he could not open them anymore.

He drifted off to the place where the subconscious breathes, but awoke again. John's body had been removed. James remained sitting on the floor, staring off into the distance.

Food was brought for him and left outside the bars where he could reach it, but he did not budge.

A part of him had died with John; his voice of hope and reason which had always helped him get back on his feet was now gone and he felt numb to life or any emotion, simply breathing because it was involuntary. He remained on the floor, motionless, except for the blink of his eyes, and more meaningless hours ticked by.

"James," Wayne called gently, close to the bars of his cell, "you need to drink and eat something."

He glanced up at Wayne, then rested his eyes on the floor again. Wayne crouched down to his level and held onto one of the bars.

"This is just a rough patch," Wayne told him. "You need to move on; I'm sure John would have wanted you to do that."

But it was a dark, desolate world James had been dragged into. A place where dreams and motivation have long been suffocated; drowned in the deep, flooding rivers of misery and sorrow. A place where notions of life are dangerously distorted; an edge, where the longer one dwells, the more death is disguised as hope.

CHAPTER TWENTY-SEVEN

Three days went by and James was heavy with sorrow. He hadn't eaten, barely drank, and Edgar injected him with salts and vitamins.

He was allowed out of his cell once a day to take a shower, and he remained standing under the freezing rainfall—cold, numb, blank—until a guard came and turned the water off. He slept a lot, lacking the will to do anything other than forget; living in the place where whatever happened never really happened at all.

He was lying on the floor in the same spot where John and himself used to spend hours talking. Someone came into the room and the cell opened.

"James?" Edgar said softly, tapping on his shoulder.

James opened his eyes, looked up at Edgar, and closed them again.

"James—you cannot just give up," Edgar said.

James couldn't be bothered—there was no point—and remained with his eyes closed.

"Hey, come on," Edgar said, pulling at his arm, wanting him to sit up. "Talk to me, James—please."

Edgar tugged at his elbow and he sat up, resting his back against the wall, Edgar crouched down in front of him.

"You cannot just give up," Edgar repeated, looking at him intently.

"Why not?" James whispered. "I don't want to be part of any of this, so why not?"

Edgar turned around and sat down next to him, his back against the wall.

"Remember when you were six years old, I had taken you to my apartment?" Edgar said. "You were very ill—"

"I wasn't ill," he corrected. "I was getting sick because you were testing how my body responds to certain poisons."

Edgar avoided his eyes and nodded.

"You're right. We were carrying out tests," Edgar replied, now looking him in the eye. "My point is, you were feeling very sick and you kept telling me you didn't want to die. You kept saying how you wanted to become a man and find a beautiful girl just like Monica and have your own life."

"I was six. Things change."

"I know. As should be. But I remember, I stayed up with you all night because you couldn't sleep and you drew this detailed picture of your future home and how many pets you wanted. You were feeling very unwell and yet you still had hope, you still had belief. But the thing that had struck me the most, was what you had said—*when you cannot control something, life is trying to teach you a lesson*. That is something to always live by and this is certainly such a time."

James was silent, remembering how Edgar had held him in his arms all night until he felt better. And how Edgar had secretly given him the antidote, even though Ricin insisted they let his body get rid of the toxin on its own, no matter how long it took.

"What happened to Monica?" James asked, recalling how concerned she had been about him that night and how she kept telling Edgar that what they were doing wasn't right.

"We had gone our separate ways. She settled down, started a family. Last I saw her, she looked quite happy—she deserves it." Edgar swallowed hard. "My parents loved her," he added to himself, and his lips sealed tight as though fighting back tears.

"What I said the other day, about your parents," James said, remembering Edgar was the only one who stuck up for him along the years, "I'm sorry."

"It's okay. Maybe it holds some truth," Edgar said, his eyes to the floor.

"They—didn't make it?"

Edgar shook his head slowly.

"I'm sorry."

"Here, drink," Edgar said, reaching out for the glass he had brought for him. "Coconut milk."

James took the glass and drank it, Edgar remained beside him.

"I need to get back to work, but I'll come by later, okay?" Edgar said, and got to his feet. "Gina prepared some rice for you—try to eat some." Edgar was about to leave but paused, "I know Ricin won't approve of me telling you this, but I'm sorry about John—I was against it. But Ricin has the final word—I'm sorry."

James nodded, somewhat appreciating Edgar's words, and watched him leave.

He lay down again, a weariness drowsing his body, and he let his eyelids close. The persistent buzz of a bee captured his attention. His eyes followed the downy insect as it danced and twirled around bright yellow and orange flowers, lifting his sight to the endless stretches of green fields that stood before him and the clear blue skies above his head.

The mellow sun was kissing his skin, a light breeze tenderly stroked his face.

"James!" a little boy called, running out of nowhere. "John is looking for you! He is in the tool shed," the boy said, and ran on in the opposite direction, leaving him confused.

The clank of a truck's engine drew his focus and he turned to it. He saw a forest-green shack and began walking toward it. The tall grass caressed his feet as he paced through it. He came to the wooden shed and peeked inside.

"John?" he called—bewildered, seeing him standing right there, selecting some potatoes in a woven basket.

"James, son! How have you been?" John greeted with a large, warm grin. "I have been waiting for you. Here, come and help me load these potato sacks onto the truck," John added cheerfully.

James gaped at him with wide eyes.

"John—are—aren't you supposed to be—"

"Come on, James," John interrupted, heading toward the truck outside the shed. "Let's load these up."

As puzzled as he was, he quickly followed John and began helping him load the potatoes.

“And we’re ready! Phew! Thanks, son!” John remarked, dusting his trousers. “We should get back to the house now, Martha is preparing a lovely lunch for today.”

“Thanks, John—but I’m not hungry,” James replied.

“No? Why aren't you eating, son? You need to eat and get your health back so when the next opportunity arises, you will be ready to take it!” John said, looking him straight in the eye.

“There cannot be another opportunity, John,” he replied, dropping his gaze to the soil beneath his feet. “There's a defibrillator, too—I can never get away.”

John wore a patient smile, his eyes full of life.

“Of course you can, son!” John affirmed. “Maybe not like you tried last time—but there is always another way; you just have to find it.”

John began walking to the house and James followed him, gazing at the vibrant flowers along the way.

“Hey, Edward!” John called, waving to a young man walking toward them “Just in time to join us for lunch. You remember my son, Edward,” John said to James.

“Hey, nice to see you again!” Edward said with a broad smile, tapping strongly on James's shoulder.

“Again?” James asked perplexed.

“The fishing trip, remember?” Edward asked. “When I caught that big bluegill but it got away.”

Edward and John remained staring at him awkwardly, waiting for his response.

“Sure; yes, of course,” he replied, forcing a smile, not to let them down.

They all headed into the house. It was a cozy home with wooden ceiling beams and rustic furniture. As they walked along the hall, the floor beneath them creaked softly, adding to the melody of joyful birds.

"I'll be right back," Edward said, and went upstairs.

James followed John down the hall and into the big kitchen.

"What would you like to eat?" John asked.

James's eyes raced fretfully around the room, the familiarity of the place tripping his anxiety.

"Isn't this Ricin's kitchen?" he said, panicked.

"Ricin who?" John asked as he sliced a red apple.

James turned around frantically—a guard stood by the door they came through, Logan posted right by the window.

"John—John you have to leave!" James said, overwrought.

"Leave?" John repeated as though confused. "But you are still here, son."

"John, Ricin is going to kill you—you have to get out, now!" he cried, but John turned to him and grabbed him by the shoulders—his grip firm.

"James, son, listen to me!" John said, holding James's gaze, "I am not afraid of Ricin and you shouldn't be either. I choose to stay here and I am not leaving you—James, Ricin doesn't want you to escape and you better not try again, because he will kill you next time. But listen carefully, son; it won't be your fault if you get caught."

"Get caught? He knows I can sense danger and avoid it."

"Of course, but if you are trapped and cannot get out, it won't be your fault," John said.

"How do I get myself trapped and caught?"

“James!” Ricin interrupted, marching into the kitchen. “James!” he called again, prodding his shoulder. “Wake up!”

James opened his eyes. He was on the floor in the cell. Ricin standing next to him.

“Get up, James,” Ricin said, impatient. “You wasted enough of my time. Do you intend to keep sleeping days away? Pull yourself together and move the hell on.”

The last time he had seen Ricin, was when he had slashed John's throat.

Ricin stood there and James got to his feet and faced him.

“I’m done working for you,” James said calmly, looking Ricin in the eye.

“Are you?” Ricin scoffed. “You actually think you have a say in this?” he asked, coming closer to James's face, eyes lined with fury. “Listen to me, you cretin! I hear you say something like that again and Matthew and his parents will be standing right here, in this room, praying to just die.”

James kept staring back at Ricin, their eyes in a fierce war.

“Grow up,” Ricin said, still face to face with him, and turned away and headed out of the room—Logan and Wayne at the ready if he dared step after Ricin.

The gate of the cell remained open, the electric door of the room locked.

James went to the basin and let the water wash off his consuming anger. His mind meandered to his last dream. What was that all about? It was one of those vivid dreams which almost felt real. *If you are trapped and cannot get out, it won't be your fault*, he remembered John say, but wouldn't it be, really? And how could he get himself trapped in the first place? But why even ponder, it was only a dream after all.

The door of the room opened again and Gina walked in.

“Hey, James,” Gina said gently, “Ricin told me to come for you and take you to the kitchen to help me cook. And I have to make sure you eat,” she said, forcing a smile.

James went with Gina to the kitchen, Logan and Wayne behind them.

“Breakfast; what do you want? Please don't tell me you’re not hungry,” Gina said, patient.

He grabbed a yellow apple from the fruit bowl on the table and took one bite.

“Breakfast—check,” he replied, putting the apple down on a napkin.

“Right—A tall, handsome boy like yourself needs fuel; that doesn't even count as a tenth of a breakfast,” Gina said, hand on hip, smile calm. “Tell you what,” she said, reaching for the blender in the cupboard, “I know this delicious recipe for a smoothie; full of vitamins and goodness, and you don't even have to chew, okay?” she said, trying not to laugh, her eyes begging him to accept.

“Fine,” he replied, knowing Gina only meant well.

She chopped up some fruits and vegetables and put everything in the blender together with some almonds and walnuts. She poured out two glasses and gave him the big one.

“It's good, right?” Gina asked, savoring the thick, green drink.

“Yeah, thanks,” he replied, and finished his glass.

"So today's menu," Gina began, trying to sound positive, "spaghetti with meatless meatballs, sound good?"

He shrugged, remembering John cooking and his passion for it.

"Hey," Gina said, grabbing his attention, "I'm not supposed to know things—I'm just the chef here; I cook, clean the kitchen, and leave. But I heard about what happened to John, and I'm so sorry. I know how much he meant to you and all I can tell you is that John was so proud of you and that he had high hopes for your future. He talked about you as though he were talking about his own son. He believed in you, James, don't give up on yourself."

"Thanks," he whispered.

Gina went to the fridge and began taking out some of the ingredients. He helped Gina cook and they even prepared a chocolate cheesecake for dessert.

At one in the afternoon, they sat down at the kitchen table to have lunch together.

"Mmmm, this is delicious," Gina said, munching on a vegan meatball. "I never thought I'd say this, but I kind of prefer it to actual meat meatballs."

"It's really good," he replied, twirling his fork in the spaghetti.

"Soooooo, you still like that girl?" Gina asked, her eyes wide with enthusiasm.

"We're too different. It wouldn't work out."

"I know what you mean; trust me," Gina replied. "Once I was dating this woman; really nice girl, but, she was a fitness instructor and obsessed with calorie counting and protein ratios, and this has too much sugar, leave the butter out next time and this is too oily. I couldn't—I couldn't handle it anymore. I love cooking because I love food. Okay, you eat healthy and exercise but come on, butter, sugar, and fat you cannot just omit from certain recipes. You know what I believe? That you should eat everything, but in moderation. I'm careful what I eat; I don't want to be unhealthy, but I so enjoy desserts and a greasy meal sometimes."

"I agree," he replied. "Life is too short to miss out."

"Exactly!"

They finished eating and he helped her clean the dishes, listening to her stories about her first job as a chef back home.

"So, you promise me?" Gina said, folding away her apron, "You are going to eat—get your full health back—and move forward, right?" She kept looking at him—her gaze expectant.

"Yeah," he replied. The heaviness in his heart was somehow lifted, his head calm. "Thanks, Gina."

"You're more than welcome, sweet," she replied with a warm smile.

A thought quickly surfaced in his mind—*trapped and caught*—it echoed. He reached out to hug her, making sure his mouth was covered with his forearm, and whispered in her ear,

"Tranquilliser gas in KJC Bank data room."

CHAPTER TWENTY-EIGHT

The guards escorted James back to the cell. The door of the room was locked but the gate of the cell was left open. Three guards remained in the room, one of them new.

James tried to keep his thoughts positive, hoping Gina had understood him clearly and would find the courage to inform the right authorities.

He lay down on the bed in the cell, staring at the protruding imperfections throughout the gray ceiling, attempting to visualize patterns and form images just to give his mind something amusing to do.

The day ticked into night and the guards changed duties. He was given some lentil soup for dinner and he ate it. Not long after, he fell asleep, but the vivid image of Matthew's throat being gashed wide open, startled him awake. He couldn't seem to catch his breath, his whole body in a cold sweat, and he got out of bed.

He went to the shower room outside his cell and stood beneath the cold trickle, calming his nerves, clearing his mind. He took some clean clothes from the cupboard and was putting on his trousers—something was in one of the zipped pockets. He reached down for it and took it out; it was the same watch Edgar had given him—the exact watch—there were distinctive scratches on one of the sides.

Someone dug it up from the seabed offshore, the last place he had hidden it. It had a tracker in it after all. So why did no one ever come for it when he was moving it from island to island? And someone therefore knew exactly where he had travelled to when he escaped; someone knew where he had been all along.

Who could it have been? Edgar? Wang Gu? But Edgar would have surely reported the information to Ricin and why would Wang Gu want to keep track of him? And hadn't Edgar said that whoever had it was lucky?

He took a closer look at it, turning it around, inspecting every piece. He tried to carefully open the back but couldn't without breaking it and decided to let it be for now, until he got more answers.

It was still four forty-five in the morning. The guards in the room stood alert, following his every move.

"May I go to the kitchen?" he asked.

The guards exchanged quick looks. Then the guard by the door reached in his pocket for the key card and opened the door.

James went to the kitchen and turned on the light. The two guards that followed him, remained posted by the door. He made a cup of tea and helped himself to some oats and cashews.

He was still sitting at the kitchen table, reading the geographical magazine that had been left on the counter, when Ricin came into the room.

"Good morning," Ricin said. "Six o'clock—nice to see you awake at such an hour and having eaten breakfast already. A jump-start a day keeps failure at bay." Ricin poured himself a coffee and turned back to James, "I see you got your watch back. Our laundry woman said you had left it here when you ran away. She asked me if she could give it back to you and I told her I couldn't care any less. Kind of suits you though—I always did like it on you; makes you look more mature."

"Who is she? The woman who does the laundry," he asked.

"Was, to be exact," Ricin said. "She just retired from the job, yesterday was her last day of work."

"What was her name?"

"Carla Lacari I believe," Ricin replied, and sipped his coffee.

James had never heard that name before, nor did he ever meet the woman who did the laundry.

"Later on today, I need you to get some work done," Ricin said, giving James an intent look. "And I might as well add—keep your opinion about the matter to yourself; you'll do everyone a favor."

Edgar entered the kitchen, his pace swift.

"Morning," Edgar said, grabbing a mug from the cupboard.

"Edgar, I need you to have a look at the report I sent to you last night. I don't trust Brian. Let me know what you think about it."

"I will have a look at it later today but first, I need to sort out that problem with Rami."

"Ah, yes!" Ricin sighed. "That other dunce."

“You’re up early,” Edgar said, turning to James with a smile. “Thought you got rid of that,” Edgar added, looking down at the watch.

“I thought I had lost it. Turns out, I had left it here. Carla found it,” James replied, waiting for Edgar's response.

“Well, try not to lose it again. It costs more than some people make in a whole year,” Edgar replied, confirming James's belief the value of the watch was only monetary and that Edgar couldn't have known it had a tracker in it.

“I need to get going,” Edgar said, grabbing his coffee off the counter. “Oh and the irony,” Edgar blurted out, pausing with his mug in hand. “One of our undercover men up north, turns out, is living right next door to Matthew's new home.”

James's nerves jolted. Matthew and his family weren't safe after all. What John had said in the dream better be right; if anything happened to Matthew or his parents, he would not be able to forgive himself.

“Matthew's father, Paul,” Edgar continued, intrigued, “believes the man is just a gardener—already paid him twice to cut their lawn. Isn't that ironic?”

“Ironic indeed,” Ricin replied, then turned to James, “Hear that?”

James glanced away from Ricin's smirk, stifling his boiling rage.

“Anyhow,” Edgar said, “got to run.”

Edgar hurried out of the room and Ricin placed his empty mug near the dishwasher.

“I got to get moving, too,” Ricin told him. “Gina won't be coming to work today; she just called in sick. I will be seeing you later.”

Ricin's phone rang in his pocket and he reached for it as he left the kitchen.

James hoped Gina was okay and that he had not compromised her safety by what he had told her. He stood up and approached Wayne who was still standing by the door.

"Am I allowed to go to the roof?"

Wayne cleared his throat, "Yes. And as long as you're still within the building, you're allowed anywhere."

He nodded—they were trusting him again.

He went to the rooftop and stepped out into the sun, Wayne stepped behind him.

He went to the stone fence and sat down, resting against it. His mind became a fierce battlefield. Opposing thoughts began stabbing one another, then survivors dragged on through all the possible trenches leading to his freedom—only for landmines to blow them up at the end of the trail. The tranquillizer gas remained his only real ray of hope.

The sun steadily rose, its warmth instilling an uncomfortable thirst. He headed into the building and grabbed a bottle of water from the kitchen before going to his bedroom.

It was just as he had left it, except for the bed that had been neatly made. His drawings were still on the desk, Cassidy's number still in the drawer. He took out the pink piece of paper and threw it away. Everything that linked him to Ricin and his businesses, he didn't want anything to do with.

He flipped through the pencil sketches, pausing on his mother's portrait. Was Edgar the one behind the idea of framing her, like he had done to Cassidy's uncle? The snake in Ricin's ear.

He sat down heavily on the edge of his bed, the sun's rays reaching him through the window. A glare on the wall, moving with his wrist, caught his eye; the reflection of his watch. It was past eleven, the second hand steadily ticking, the digital display bright. A red flicker at the bottom of the dial grabbed his attention. He had never seen it or noticed it before, and it was only visible when the sun was hitting it at a particular angle. He went to the window, slowly moving the face of the watch until the sun was illuminating the small, red inscription at the bottom.

'Truth within' he read silently to himself. Was it just a slogan or was it purposefully put there to mean something else?

"James!" Garth called, pushing his bedroom door wide open. "Come on."

James had no choice and left with Garth. He was taken to the third floor. Ricin and Edgar were already gathered around the teak table, the smell of fried food filling the air.

"Have a seat; join us for an early lunch while we go over some details for your next job," Ricin said.

It was one of Ricin's ways to still get what he wanted; lunch together, as though everything was just perfectly fine. James had to take a chair and Garth took the one opposite to him.

"The orange sauce is the sweet and sour," Garth said, uncovering the foil containers on his side of the table while Edgar opened the others.

"What is it about their spring rolls, huh?" Ricin said, biting into one. "I was never a fan but theirs are something."

"The spices they use are the perfect blend," Edgar replied. "And they don't add any chili," he added to James.

James's plate was still empty—eating with Ricin was the last thing he wanted to be doing. The others helped themselves, filling their plates with the various types of noodles and rice. Ricin then handed him one of the noodle containers and kept looking steadily at him, expecting him to take it.

He took it from Ricin's hand and scooped a small portion onto his plate with the fork.

"You got to try this," Garth said, placing a rice dish in front of James. "Funnily enough, it's called Snowflake—got to do with the coconut flakes I suppose, but hey, it's got your name," Garth mocked.

Ricin gave a small laugh. Edgar remained quiet.

"It does have a cool edge to it though, right?" Garth said. "Snowflaaaaake."

Truth of the matter, he'd rather be called Snowflake than James and what it stood for.

"So," Ricin began, chewing his food, "your dumb decisions have put us behind schedule once again," he said, looking at James. "Today, you are going to interrupt a business deal which I am not in accord with."

Business deal? What about the bank job? His heart missed a beat, doom creeping up on him again.

"James?" he heard Ricin call. "Are you paying any attention?"

“The bank job?” he voiced, wanting to know if he was still going to get to do that.

“That job is being done by my special undercover crew since you wasted so much time trying to be such a hero,” Ricin replied, reaching for his glass of water.

James's face dropped, screaming internally—that was his only chance; his only safe way out.

“Can you just pay attention?” Ricin snapped.

James looked up again, his leg jiggling nervously—he was back at working for Ricin; this was not what he wanted.

“As I was saying,” Ricin said, “this mission—”

“What about my replicant; isn't he ready to work?” he interrupted, wanting to know if that process was proving to be successful.

Garth paused mid-bite, his eyes bounced between James and Ricin. Edgar glanced up, then lowered his gaze to his plate again.

Ricin kept staring fixedly at James.

“I'm just—asking,” James said, the unexpected tension dominating the whole room.

Ricin picked up his glass again and drank some water.

“The replication process of your human body is coming about perfectly,” Ricin said. “However, none of the mutant genes are generating successfully—I already killed two of you,” Ricin added in a solemn manner. “Two teenage boys identical to you—same exact everything—except they don't see what's coming to them.”

Garth chewed quickly and picked up a napkin.

“You know what the irony about that is, James?” Ricin asked with a long pause. “I'm not sure if killing them point-blank was satisfactory because it felt like I was killing you—or because deep down, I don't really want another you."

Ricin's lips sealed tight and James escaped his gaze.

"If only you could see what I am willing to give you—son," Ricin said, and grit his teeth. "Maybe one day—you'll finally get it. Until then," Ricin said, shaking off the tense aura with a loud, indifferent sniff, "jobs will proceed as necessary—this mission in particular, has long been coming. It's between two rivals of mine, Gustav and Dune. Not that they ever stand a chance against me, but I have always believed prevention is better than cure. They are meeting tonight, just before the tunnel. You will wait for them there until they both show up. Dune is going to have a case in which he'll be carrying a very rare substance the other intends to buy. Not that I myself am in current need of such a substance, but I cannot allow Gustav to have it. Wait until Dune is handing over the case to Gustav, so that we'll be sure it's the real thing, then grab the case and make a run for it. No doubt, expect a heavy fusillade. Once back in the car—vehicle is bulletproof, tires are too—Garth will drive off. Any queries?"

James said nothing. At least no innocent civilians would be involved.

"Great," Ricin remarked, helping himself to more noodles. "And James," Ricin added, pausing to look him squarely in the eye, "dare to even take a single step in the opposite direction I tell you to, and I will get you back to watch me slash Matthew's throat wide open and then, I'll teach you the lesson of a lifetime."

Ricin's expression pierced James's heart. He could feel the intense throb all the way to his throat.

"It won't come to that," Edgar said confidently. "Right, James?"

He looked up at Edgar, then gave a slight nod.

They continued eating. Ricin and Garth discussed the last soccer match. Edgar lost in his own thoughts, occasionally glancing at James.

Soon, James was in the front passenger seat, Garth behind the wheel. The sun shone and a flock of birds raced beneath the white meringue of clouds.

"Weather's nice today, right?" Garth said as he drove on, "Not too cold not too warm; just perfect."

James paid no attention to him.

"Will be going for a motorcycle ride with a friend of mine later today—should be fun," Garth added, tapping to the rhythm of the song playing on the radio. "Do you still remember how to drive one?"

James kept staring out of the window, a plane was passing right over their car.

"I'm sure you still remember," Garth said. "Maybe Ricin would agree to let us ride one for your next job. What do you say?"

A couple drove past their car, their voices, singing along to the radio, picked up then tailed off as they went by.

"You are such great company," Garth said, and increased the volume of the radio.

They arrived at the place and Garth parked the car a few meters away from the tunnel—far enough to avoid arousing any suspicion.

They waited quietly in the vehicle and it started to drizzle. Tiny drops pitter-pattered onto the car window; transparent worms slinked down the glass, engulfing others in their paths to grow longer and faster.

"James, not that you have a choice," Garth said, straightening his posture as he turned to face him, "but I'm guessing Ricin never told you what this mission really is, huh?"

"What do you mean? He said it's a substance he doesn't need."

"I have to say," Garth snorted, smiling as he returned his gaze to the road, "he is truly admirable Ricin; such a commendable genius."

CHAPTER TWENTY-NINE

This had to be the last piece Ricin needed to begin the biological war. A tornado of adrenaline engulfed James.

"This is what he needs to start that war, right?" James asked.

"If he didn't tell you; I'm not saying anything either," Garth said, peering through the rearview mirror to see if anybody was driving up the road.

James's mind raced chaotically; maybe he should pretend to trip and make a noise, alerting the business dealers of his presence; they'd retreat and postpone the deal. Or maybe he should allow himself to get shot and lose the case in the process.

"Don't even think about it," Garth warned, as though reading his thoughts. "You get the case and we go back to Ricin with it. I'm sure you don't want to add Matthew's gravestone on your conscience now, do you?...That's what I thought."

"Garth," Ricin called through the speaker on the dashboard, "any sign of them?"

"No. Nothing yet," Garth replied, checking the road again.

“They’re late,” Ricin said.

“Who gave us the information about this deal?” Garth asked.

“Greg. And he will be sorry if he got it wrong.”

“I don't trust that guy—never did, Ricin,” Garth said, “and I had warned you about him.”

Ricin sighed, “You did. Wait a few more minutes and if they don't show up, head back to drop James off and go pay Greg a visit; you know what to do.”

“Sure. Consider it done,” Garth replied without hesitation, and they all went quiet again.

James's nerves were on a razor's edge, though dulled with every passing minute where nothing happened. The drizzling rain let up in the silence.

“Greg has it coming; that idiot!” Garth said, and started the engine.

James sighed in utter relief; luck was on his side this time. He leaned back in his seat, his head up to the peaceful skies, and tried to enjoy the car ride.

***

Back at Ricin's, the night turned into day several times over. Gina had not yet returned to work and Edgar had gone away for a few days on a business trip.

James practiced with Garth every day; programming simulations in the morning, target practice with new weapons including different blades, in the afternoon.

He kept trying to think of ways to get away from Ricin; none promising. The nightmares—involving Matthew's family—reminded him of the high stakes.

He had just finished eating lunch in his bedroom and was looking out of the window. A young sparrow was attempting to fly to higher branches, only to flap its way back down to the ground.

"Change of plans!" Ricin said as he stood in his bedroom's doorway. "And for once, it's actually not your fault, James. I have two failed missions," Ricin continued as he stepped into the room, his expression vexed. "The business deal, which I'm still waiting on for information, and the bank job."

The bank job? James's heart leaped for joy, his face maintaining its composure.

"It seems those particular undercover were after all not capable of getting to the data room without being arrested, so you are going to get that job done this time. Meet Garth on ground floor, near the elevator, in an hour. Make sure you get it done," Ricin warned.

James went to the cell and sat on the edge of the bed, gazing around the room—hoping that was indeed the last time he would ever be in it. His eyes rested on the floor outside the gate where he had last seen John cough through his final breaths. *I'm going to make it, John; I'm going to get out of here*, he said silently to himself, trying to be positive and have faith in Gina.

***

James waited near the elevator, Wayne and Logan with him.

"Snowflaaaake," Garth called with a smirk as he approached. "Ready to roll?"

Garth pushed the elevator button and turned to Logan and Wayne.

"Gum? Mint," Garth said, holding a pack of gum out to them.

Both Logan and Wayne took one and then Garth offered to James.

"No, thanks," James said.

"Remember?" Garth asked him, "When we had each chewed on a whole pack of bubble gum at one go, to see who could blow the largest bubble?"

The elevator door opened and they all stepped inside.

"Yeah—you nearly choked," James replied.

"I did not," Garth objected. "I was laughing so hard when the bubble burst in your face and stuck to your hair —I just gagged."

The gum had stuck to the hair on James's forehead and he spent hours getting it all out.

"And that other time with the marshmallows," Garth laughed. "We should try it with chili mints."

Garth's eyes were bright with competitive enthusiasm, as though oblivious to what they were heading out to do.

They all got into the car and soon, they were parking close to the bank. James's hands were sweating profusely, his mouth awfully dry

"Keep your cap on and your head low until you get to the roof, understood?" Garth said, attaching the mini camera to his t-shirt, making sure it was angled properly.

"Yeah," he replied, putting the aural device in his ear.

"Remember, wait on the roof outside until you hear the fire alarm go off. As soon as I'm done downstairs, I'll be right up to make sure you have finished the job," Garth said, putting on black leather gloves.

James nodded—the gas better be pouring out quickly; he could not upload that virus into the system.

Wayne and Logan remained in the car. Logan took Garth's place behind the wheel, ready for when they got out. Garth headed to the front door of the bank and James made his way to the side of the building.

He climbed up to the roof and waited, a tremble of angst ran through his whole body. The sun had set, the skies' light faded away, a darkness ready to take over.

The fire alarm went off. He quickly climbed down to the closest window in the internal yard, entering the fourth floor. He hurried to the data room and opened the door with the fake pass Garth had given him. No one was in the room and he went to the main computer.

"Be quick, James," Ricin said in his ear, as he began to hack into the system.

He continued clacking at the keys, hoping the gas would start pouring into the room and the bulletproof door be unresponsive to the keycard. But more seconds ticked by and nothing happened.

The virus was nearly uploaded, only a few more commands left to get it up and running. Why wasn't anything happening? Why wasn't he being trapped and caught?

Maybe Gina was too afraid to inform the authorities, knowing the consequences if she got caught; she too had people she cared for and had to protect.

A pyroclastic flow of rack and ruin hit James hard, reminding him that his whole existence was ill-fated, and that no matter how hard he tried to get away from Ricin, his own destiny was always against him.

He had to do something; he couldn't upload that virus, but Garth would be there to check he had finished the job.

"You done?" Garth soon asked in a hurry, standing in the doorway.

"Not yet," he replied, still inputting codes.

“Not yet?!” Garth snapped. “Get on with it, James!”

Garth guarded the door, keeping it wide open. But for the gas to work, that door had to be shut and locked.

James began to panic, sweat trickling down his forehead.

“Garth!” he called. “Something's wrong; it's not letting me proceed,” he lied.

“What do you mean?” Garth asked, running to James's side, the door closing behind him.

“The system is not—”

“What the hell, James!?” Garth snapped, taking over the keyboard, and started rewriting the last command codes he had inputted. “You’re doing it wrong!”

“James,” Ricin growled in his ear, “I know you know how to do this, boy.”

James couldn't let Ricin believe he was purposefully not doing the job. He grabbed the keyboard from under Garth's hands and continued typing.

“I got this,” he told Garth, and his fingers continued inputting information much faster than Garth could—he could not give Ricin a reason to go after Matthew or his family.

“Make sure you get it done right,” Garth ordered. “I’ll guard the door.”

Garth turned to walk away. James continued typing, his frustration driving his hands to work even quicker, his guilt goring him.

Garth was almost at the door, James about to input the final command code, but his warning reflexes heightened.

A forceful cascade of white gas began pouring into the room from the vents, rapidly concentrating the air. It was happening! A peaceful happiness took over him; his life was about to change.

Garth ran to the door but it would not open, and he repeatedly shot at the locks, trying to get the door to move—all his efforts in vain.

"We're locked in!" Garth shouted, distressed, pulling up his shirt to cover his nose and mouth.

"Locked in?" Ricin exploded. "What's going on?!"

"We're trapped! And this gas is pouring out from everywhere," Garth explained, trying to barge open the door once again.

James hurried to the door, and pretended to help Garth attempt to open it, but a profound weakness was already starting to take over.

"This is your fault," Garth yelled, turning to him with hellish fury.

"What?!" James voiced in complete shock.

"I was supposed to be guarding the door—keeping it open—not—not—"

Garth collapsed onto the floor. James light-headed.

"James!" Ricin roared in his earpiece, an accusatory tone.

"No—No!" James protested. "The system—"

"You were stalling—"

"No! There was an error—the system—it—it was—"

James's mind could no longer function. He stumbled as his feet took him a step back and he blacked out.

***

All was perfectly quiet. The air clean and light. His head heavy, his eyelids too leaden to keep open. Around him was brightly lit but everything was just a blur. He couldn't remember anything, nor recognize where he was.

“James?” he heard a male voice say, but he was too giddy to focus and drifted off to golden sands and a salty breeze.

His eyes opened again and everything that happened flashed before him.

“Matthew!” he gasped, sitting up abruptly, about to jump out of bed.

“Hey, James; calm down,” a man said, “you are safe here.”

Another two—a man and a woman—were also in the room.

“I have to go,” James blurted in panic as he attempted to get out of bed. But he was still rather weak and the men quickly held him.

“No! Let me go, please! You don't understand!” he cried, struggling to get free from their grip. But his body had not yet recovered from the effects of the gas and they managed to pin him down in bed again.

“James, I need you to calm down; everything is okay,” the same man said in a reassuring manner.

But all James could picture was blood gushing out of Matthew's slit throat and he resisted even harder.

“Please! My friend is in danger because of me!” he yelled, managing to pull one of his hands free.

“Get the sedative. NOW!” the man told the woman, and she rushed out of the room.

James couldn't get up, his body weary, their hold strong. His reflexes warned him and the man injected a warm liquid into his arm while the others held him steady.

“No—please!”

"James, everyone is safe," the man repeated, patiently. "I promise you; everything is going to be okay now."

"Ricin's going to kill him! He's going after Matthew and his family! Please—I have to—I hav—" The sedative kicked in, his mind diffusing blank, and everything around him faded.

***

The smell of chocolate and pastry teased him; thoughts calm, meandering with the wind.

His mind yelled, startling him awake; *Matthew!*

"James; James it's me. I'm okay," a familiar voice rushed.

It was Matthew; he was sitting right beside his bed, mug in one hand, croissant in the other.

"Matt, you're not safe!" James said, chasing his words. "Ricin is—"

"It's okay," Matthew cut in with a smile. "I am safe; my family is safe. You're going to be okay, and they know about the tracer and they are taking care of that too."

"Defibrillator," he voiced, his mind racing ahead of him. "I have a defib—"

"Yeah, they know."

"They know?" he asked, confused, his head spinning.

"Yeah, everything is going to be okay," Matthew repeated.

James's thoughts were still fogged, his heart pounding.

"Matt," he began, and swallowed hard, "John—"

"He's dead. We know," Matthew said, his tone calm.

"How—how do—"

"We were not given any details," Matthew said, carefully keeping his voice down, "but Ricin is not the only one who has undercover people working for him. Someone from the government is working on the inside; they have eyes and ears with Ricin."

A long pause. Matthew's words hard to grasp.

"Do you know who it is? Is it Carla Lacari?" James asked.

"We're not allowed to know," Matthew replied, shaking his head. "And that bomb you—"

"I didn't know it was a bomb."

"They're alive; it was all a set-up," Matthew said in a hushed tone.

James opened his mouth but words would not come out.

"They knew Miller's house was bugged; they told me to go speak to Miller at his house. Cameras were looped after you left and the family hurried out safely."

A huge heaviness lifted off James's shoulders; Miller's family was safe; those children were still alive! And he was not a murderer after all. Relief drugged his body and he fell peacefully silent.

"I'm glad you made it out," Matthew told him, smiling.

"Matt, I'm sorry about John. I did everything I could to get him out of there and he was free to go, but he…"

"He decided to stay," Matthew said, finishing his sentence. "We got a letter from him. He told us what happened and we understood his decision. He knew Ricin would eventually kill him."

"I'm so sorry, Matt."

Matthew nodded, his face to the floor, a sorrow upon him.

“Hey, they told me I need to let you rest,” Matthew said, changing the subject.

“It's okay; I feel fine.”

He felt more than fine—as though he could breathe easily for the first time in his life. He inhaled deeply and let his body relax and sink into the soft pillows behind his back.

“Hey, James, how are you?” It was the same man who had spoken to him before. “I’m Stephen Patai,” he continued with a warm smile, coming closer to the bed. “I’m a medical consultant. It's a great, great pleasure to finally meet you.”

The man was tall and broad shouldered, probably in his late thirties, and had the emerald eyes which complemented his peculiar accent.

“I’m so sorry I had to sedate you again but we couldn't let you leave,” Stephen continued. “Matthew is safe and sound, as you can now see for yourself,” he added with a grin. “Would you like something to eat? Or are you still nauseous from the sedative?”

“Thanks. I’m not hungry.”

“No problem. Whenever you want to eat, just let us know, okay? I understand that you have been through—a lot—and you need to rest, and recover from all the trauma. Just need to tell you; that patch on your chest; don't take it off as it is interfering with the signals so Cole cannot detect your location or activate the defibrillator. We are still monitoring your vitals just in case, but I want you to know you are safe here and Cole cannot get to you. When you are well enough, we will surgically remove them. Until then, just relax; you not only need but deserve that. I’ll be in the adjacent room, if you need anything just holler—kidding—don't holler, just press the orange button right there."

"How have you been doing?" he asked Matthew, when Stephen had left.

"Okay, I guess. Mom is still recovering from everything but she's feeling better every day. We still haven't done a memorial service for Grandpa; mom keeps postponing it—saying that she has to come up with something special since it's without his body, but I'm sure it will give her the closure she needs. In the meantime, Dad and I decided we are going to help her open up her own bakery with a little cafe; just the way she always imagined it. We're naming it after Grandpa; Melwin."

"That's really nice."

"Yeah; we're all excited about it. We'll soon be settling the papers and we can start renovating the place. What about you? How have you been holding up?"

"I'm just glad it's over and if this works out, I couldn't be better. Where are we exactly?" he asked, really looking around the spacious room for the first time.

Blue drapes with golden yellow tassels embellished the windows, large ceramic pots with plants filled each corner.

"We are in the president's residence," Matthew replied, himself amazed.

"Seriously?"

"We are," Matthew nodded. "And the president is more than glad to have you stay."

CHAPTER THIRTY

It was the first time James slept through a whole night, and he woke up feeling more energized than ever.

He sat up in bed, had barely rubbed his eyes, when Stephen walked in with a breakfast tray.

"Good morning to you. Rise and shine!" Stephen greeted merrily. "How are we feeling today?"

"Great, thanks. I have never slept so well."

"That's good! That's really good," Stephen replied. "I brought you some breakfast; oats cereal with nuts and some fresh mixed fruit. Is this okay?" he asked, lowering the tray for him to see.

"Yeah; it's perfect, thanks," he replied.

Stephen put the tray down on the nightstand beside James.

"Feel free to freshen up," Stephen said, pointing to the en suite. "You've got clean clothes on the shelf. Oh! And it doesn't matter if you wet the patch on your chest, just don't take it off."

"Thanks."

"And yes, um, whenever you feel comfortable, the president would like to speak to you."

"Sure. Everything okay with Matthew?"

"Yes, of course," Stephen answered with a reassuring smile. "Him and his family are on constant security watch. I'm sure Matthew will soon be escorted here. Last I checked, he was still asleep."

"Thanks for everything."

"You are more than welcome," Stephen replied cordially. "I'll leave you to have breakfast in peace. If you need anything, just let me know."

James ate breakfast and had a warm shower—everything still seeming so surreal.

"Look—at—you!" Matthew remarked, as James stepped out of the en suite. "First time I am actually seeing you in such cool clothes. Except when I let you borrow mine, of course."

"They are nice, aren't they?" he agreed, looking down at his polo shirt. "Everything okay?"

"Yeah; I have my own driver now—how dope is that?"

"Still keep your eyes open, Matt. And be careful who you—"

"James," Stephen cut in, popping his head through the doorway, "sorry to interrupt but if it's okay with you, the president is free to talk right now. What do you think?"

"Yeah, sure. Matthew can join, right?"

"Of course. Follow me then," Stephen replied.

Stephen showed them down a wide hall with checked marble floors. There were busts on each side along the corridor, large portraits of men and women hung on the wall at the pillar intervals.

"After you," Stephen said, stopping in front of a brown, double door.

The sun was glistening on the glass coffee table. Mint drapes danced with the zephyr at the large windows. The three tier chandelier hung low in the middle of the room.

"James," the president said with a formal smile, getting to his feet to greet them. "This is a much better setting for an encounter than our previous one, right?"

"Mr. President," James replied, "I am really sorry for what happened last—"

"James, it's okay," the president said, "I know your hands were tied. My leg healed perfectly well. And do call me Miguel, please," he continued with a broad smile as he held out his hand.

James shook Miguel's hand and Matthew did the same.

"Please, have a seat," Miguel said, and sat back down on the armchair he was on.

Matthew and James sat on the sofa facing Miguel. Stephen began pouring glasses of water for everyone.

"This is Jeffrey by the way, a good friend of mine," Miguel said, pointing to the old man who was sitting on the other armchair, a cane right next to him, his left hand with a tremor.

Jeffrey nodded to the both of them as a sign of acknowledgment and they reciprocated the gesture.

"So," Miguel began, "Cole Miller." His lips paused to seal tight. "That man has been at the top of our priority list for quite a number of years now. Thing is, he is more of an asset out there as a way of keeping the underworld under control and as a gateway to bring some of them down, rather than behind bars. We have had eyes and ears on his operations and have intervened whenever we could. I heard Matthew told you that already."

“So you knew about John?” James asked, incredulous. “Why didn't you do anything?”

“Unfortunately, some things are still out of our control,” Miguel replied. “These affairs are very delicate and way complicated. Cole is still one powerful man; he rules the underworld—don't for a second underestimate the threat he is to society. But as I have explained, for now he is serving as a crucial pawn. May I add at this very moment that whatever we are discussing is strictly confidential. If Cole suspects we have eyes and ears, he is the type of man who will readily kill his whole crew just to make sure he nails the rat.”

Miguel reached for his glass of water and took a sip.

“How long have you known about me?” James asked.

Miguel sighed, as though to say he was sorry, “Years—from the day you were born to be exact.”

James stared fixedly at Miguel, shock and anger setting in.

“All those years,” James whispered. “Everything Ricin put me through; all those tests and punishments.”

“Believe it or not,” Miguel said, “we have tried several other times to get you out of there before, but to no avail. And the tranquillizer gas plan was in place for years but we never had the opportunity to get to use it to get you out.”

“Do you know who the person on the inside is?” James asked.

“No; and only a handful of people know the answer to that. And that is how it has to remain for the operation to go on safely.”

“Did you know I was going to break in and get that file from you?”

“No—we did not,” Miguel replied with a nervous chuckle. “We only get information when there is a threat or we need to be positioned somewhere. Whoever is in there, doesn't see you as a threat.”

“Right,” James replied, and got lost in his own head.

“James,” Miguel said, grabbing his attention again, “another matter I wanted to discuss with you, is about the tracer and defibrillator you have attached to your heart muscle. I understand you are keeping a patch on your chest to interfere with the signal, but that cannot be the permanent solution. We believe removing them is of utmost priority if we are to keep you safe and free from Cole. Do you agree?”

“I guess; though he might still get to know my whereabouts as his undercover people are everywhere.”

“So I have heard,” Miguel concurred. “But then again, you need not worry about the people in here— my staff— their backgrounds are regularly checked and updated and I can assure you; you can trust them.”

“Good to hear,” James said politely, still convinced Ricin would find out where he was, one way or another.

“So you agree that we need to surgically remove the tracer and defibrillator,” Miguel said, and leaned forward in his seat, resting his elbows on his knees, locking his hands together. “We were thinking however, and please, I really do hope you don't take this the wrong way, but we were considering if it would be wise to replace Cole's tracer—with one of ours.”

A deafening silence took over the room, James's breathing suddenly uneasy, his heartbeat tripling.

“That way, if—and I hope not—but if, something goes wrong with our person on the inside and Cole manages to get hold of you again, we will know where to come for you," Miguel explained. "What are your thoughts on that?"

James's heart kept racing vigorously and something in Stephen's pocket began beeping.

"You don't have to give an answer right now," Stephen told him, having turned off the beeping sound, "Take all the time you need to consider it. Just remember, the purpose of our proposed tracer is solely for your safety."

Was it? Having their tracer in him could easily make him their prisoner instead.

Miguel leaned back in his seat, Jeffery's brow furrowed in thought. All eyes fastened on James.

"Um," James voiced, his mind revving to think of what to say without coming across as being extremely upset. "I don't think that would be—I…um…understand what your concerns are but—the idea of still having a tracer in me—umm..." He couldn't find the right words to explain his objections and paused.

"Take your time; think about it," Miguel replied, aware of his disappointment. "I know you've been through a lot of mayhem. Our only objective to know where you are, is to keep you safe," he repeated with great honesty. "We have also thought about maybe inserting a subcutaneous tracer in you," Miguel said, turning to Matthew. "Let me explain; if we are to keep track of where you are, James, we will have to place your tracer somewhere where Cole will have to spend some time to remove it, thus allowing us to get to you at once and well, the heart is a good location. With Matthew we can do it subcutaneously, that is, under the skin; Cole will not suspect that and we can still know where Matthew is, if Cole manages to get hold of him to threaten you."

"Right," James uttered unconvinced, everything whirling dramatically.

He had never really thought about what his life would be like when he got away from Ricin and all the world knew about him. But he had liked to think that being free from Ricin meant he would be able to live a somewhat kind of normal life; the life of a normal teenage boy, and not that of a traceable person under constant surveillance. He knew he could never go back to living on the run now—everybody knew his face—but the reality of his present new life sounded too restricted and simply another trap.

"You okay?" Stephen asked him, concerned.

"I'll think about it," James replied in a low voice, not wanting to raise any issues, but concluded to himself that another tracer merely meant another prison.

"I'm fine with doing mine," Matthew blurted out. "Even on my family; anything to be able to prevent Cole from using us as incentive."

"Glad to hear that, Matthew," Miguel replied, then turned to James again. "Don't worry. You let us know when you decide, okay?"

James gave a slight bob of the head, ill at ease.

Miguel forced a smile and stood up.

"It was a pleasure talking to the both of you but I have an important meeting now which cannot be postponed. I'll get back to you two later," Miguel concluded with a warm grin.

They both shook Miguel's hand. Jeffery, still slumped in his armchair, now smiling and nodding at them.

Matthew and James left the room with Stephen and began walking up the corridor.

"You okay?" Stephen asked him again. "You look worried."

"I'm—I'm fine—I just wasn't expecting that."

"I understand. Think about it; no pressure," Stephen replied calmly.

But he had already decided he did not want another tracer; be forced into another cell. What he had to actually think about, was how to make sure they did not insert theirs when operating to remove Ricin's; because he would be sedated for hours, they might as well be putting their own shackles on his heart—and he wouldn't even know it.

CHAPTER THIRTY-ONE

Stephen had shown them to the internal courtyard and they were strolling along one side, beneath the lemon trees. The sun was high, the skies a radiant blue.

"Why do you think it's a bad idea? Their tracer," Matthew asked, breaking the silence between them.

"I get why they would want to have theirs inserted in me; just in case," James replied, his eyes downcast in thought. "But I doubt that is their only motive and if it's not—I'll have nowhere to go then."

"I'm not following; what other motives could they have? These people are not Ricin."

"I'm sure they would want to study my mutant genes. What if they would want to use that information for the wrong intentions? Maybe military purposes. Ricin might have killed some innocent people but this could mean killing whole nations and I cannot be part of that."

"You sound as though Ricin is better than the president," Matthew said, confounded.

"If Ricin has taught me anything about people, it's that no one can be trusted—not even the president."

"Not everyone is as sick or as reprehensible as Cole. And I'm sure the president doesn't intend to use you like Cole did. I know it's hard for you to trust people but it's not like they forced you to do it; they made it quite clear this is your choice to make."

"Is it really, though? I'll be sedated for hours; they could be doing anything during that time."

Barking of dogs redirected their attention. Three small, fluffy, white dogs raced up to them, two with a fancy bow on top of their head.

"Hey! Come here!" a middle-aged woman called behind them, but the three dogs continued running toward James and Matthew, and jumped at their feet.

James stooped in an attempt to pet them, but they were hysterical whirligigs.

"Look at those eyes," Matthew said, petting the one without a bow. The dog leaped even higher and Matthew picked it up. "Cuteness overload," Matthew said, the dog licking his face. "By the way, I persuaded mom to keep Julie. Remember? The black cat at the garage? Her favorite spot is on my pillow."

James smiled. That cat had seen him through many anxious days and sleepless nights—the only one that could hear all he could never say.

"Glad you took her in," he replied. "But Julie, really? Long lost crush?" James chaffed.

“Hey, mom picked the name; that was the deal.”

“Looks like you two like dogs, huh?” the woman said as she approached them, her blonde curls up in a loose bun. “Sorry about that; I didn't know anyone was out here. Would have kept them on a leash.”

“Not a problem at all,” Matthew replied.

The dogs calmed down and wandered off, sniffing the ground, following each other closely.

“Hey you’re—you’re James and Matthew, right?” the woman said.

James gave a slight nod while Matthew reached out his hand.

“Pleased to meet you,” Matthew said.

“Oh, wow!” she replied, shaking Matthew's hand and then James's. “I’m Nancy. Pleased to meet you both and welcome aboard,” she continued with a broad smile. “I’m the pet sitter and trainer. Miguel has these three little rascals, adopted recently, and two red-footed tortoises. He loves them pets.”

“Cute,” Matthew said. “How old are the tortoises? Are they big?”

“Oh, they are only three years old—about this big,” she replied, her fingers almost touching as they formed a circle. “You could come see them if you like—they got their own little garden at the back. Cupcake and Ice-cream are their names; Miguel's nieces named them.”

“Boys,” Stephen cut in from behind them. “Hey, Nancy, how's the training going?”

“Well, as you can see,” Nancy replied, putting both her hands on her waist as she looked out to where the dogs were, “I got a looong way to go, Stephen. Wish me luck. HEY! Georgie! Stop that!” One of the dogs was digging in the soil, uprooting flowers. "Please, do excuse me," she quickly added as she hurried away.

"Hey, want to play some ball?" Stephen asked. "There's a pretty sweet indoor court."

"Sure!" Matthew replied. "Come on, bro—let me remind you how to practice not being a sore loser."

"Last I remember, it was the other way round," James said.

"Not today, bro; not today," Matthew replied, his determination overly pronounced.

Stephen took them to the indoor sports court. It was huge, well maintained, and had a volleyball net as well as basketball hoops.

"Balls are there," Stephen said, pointing to the storage shelf unit.

A bubbly ringtone began playing and Stephen picked up his phone.

"Hey, Samy," Stephen answered. "Yeah, I'll be there by eight. Tell mom I said *thanks*. Okay, see you later, sweetheart, love you."

"Do they play here? As in, real teams?" Matthew asked eagerly when Stephen hung up.

"Yes, sometimes; on special occasions," Stephen said.

"Cool!" Matthew replied, looking over at the stadium seating.

"Shoot! I almost forgot," Stephen said, frustrated with himself. "I got to make a phone call but I'll be right back —join you for a game. I might be older but hey; I still got it," he said, pointing both his index fingers at them, then turned around and left the court.

"This is awesome, right?" Matthew remarked as they went over to the shelves. "You ever played hoops?" he asked, grabbing a basketball.

"Not really," James replied, his mind taking him back to training sessions with Wang Gu. "You?"

"At school, for fun. To get girls' attention."

"By losing?"

"Haha! Actually, I've got a pretty good aim," Matthew said, dribbling the ball toward the hoop. Matthew paused, aimed, and threw the ball. "He shoots—he scores!" Matthew shouted triumphantly.

James grabbed a basketball and began bouncing it. The distinct feel of pebbling against his fingertips took him back to Ricin's courtyard. Blindfolded, he had to rely on his senses and reflexes to try and take the ball away from Wang Gu.

Wang Gu would keep moving around him stealthily, occasionally giving the ball a bounce. He used to listen for any shuffle, any breathing other than his own, then target Wang Gu and approach him, cautious to avoid Wang Gu's strikes with deer horn knives. *Not fast enough. Again!* Wang Gu repeatedly said when James grabbed the ball, avoiding the blades.

"He shoots? He doesn't score?" Matthew voiced, pulling him back to reality.

James dribbled the ball further away from the hoop than Matthew was, and tried a shot.

"And he misses!" Matthew said. "The girls would go awwwww!"

Matthew tried another shot and scored again.

"Two-zero, bro!" Matthew stated, his grin victorious.

James shook his head at Matthew, his competitive side kicking in. He moved further back, nearly to the center of the court and bounced the ball in concentration.

"Oh, bro! You kidding me? You didn't even score from here, man," Matthew teased.

But James bounced the ball, focused on the size and weight of the sphere beneath his hand, noting his distance from the hoop. *Focus!* Wang Gu's voice echoed in his memory. *You either focus or you get cut. Small cut, big cut; you get no food for two days. Second day, weak, probably cut again; another two days no food. Cycle! FOCUS*! Wang Gu's voice yelled in his ear, and James shot the ball toward the hoop with precision.

"And he scooooores! Whoop! Whoop! That was awesome!" Matthew cheered. "I got to try it from there," he added with a smug smile, and stood next to James.

Matthew began bouncing the ball low, eyes focused on the hoop.

"I'm going to score; I can do this!" Matthew encouraged himself, his voice lacking any confidence, and bounced the ball even faster.

James watched Matthew, struggling to suppress his laughter—Matthew's face made odd frowns and lip twitches, doubting his ability to score from such a distance.

"I can do this!" Matthew repeated, determined.

James watched on, stifling his laughter. But then, his reflexes startled in alert. He swiftly turned around, trying to detect from where the harm was about to strike. But the warning was familiar; the harm inevitable. Sharp pain pierced his heart and his knees gave way under the intense agony.

“James?” Matthew shouted, rushing to grab him, preventing him from collapsing onto the floor. “James?” Matthew cried out loud. “Someone help!!”

“The defibrillator,” James whispered.

“What?” Matthew asked in panic.

But the pain in James's chest intensified, the tightness smothering.

“James? James, what's wrong?!” Matthew grabbed James's face, trying to seize his attention.

But James couldn't draw in air, around him in a fog, his vision fading until finally, he lost consciousness.

***

It was a distant voice that woke him up, words muffled. A familiar clink sharpened his ears and he recognized the voice—Matthew's. His eyes slit open, the rest of his body numb. Matthew was slouched on an armchair beside his bed, talking on his cell phone.

“Hey,” Matthew said, leaning forward. “Mom, he's up, I got to go. Will call you later, okay? Bye.” Then to James again, “Hey, how are you doing?”

“What happened?” James asked weakly.

“Cole he...ummm...managed to activate the defibrillator, so they had to operate on you and ummm... remove the stuff.”

Stephen entered the room, “James! How are we doing?”

“Numb,” he whispered.

“It's the pain medication. We can change the dose if you prefer; which I don't recommend for now,” Stephen replied, checking the rate of the flow in the drip.

“It's okay. Thanks.”

“We, should leave you to rest,” Stephen said, looking over at Matthew rather oddly.

“So I don't have anything—any tracer in me now?” James asked.

“No, nothing,” Stephen replied with a smile.

Pure relief. His heart free to beat wherever it wanted.

Matthew stood up, avoiding eye contact.

“I’ll leave you to rest,” Matthew said, his head still bowed. “I’ll come by later, okay?” he added, lifting his face, struggling to look him straight in the eye.

“Thanks,” James replied.

Something was off with Matthew—he seemed to be purposefully holding back what was on his mind. But James was too exhausted to ask him, besides, nothing really bad could have happened; Matthew didn't look sad, just worried; maybe because of the surgery itself.

He watched them leave and when Matthew returned later that day, he was back to his normal, humorous self. It was the surgery Matthew must have been worried about.

Three long days went by, but James was already much better and able to go for short walks in the interior courtyard.

“I can't believe I’m finally free again,” James told Matthew, hands in his pockets, enjoying the stroll in the afternoon sun.

“Glad you are recovering well,” Matthew replied, head to the ground.

“But there is something you’ve been wanting to tell me, right?” he asked, seeing Matthew avoid his eyes again.

"James, I—" Matthew began, pausing to look straight at him. "I couldn't tell you because you were too weak after the operation and not because they told me not to. Stephen still thinks it's too early for you to know."

"Know what?" he asked, tense.

Matthew sat down on a bench and waited for James to follow.

"When they were doing your surgery," Matthew said, moistening his lips anxiously, "they decided it was best for your safety to know your location at all times."

James's heart quickened, his fury rocketing, anticipating what Matthew was about to say.

"They did insert their tracer in you; just as a precaution."

James looked away.

"I know you were against it but there was nothing I could do; you could have died if they did not carry out the surgery right away; I only got to know after they did it."

"It's not your fault," James replied, frustration driving his thoughts.

"James—"

"This is exactly what I feared," he snapped. "They seem to be giving you a choice but in reality, they are not so different from Ricin. I cannot live my life if someone is always making decisions for me! I'm back to being a prisoner; just in a different cell."

"Hey, listen, these people are not Cole; you can talk to them. Stephen seems like a genuinely nice guy."

Talk to them?! They clearly weren't even bothered to hear his opinion, let alone value it.

"Hey, bro," Matthew said, his voice empathetic. "It might feel like you're not free but this is different. These are good people and as hard as it is, you need to trust them if we are to move forward together to bring Cole down."

James remained silent, eyes rested on a pile of leaves, his head reeling. There was not much he could do now was there? Their tracer was already in him; his freedom permanently snatched away from him.

He followed the foliage as it began playing *Ring Around the Rosie* in the breeze, twirling around and around until all the leaves fell down.

"What are you thinking?" Matthew asked with concern.

"I didn't want this," he replied under his breath.

The overcast sky split open and rain tumbled from the abundant clouds. James and Matthew hurried inside.

They walked down the corridor and Stephen showed up, coming in their direction.

"Hey, boys," Stephen greeted with a cheerful smile.

But James's face remained grave.

"Everything all right?" Stephen asked, stopping next to them.

"He knows; I just told him," Matthew replied bluntly.

Stephen paused, rather thrown off balance.

"Can we talk, James?" Stephen said.

"About what? The tracer or the lies?" he replied.

"Can we sit down? Please," Stephen insisted patiently, glancing at Matthew. "Please, come to my office."

Stephen began walking down the corridor, looking over his shoulder, expecting them to follow. He took them to a spacious room and pointed to the white sofa.

"Have a seat," Stephen invited.

They all sat down and Stephen switched his cell phone to silent mode.

"James, we would have much rather had our decision include your approval beforehand," Stephen began, "but given the circumstances, we had to think fast and act quick. The operation is definitely not a minor one and having to redo it comes with a lot of risks. We believe that being able to trace you if something goes wrong is the most important thing to keep you safe. And that is the only reason for inserting our tracer."

"But couldn't there be another way?" James said, annoyed. "I appreciate your concerns for my safety. But that's what Ricin used to say too—everything done for my protection—and I'm skeptical that is your only motive," he added, a steady gaze on Stephen.

"We overheard your conversation the other day," Stephen answered openly. "And I do not blame you for thinking we would like to study your advanced abilities, because we do; I myself as a scientist would love to. However, your abilities are yours and whether or not you allow us to study them is your decision and nothing will change that. The reason we are interested in studying them is because we believe they might shed light on cures to certain illnesses; that's all, and I give you my word on that."

The idea of trust was a naïve thought for James. He stared at Stephen with no expectations he'd fulfil that promise.

"You don't seem convinced," Stephen said, patient. "And after all you've been through, I don't blame you at all, but I really wish you'd give me the chance to prove it to you."

There was a wooden, coffee table in front of them made from the same teak timber as the table at Ricin's headquarters—as though incarceration wasn't enough, they had to instil the same sense of dread.

"If you think this tracer would hinder our way forward together," Stephen said, his hands locked together, his right thumb rubbing over the other, "when Cole is behind bars, we can remove it again."

James lifted his face. The idea of Cole behind bars soothed his rage, even though his own freedom still seemed to be lost forever—because would they really remove it?

"Did they insert your tracer too?" he asked, turning to Matthew.

"Yes; I asked for it." Matthew replied. "I don't want to be used by Cole and that is the only way I think is a good prevention."

"I don't know what kind of tracer you used," he said, "but the first tracer Ricin had inserted interfered with my pulse when my heart was under stress. That is why he had to change it and added a defibrillator."

"We were informed and made sure our tracer won't cause any such problems," Stephen replied with confidence. "And there is no defibrillator—you won't be needing that."

"Good to know," James replied—at least he would be able to run away if he had to—but where to? The tracer would pick up on his whereabouts even in the deepest sea trenches.

"James," Stephen said, and waited for him to look up, "I am a father of three daughters and my only aim in life is to see them happy and make them proud of their dad. I would not have enrolled for such a position if I knew or thought there was the slightest possibility that I would be involved in anything that is morally wrong." There was honesty in Stephen's voice and eyes; he couldn't be lying. "So all I am asking of you, is for a chance to make it right for you."

James swallowed hard and rubbed his hand nervously against his trousers. Stephen's gaze intent, awaiting his reply.

"Okay," James forced himself to say.

Stephen's shoulders dropped, failing his attempt to conceal his silent sigh of relief.

"That's great!" Stephen said. "I won't let you down."

It was more than a promise; there was dignity of a father.

"Wow," Stephen said with a light chuckle, "I might be better at talking to boys because you know? With my girls." Stephen shook his head as though confused, "You never really know if you're getting through to them—or actually pulling out the safety pin of a grenade."

Matthew laughed and James put on a smile.

"My two eldest are twins, nearly your age. Some days, I really don't know how to talk to them at this point, especially Alba. One day all's well, the next, whatever I say is a trigger."

"That's it," Matthew said, lost in his own thoughts, "So *I* wasn't the problem with the girls I dated after all." Matthew nodded to himself and Stephen laughed.

“We got our flaws; many of them,” Stephen said, “but women definitely ain’t perfect either. Keeps one on his toes; never a dull moment.”

Stephen looked at James again, “We should let you rest; your body is still recovering. And if there is something—anything—we can do for you, please let us know.”

“Thanks,” James replied, then hesitated, “Since you are mentioning that; there is something you could do—for someone else.”

CHAPTER THIRTY-TWO

James tried to conceal his conflicting emotions as he got dressed in a black suit. He was torn between unmeasurable rage and yet a peaceful calm, between regret and guilt, and yet a sense of great attainment. *Guess John was right*, he thought as he wore the black tie; *irony is truly the mother of life.*

"We are all gathered here for a very special person," the pastor began, as Matthew and his family, some relatives and friends, Stephen, the President, other staff members, and James, stood in the garden of the residence around a beautiful memorial stone with a large sculpture of an angel. "A father, a grandfather, and a dear friend. A person who not only served as a light of hope and guidance, but also as the man who was ready to sacrifice his own life so that others could live and have a bright future. A person who was not only a real shoulder in moments of most need, but also the anchor of truth and righteousness. We are thankful to you, John Edwin Meli, for all the love you gave and the unforgettable difference you made on this Earth."

A memorial service for John was the least James could ask for, for Katy and Matthew. John's body was not there but his presence was with all of them; his memory engraved not only forever in their hearts but also on the eternal stone.

There was a moment of silence and the sweet chirrup of birds harmonized the air. Katy's tears streamed silently, her eyes fixated on the marble angel as those present laid beautiful bouquets of bright flowers in front of it.

"I'm so sorry," James told Katy again, when the memorial service was over.

"It's not your fault," Katy replied with a weak smile, and hugged him tightly. "And whenever you want to come over; our door is always open for you, okay?" she added with a tap on his shoulder.

Paul stood next to her, his lips pursed tight, his expression speaking for itself—James was clearly not welcome in their house. But could he really blame Paul? It was because of him Paul's family were a living target, John already taking the fall.

After the ceremony, Katy and Paul were invited to the president's residence for tea but Paul refused and they left.

Matthew remained with James and after a stroll in the garden, they headed inside the residence. A gloom shadowed James, his thoughts dark.

"You okay?" Matthew asked as they walked through the corridor.

"Don't really know," he replied, almost whispering. "I keep thinking and replaying events in my head—maybe, if just maybe I had done some things differently than I did, then John might still be alive. He might—"

"Don't," Matthew cut in, looking steadily at James. "You're not the one to blame. And you did whatever you felt was best at those particular times and places. Cole killed him, and whatever had to happen, would have happened anyway—Grandpa gave up his life for yours because he saw great value in that. Carrying these thoughts of guilt and regret will only weigh you down and diminish that value."

"He didn't deserve to die the way he did," James replied.

"I know. But just like mom keeps saying; try to remember him as a blessing that happened in your life, not as a loss—he would want that."

"Yeah. Thanks."

They came to the end of the corridor and stopped next to the elevator.

"Thanks for asking for the memorial service," Matthew said. "I really appreciated it; it was as special as mom wanted it to be. Thanks."

James shrugged—it was the least he could have done.

"You should get some rest; you're still recovering," Matthew said. "Oh! And mom wanted me to give you this," he added, reaching down in his pocket. "It's a letter from John. We received it with ours, it's for you."

James took the letter. He never thought he'd actually hear from John again; the irony was bittersweet.

"I'll see you later," Matthew said. "Get some rest."

"Yeah. I will. See you, bro."

James went to his room. He sat on the edge of the bed and opened John's letter. It was in John's handwriting, the blue ink occasionally wavering where his old hand had shaken.

Dearest James,

If you are reading this, it means I did not make it, but it also means you have made it out of here and have a bright future ahead of you. I cannot be more glad about that.

Ever since I met you, I knew you had the kind of heart that every father wishes his son to have. You are a person of value, with great morals that I have no doubt will stand the test of time.

I'm glad I remained by your side and I will never regret I chose to stay. You once told me I have taught you a lot about life but I can say the same about you.

Always strive to be more of yourself and less of what others want you to be. In the end, you are the one who has to live with the choices you make; be sure to make the right ones.

Life will never be easy; it's that way for everyone. It will bring you down to your knees, to teach you to be humble. It will take you through pain, to teach you to appreciate the good times. It will throw at you more than curveballs and daggers, making sure you continue to grow and move on the right path.

Whatever your life's path puts you through, never give up, never lose hope, and always try that one more time.

Look out for Katy and Paul, and especially Matthew; you mean to him, the brother he means to you.

I'm proud of you, son, and I'll always be with you.

Love,
John.

A warm tear escaped the corner of his eye, John's wrinkled smile vivid in his mind. He folded away the letter and put it in the first drawer of his bedside table. His watch was in there and he picked it up. He had forgotten all about it and the small, red inscription—he had to get the watch opened and have a good look inside.

"Hey, James, how are you, fine?" a woman asked as she hurried into the room with a stethoscope around her neck.

"Not bad, thanks."

"I'm Abigail. Stephen sent me to take your blood sample, to run a few tests; to check that everything is okay," she continued with a vague smile. "Hope you don't mind, it will just take a minute."

"Sure," he replied.

"Okay, relax your arm…There we go," Abigail said as she drew some of his blood into a large syringe. "And that's ready. It didn't hurt now, did it?" she asked, putting the cap back on the needle.

"No."

Abigail forced a formal smile and headed toward the door.

James stood, then crouched to tie his shoelace. Abigail paused in the doorway, looking his way.

He looked up and their eyes met; her expression demonic. Her lips slithered into a sly smile and his reflexes tripped—the harm was inevitable. What had she just done to him?!

"Take care, while you still can…Snowflake."

About the Author

Marie Therese Aquilina was born in 1987 in Malta. She is a wife, and mom of two daughters. She studied sciences and graduated as a biology teacher. She is a huge animal and nature lover. Her favorite place to be is by the sea.

Writing has always been one of her greatest passions and James's story initially came to her when she was only eleven years old. The story continued to unravel in her mind over the years and led her to write *The Snowflake Series*.

You can follow Marie Therese Aquilina on Twitter (@Marthese Bonaqui)

www.ingramcontent.com/pod-product-compliance
Lightning Source LLC
Chambersburg PA
CBHW020335180626
46812CB00001B/210
9781949193626